Under Pink Skies

I0773082

Copyright © 2025 by Hallie Anne

This book was previously published under a different pen name.

All rights reserved.

No part of this publication may be reproduced, distributed, or transmitted in any form or by any means, including photocopying, recording, or other electronic or mechanical methods, without the prior written permission of the publisher, except as permitted by U.S. copyright law.

No generative artificial intelligence (AI) was used in the writing of this work. Without in any way limiting the author's exclusive rights under copyright, any use of this publication to "train" generative artificial intelligence (AI) technologies to generate text is expressly prohibited.

The story, all names, characters, and incidents portrayed in this production are fictitious. No identification with actual persons (living or deceased), places, buildings, and products is intended or should be inferred.

Published by Aspen & Ivy Press

Cover Design: Yummy Book Covers

Editor: Alyssa Daily Editorial

Proofreading: Meghan Monarch

1st Edition published November 2024

eISBN: 978-1-965506-06-6

ISBN (paperback): 978-1-965506-07-3

Dedication

For Kat, Sophie, Victoria, Harry, Clay, and Ed

Also by Hallie Anne

Watford Sweethearts Series
Under Pink Skies
Sunny Skies Ahead
Through Stormy Skies [Nov 2025]
Anthologies
Love in Appalachia

Content Notes

Under *Pink Skies* deals with heavy themes. There are in-depth discussions of alcoholism and alcoholism recovery, addiction recovery, emotional abuse, parental death, grief, and abandonment. There are on-page references to childhood abuse, neglect, and domestic violence, though there are no graphic depictions of any. There are references to a car crash, which occurs off page, and a hospital stay with police interactions, which occur on page. Take care of your mental health, and reach out to the author with any questions.

Playlist

- Something in the Orange – Zach Bryan
- Mean Old Sun – Turnpike Troubadours
- Dawns (ft. Maggie Rogers) – Zach Bryan
- Remember That Night? – Sara Kays
- This Love (Taylor's Version) – Taylor Swift
- Losers (ft. Jelly Roll) – Post Malone
- Orange Juice – Noah Kahan
- Nine Ball – Zach Bryan
- The View Between Villages – Noah Kahan
- Shake the Frost (Live) – Tyler Childers
- Overtime – Zach Bryan
- Mountain Song – Flatland Cavalry
- Something I Need – One Republic
- The Outskirts – Zach Bryan

- Lose It – Kane Brown

- Beneath Oak Trees – Dylan Gossett

- So High School – Taylor Swift

- All Your'n – Tyler Childers

- The Good I'll Do – Zach Bryan

- The Alchemy – Taylor Swift

Listen on Spotify

Chapter 1

Abbie

Running a general store in a remote mountain town had always been a crap shoot.

But today, everything was falling apart.

Literally.

"Crap," I muttered, rubbing my chin with my thumb and forefinger, trying to figure out what kind of ragtag solution I was going to come up with for the steady drip of water leaking from the ceiling in aisle three. The aisle was mostly stocked with canned goods and boxed camping provisions, and yet another leak was a reminder of everything that was breaking down around me.

Expensive breakdowns that would require extensive repairs to fix, with money we simply didn't have.

Double crap.

I placed one of the smaller feed buckets beneath the leak, hoping to at least prevent the water from further damaging the wood floors beneath it. We hadn't had new homesteaders come to Watford, Washington in years, and it's not like anyone in town was lining up to order their equipment directly from us. If there was anything the last few years had taught me, it's that "buying local" only goes so far. If people could get it cheaper, they would. I didn't fault them for that. Times were hard, and money was thin, especially in a small town like Watford, where industry was scarce.

It simply sucked that it affected my family so deeply.

I returned to my work desk, which was long slabs of wood stacked onto several thick planks with wooden shelves carved into the bottom. My father's family had made beautiful heirloom woodworking, and this counter was a testament to the incredible things my father could create with his hands, a piece of wood, and a sharp tool.

Not that he had touched any of those things in recent years.

Cancer had a way of sneaking up on the most unsuspecting of families. Ours was no different. No family history of breast cancer, and by the time they'd discovered my mom's, it was advanced. We had several beautiful months together as a family.

And then she was gone.

I squeezed my eyes shut as unbidden memories of her funeral rammed into my mind.

I didn't have time to dwell on the past. I had to keep moving forward. If I didn't, I would break down.

"Abbie?"

The delicate cadence of Imogen's voice immediately calmed my frayed nerves as the door to the store opened.

"Behind the counter."

I didn't recognize my voice, and as I schooled my face into a neutral expression, I prayed Imogen wouldn't ask too many questions. As I glanced back down at the countertop,

I noticed the IRS letters I had been examining last night were still laid out.

As if dealing with my drunken, grieving father, and attempting to keep the family business afloat wasn't enough, the IRS was now breathing down my neck because my father never thought hiring a bookkeeper could serve us well in the long run. I didn't know how deep the IRS hole went, but it was enough to result in a pile of paper mail on my kitchen table. Add that to the weekly phone calls and a barrage of emails from various debt collectors looking for my father, and I was at my wit's end.

"Ah, there you are," Imogen said, rounding the corner and throwing me a dazzling smile. I'd known Imogen for years, and it still surprised me how genuine of a person she was. She hauled with her a gigantic cardboard box full of dozens of farm-fresh eggs.

"I'm worried that box is going to fall apart on you," I said, and Imogen immediately waved me off.

"Nonsense. I've been using this box to carry eggs from the homestead to your store for over a year now, and it hasn't failed me yet."

I couldn't help but smile at her comforting mountain drawl and the way she naturally fell into rhythm. I grabbed the clipboard from its nail against the main post, handing it to Imogen. She signed it with a quick flick of her wrist and set about putting the eggs into the main fridge.

We only had two industrial fridges, but given the tiny amount of refrigerated goods we kept on hand—eggs, milk and cheese, and fresh produce during the harvest season—we didn't need to expand. The two fridges pressed right next to each other against the back wall, subtly hiding the staircase that led to the upstairs loft where my father now lived.

"So, have you heard anything from your lawyer?" Imogen didn't look up from where she was busy examining each carton to ensure the eggs had survived the trip from her farm, but she knew my smile faltered by the waver in my voice.

"I'm sorry?"

"For taking on the IRS. Have you hired a lawyer?"

I huffed out a dry laugh. "I don't think a lawyer would do me any good. At least, I hope we're not at that point yet. I've reached out to a few accountants in Spokane but haven't found one willing to work with us. Turns out not filling out a single piece of paperwork, including anything tax related, for several years, is a nightmare for bookkeepers to sort through."

Imogen knew I was struggling financially to keep myself and the store afloat, but even she didn't know exactly how badly we were hurting. My father was the only one who knew the intricacies of the mess we were in, but he was barely sober enough to stand most days. Asking him to find an employee's W-2 form from the first year Watford General was operational would only end with him laughing in my face and smashing his bottle against a wall.

"You know Cassie is a lawyer at a large firm in Seattle now, right? I could call her. I'm sure she'd be happy to look over your documents and give some suggestions."

I smiled, but shook my head. "Your sister has enough on her plate right now."

Imogen made a small hum of consideration and acknowledgment.

A loud crash from above us shook me from my thoughts. The wooden floor of the ceiling creaked under the weight of my father's feet, and I heard the muffled sounds of him stumbling and cursing, trying to find his way to the door.

Triple crap.

Today was not my day.

Imogen turned her head toward me, her lips parting in a silent question. I looked away quickly, not trusting myself to meet her eyes without crying. I silently sent a prayer to whatever God might be listening that my father wouldn't make a fool of himself in front of my last remaining friend.

But God had turned a blind eye to my family a long time ago.

My father, in all his hungover glory, stumbled his way down the steps, leaning against the wall for stability. Even though I was standing well over ten feet away from the landing, the smell of stale beer, vomit, and a severe lack of showering hit me like a freight train. Malcolm's black hair was stringy and overgrown, and his beard was patchy. Shabby clothing that was positively filthy completed his disgusting aesthetic. I barely swallowed my gag, even as distant tears stung the back of my eyes.

Imogen would never speak of this. I trusted her with every dark part of me, and she did the same for me.

But knowing she was seeing this part of my life—the part I tried so desperately to keep hidden from my customers, from Watford, from everyone—made me vulnerable in a way I hadn't allowed myself to be in years.

Imogen stood frozen in place as Malcolm greeted her with a grunt. She clearly wanted to intervene, but didn't know how to do so.

I expected myself to be embarrassed by my still-drunk father heading toward the store's beer cooler, but rage filled my veins.

How was it I had lost my mother, but no one had allowed me to grieve? My father had found a broken solace at the bottom of a whiskey bottle and left me to fend for myself against the weight of the world.

I'd been struggling for the last five years to pick up the ruined shards of my family and the business that sustained us and our presence in Watford, all while trying to piece the jagged pieces of my heart after *he* left.

Because he'd left me. Days after my mother's funeral, the person I'd sworn I'd live the rest of my life with abandoned me.

I swallowed the lump in my throat once more.

Not here. Not now. Never.

I couldn't let these emotions out.

If I did, the entire world would fall to pieces. That, I was sure of.

"Imogen," my father said, smiling as he inclined his head toward the black-haired female to my right. I took a small step toward her, ready to push her out of the way if my father suddenly stumbled or flew into one of his all-too-common drunken tirades. "It's been a long time since I've seen you."

Imogen replied with her own tight-lipped smile. "It's nice to see you too, Mr. Malcolm. My mother was just asking about you the other day."

The understatement of the century. Malcolm Collins had become an enigma since Tilly had died. No one, save for me, Imogen, and the bartenders at the Roadhouse, knew anything about what my father and I were going through. And even Imogen had never seen him like this.

My father had a talent for presenting his best face when we were in public, saving the worst of his moments for his family. And the days when he couldn't pull his shit together enough to keep up the facade? He simply didn't go out. He barricaded himself inside the walls of his house and created chaos there instead.

I'd noticed his alcoholism was getting worse, particularly after the anniversary of my mother's death, but this was something different. Imogen sensed it, and I wanted to crawl into a hole and leave this place forever.

"Ah, your mother, such a lovely woman."

I rolled my eyes. Using the term "your mother" rather than Kayla meant the drunken fool couldn't remember my best friend's mom's name. I opened my mouth to speak, but my jaw hung open in shock as my father ripped open the door of the beer cooler and grabbed a bottle of Corona straight from an unopened six-pack, gripping it in his filthy fingers as if he held a claim to it.

"Dad," I said incredulously, taking a step toward him. "Those are for paying customers. We can't afford—"

"I'll tell you what we can't afford."

The harsh tone of his voice made me flinch. He hadn't changed clothes or brushed his teeth, had barely made small talk with the two lowly human beings he encountered on his way to salvation: no, he'd woken up, stumbled his way downstairs, and made a beeline for the beer fridge.

Bottle still in hand, he stalked over to the storefront counter that held the cash register and scanner.

I had to put in a lot of effort to get that scanner so that my life would be easier during the tourist season, but even now, I could tell he didn't value many of the decisions I made for Watford General Store in the last few years.

The scanner was the least of his worries, but the scathing look he shot in my direction made my insides twist with a shame that had taken root in my soul. I briefly searched his hazy eyes, trying to decipher which lecture I'd receive this time.

"What we can't afford is you trying to tell me what I can and can't do in my own damn store. I built this place from nothing. You've gotten way too comfortable as the acting manager."

Acting manager. I bit back my laugh. I was the "acting manager" because he could barely find his way around his bedroom these days, much less count back change or hand a receipt to a customer. I had been the "acting manager" for the last five years, had brought us back from the brink of bankruptcy, and had done it all without complaining.

It was always the same argument.

No one—including me—had the right to criticize him about anything.

Even if that argument meant he ran the store and both of our financial lives into the ground.

"That doesn't even make sense, Dad," I replied, pinching the bridge of my nose.

I prayed Imogen snuck out the front door amid the chaos so she wouldn't have to witness this firsthand.

"It's expensive to import beer and wine this far into the mountains, even with the savings we get from going half-in with the Roadhouse. I don't have to tell you this. Please stop."

He grumbled in reply. He tightened his grip on the bottleneck and went back upstairs, mumbling gibberish to himself the entire way up. His decision to move into the attic space above the store was one I'd fought against. When he and Mom built the store, they'd created the loft attic space for me to have a place to go when they pulled long hours during tourist season, completing inventory checks and making small repairs and upgrades to keep the store running.

If anyone else in town had been aware of how bad his latest "slip up" had been, I'm sure they would have agreed with me about not wanting him above the place where all the goods were stored.

But my father always did what he wanted.

"Are you okay, Abbie?"

Imogen's voice was far less comforting this time, given what she'd just seen.

I stayed quiet, not trusting my voice to speak.

I wasn't okay. I wanted so badly to spiral. To fall apart. To let someone else shoulder these burdens. If only so I could know a moment of peace.

"I'm here for you, honey."

When she pulled me into her side for a tight hug, I still refused to speak, but I let silent tears run down my cheeks, creating dark marks on the dark pink fabric of her blouse.

Chapter 2
Connor

I felt like I was missing the punchline of a bad dad joke.

"Crap."

"You can use a stronger word than that, Harvey."

I ignored the barb and gestured toward the Winding Road Farms barn, a tall building worn down by time. The red-painted wood was now faded and weathered by years of sun and rain, held in place by rusted hinges original to the building.

I was trying to see the vision, but I couldn't see past the heaping mass of work.

"Are you seriously trying to turn this dilapidated pile of wood into a wedding venue?"

Kameron laughed beside me, shaking his head as though I was the one incapable of seeing the grand vision here. Despite the absurdity of the moment, I felt a pang of gratitude in my gut because I'd gotten out.

I escaped my hometown. Seen the world. Or at least the parts the Marine Corps sent me to. I had a host of life experiences I knew would serve me well in this next chapter of my life. I met some of my best friends, including Kameron, who'd left the Corps the year before me.

My plan had been the Marine Corps until I woke up one day and realized that I'd already accomplished what I'd set out to do. I'd gotten out of my hometown. I'd made something of myself. Even though I was ready to leave the active duty world, I didn't have a clear direction for my next step. It's not like spending four years in the Marine Corps infantry left me with many options.

So I'd done what any rational person would do and called up my best friend, Kameron, and practically begged him for a job. His response had been straightforward.

"As much as I enjoy seeing you grovel, Harvey, you don't have to beg. Of course, there's a place for you here."

While I was one of the stereotypical shiny new vets who had no plan or vision for their life, Kameron was the opposite. He'd lost his father, a first responder of over thirty years, to suicide several years ago, and since then, he'd made it his life's mission to open a regenerative farm with an emphasis on holistic healing for veterans and first responders with PTSD. Kameron had never gone out drinking with us on deployments or done anything that cost him a dime more than he absolutely had to spend. He saved every cent of his active-duty paychecks and, at the end of his four years, he took that money, along with the inheritance from his father, and bought the Winding Road farm, a sprawling expanse of farmland and forest.

In the month since I'd left active duty, I hadn't felt the impulse to curse. I worked with my hands every day, rebuilding infrastructure on the homestead, tending to livestock, and moving in a positive direction in my life.

With Kameron's help, I'd been sober since the last year I was on active duty, which was no small feat, considering how far gone I'd been when I got off that plane at Camp Pendleton, a freshly minted Marine who was more than ready to dive headfirst into the high life.

In a way, I had everything I could have dreamed of as a teenager.

The only thing I didn't have was *her*.

I didn't ask many questions when Kam offered me a job working on his farm. I'd been desperate, and my previous job as an infantryman didn't lend itself to many civilian opportunities. I didn't ask questions when Kameron booked me a flight into Portland and bought me a bus ticket to the mountains of eastern Washington. My naive, foolish self hadn't even thought to check a map to see just how close Kameron's new homestead operation was to my hometown.

As it would turn out, they were less than an hour apart.

Kameron's final chuckle brought me out of my thoughts.

"Multipurpose venue," Kameron corrected, wagging a finger in my face. "We'll host weddings, of course, but also private events and nonprofit training. We're going to restore this barn. The best one Watford County has ever seen."

I rubbed my temples. Watford County, Washington, already had many, *many* barns.

"This thing is falling apart, Kam."

"You can't see the vision, Harvey," Kam said, shaking his head. "We keep the original frame of the structure, an open-concept floor, with a hayloft above where guests can take pictures, store gifts, or do whatever else people do at weddings."

I laughed, unable to stop myself. "Have you researched this? Watford County is fairly remote . . . I can't imagine there's a large market for wedding venues that are literally in the middle of nowhere."

Kameron waved my concerns off with his hand, gesturing for me to follow him inside the barn.

"The space won't be limited to weddings. People could hold concerts and baby showers and all that shit here, too. It's a *multipurpose space*. One that will bring in income we can use to fund program expansions for Winding Road Recovery."

I smiled as Kam grabbed the rusted handle and pulled the door open. My grin widened as the handle fell off in his hand.

"I never said it wouldn't take work," Kam defended himself, dropping the handle and kicking it off to the side. He shoved his index finger into the middle of my chest. "Wipe that grin off your face and help me measure these pillars."

I held my hands up in mock surrender before grabbing the pencil that was tucked behind my ear and taking the measuring tape from Kam's outstretched hands. He barked orders, telling me what he wanted measured, so he could buy the building elements to make his grand vision happen. This was what I was used to, where I thrived: having a clear-cut task and being able to fulfill that task to the best of my ability.

My cell phone rang out in the barn's silence. Kameron gave me a *seriously, dude?* glare from the other side of the barn, where he was taking pictures of the original stain color, no doubt trying to preserve as much of the original look and feel of the barn as possible during the remodel.

I shrugged my shoulders and silenced my notifications without looking. Despite no longer being on active duty and having my phone notifications silenced most of the time, I must have forgotten this morning. I was still operating on an iPhone 8, which made me a boomer, according to Kameron and Lucas, another active-duty stray Kameron had taken under his wing.

We continued to take measurements and discuss Kam's vision for the "multipurpose venue," until my phone rang again a few minutes later.

"Are you going to get that?"

I pulled my phone from my front pocket and flipped Kam the bird as I looked at the screen.

"It's an unknown caller."

"They had to have called you twice in two minutes to have gotten past your 'Do Not Disturb' setting," Kameron pointed out. "You should probably answer it to be on the safe side."

I grimaced, but given the greater context of the situation, I decided answering it probably was my best bet.

"Hello?"

"Hi, is this Sergeant Connor Harvey?"

I froze.

"Yes, it is," I said cautiously. "Who is this?"

"This is Amelia Pollock from your credit union," the woman said, far too cheery for someone who worked in the finance industry. "I must say, you're a hard man to get a hold of, Mr. Harvey. We've been trying to get in touch with you for some time."

My fingers tightened around the phone. I had an inkling of why someone from my bank would call me, and I wasn't keen on talking about it in front of an audience. I glanced to where Kameron was measuring the inner width of the barn door, and I stepped back outside for whatever sliver of privacy that would grant me.

"Apologies," I forced out. "I just transitioned, and—"

"Yes, I can see that in your file," Amelia chirped.

"Right," I said, already over this conversation. At boot camp, you got two options for bank accounts, one being some small credit union in southern California that didn't have an on-base presence at Pendleton, and the other being this institution. Not exactly a wealth of options.

"I'm calling because you've had a rather large balance sitting in your checking account for several weeks—well, actually months," Amelia said, and I could practically see her eyes bulging out at the amount. I bit the inside of my cheek. "We wanted to discuss your investment options if that's something you're interested in."

"Not really," I replied, trying to calm my racing heart while also not flipping out at this poor woman who was just trying to do her job. "I'm still . . . considering what to do with the funds."

It wasn't necessarily a lie, but it certainly stretched the truth. Uncle Ellis had passed away just a few short weeks before I was set to leave the military. And because the Marine Corps still had their meaty claws in my life, it hadn't been hard for the Veterans Affairs office to find me and walk me through the process of signing all the legal paper-work to assume his benefits.

Because in an eternal "screw you" from life, my worthless uncle—for reasons I would never understand—had named me as the sole beneficiary for all his veterans' benefits.

The six-figure deposit came less than two weeks after I had begrudgingly signed the paperwork, and I hadn't touched it. I didn't want my uncle's blood money. I didn't want a reminder that man had ever been part of my life.

And I really, *really* did not want reminders of my child-hood or my life before I joined the military.

"We could help you sort through your options," Amelia continued. "What time this week works best for a phone call with our wealth management banker?"

I had to give it to the girl. She'd really taken that annual sales training to heart. I smiled despite myself.

"This week isn't a great time," I said. "I'll give the branch a call when I have the time. Thanks for calling."

I quickly hung up the phone. That was polite enough, right? It would have to be enough.

"What was that about?" Kameron asked, balancing rather precariously on the top of a ladder that looked like it had seen better days.

"Just my bank calling," I said, shrugging. Kameron gave me an odd look I couldn't decipher. Kameron knew my history before the Marine Corps was difficult, but even as close as we were, I couldn't quite get myself to talk about it.

The only person who'd heard the full story was Anna, my therapist. We'd slowly been working toward sharing more about my childhood, and while it was the hardest thing I'd ever done, I felt lighter after every session. It was extremely painful to revisit those memories, but in a way, letting go of that burden was making it easier for me to make progress, even if that progress was slow.

Kameron shrugged and returned to taking pictures of the scaffolding. My thoughts were scattered. I inhaled deeply, crossing my arms over my chest as an idea suddenly struck me. Amelia had been right about one thing: that money had been sitting in my checking account for far too long. At this rate, it was probably more of a fraud risk than anything.

After talking to Anna, I realized I wanted the money to be used for a good cause to counteract the negative emotions my inheritance brought up for me.

Kameron climbed down the ladder, pencil between his teeth, and he gestured for me to follow him back to the main house. I watched him exit the barn, and I took one more look around the space. The structure was still falling apart, but for a second, I saw this place for what it could be: a beautiful space that brought people together and helped Kameron expand his program's outreach.

"Hey Kam," I called, a sense of rightness settling over my body as the idea fully took root. There was a way for me to do something good with the money I didn't want or need. I was standing in it.

"Are you looking for investors for Winding Road?"

Chapter 3

Abbie

"**T**hank you, have a good one!" I called out, while I stuffed cash into the till. Kelly and Joe Sakis waved goodbye as they left, the door's bell jingling to mark their absence. They were some of my best customers these days, often placing special orders for seeds they didn't have stored up on their homestead. Every once in a while, Kelly got an exciting, all-consuming idea for a new addition to their tiny farm, and Joe would fork over some serious cash to procure the wiring, wood, nails, power tools, and safety mechanisms necessary to make her dreams come true.

Even then, it had been months since Kelly had a new idea, and with that, it had been months since anyone in town had needed to place a special order.

I looked to the stocked aisles and sighed heavily. The store had been in hot water long before I took over as the acting manager, but with each passing day of minimal customers and even more minimal income, the future looked bleak. I tried my hardest in recent months to focus more on stocking non-perishable, non-food items that had longer shelf lives, but that inventory didn't move as fast as the food. Being the only true grocer in town outside of individual farms made Watford General a central location for people to come to for things like milk, eggs, and seasonal vegetables, as well as the occasional fruit and fresh cuts of meat during the right season. The two commercial refrigerators lining the back wall of the store had been the best investments I could have made for the store.

I finished counting the cash and wiped my forehead with the back of my arm. I had a sinking feeling that the window unit air conditioner—the only source of airflow in the entire store—was on its last legs. Not only would it make me miserable, but it would also put undue stress on the refrigerators and freezers. If they went out on me . . . I couldn't let myself go there.

When he was sober, my father had told me to never borrow tomorrow's problems. I let out a sarcastic snort as I picked up my inventory clipboard to update the spreadsheet later on tonight. Just as I rounded the corner of the main counter, the phone rang. The sound jolted me from my thoughts; my pulse quickened as the all-too-familiar anxiety about who was on the other end of the line crept back in.

I picked up the receiver where it hung against the pillar, taking a deep breath and exhaling slowly and quietly.

"Watford General, how can I help you?"

"Hello, is this Abbigail Collins?"

I inhaled sharply. Now that was a voice I hadn't expected to hear.

"This is her," I said, feigning nonchalance. Watford General wasn't the only thing in hot water. My own financial future was at stake. I'd poured every cent of my personal savings into trying to keep the store and my father afloat. "I have to say, Councilman Kaser, I wasn't expecting to hear from you."

"So formal," the man said, giving a polite chuckle. "We've known each other practically our entire lives, Abbie. We can have a laid-back conversation."

I rolled my eyes. "As you wish, *Trent*. How can I help you?"

"I'll cut right to the chase here, Abbie, as I know your time is valuable and so is mine, of course."

I would never understand how the baby-faced kid, who was several grades older than us, turned into this arrogant douchebag, but I kept my mouth shut.

"The Watford town council has been brainstorming ways to drum up the local economy. As I'm sure you're aware, it's been a rough few years for economic development, and as your local government officials, we want to do something about it."

I couldn't stop the scoff that escaped my lips. "With all due respect, it's been several years since the pandemic knocked everything off-kilter around here. Why has the council decided now is the time to revamp things?"

Trent paused, either taken aback by my bold response or considering the right answer to my question. "That's a valid question. I'm sure many other small business owners share a similar sentiment. For transparency's sake, Watford has received a rather large grant from the state of Washington, specifically for bolstering rural economies and promoting local small businesses. For the last several weeks, the council has been deliberating on the best way to use these funds. I believe we've come up with the perfect idea."

"I'm listening," I said, biting my bottom lip to keep the frustration from my voice. I really did not have time for this.

"Do you remember Founder's Day?"

The doorbell above the main entrance jingled, and one red-faced, sweaty Kevin Phillips appeared, mouthing *sorry, sorry* as he threw his backpack over the checkout counter and grabbed his apron. I threw my hands up in a *what the hell, Kevin?* gesture, but he paid me no mind, grabbing the inventory clipboard and the box cutter and getting to work. Hire local teenagers, the small business blogs had told me. Invest in your local workforce. But at what cost to my sanity? I'd thought hiring Imogen's brother was a safe bet, but Kevin was still a teenager through and through.

My brow furrowed, and I rubbed my temple, trying to focus on the conversation at hand.

"Of course, I remember Founder's Day. I've lived here my whole life. It's been several years since they held that celebration."

"It's been ten years, to be precise," Trent said cheerily, and my heart sank.

"A lot can change in ten years," I choked out.

"Indeed," Trent replied, "and much has changed with our town. That's why we want to bring back Founder's Day this October. It will actually be the fifty-fifth anniversary of Founder's Day, so the timing is ideal. And we all know how beautiful Watford is in the fall."

My jaw hit the floor.

"October?" I sputtered. "You want to put on a massive festival in October? That's less than three months away."

Trent laughed on the other end of the line while I stood there gaping like a fish out of water. Either he'd said something funny, and I missed the joke, or my shock was the joke.

"It's a short timeline, yes, but we had to wait for the Washington State Treasury Department to confirm that they had dispersed the grant funds. This is our 'building back' year for the festival, so it doesn't have to be large, but we want it to be impactful. We want to draw attention to all the lovely small businesses in Watford and the campsite Noah Wilkinson has just remodeled and expanded."

A dull ache formed in my temples.

"Why not just cut checks to all the local businesses in Watford that the pandemic and subsequent economic downturn has affected? Why funnel all that money into one event?"

"Because that wouldn't be as glamorous, Ms. Collins."

Now it was my turn to laugh. Trent Kaser may have been born and raised in Watford, but he certainly wasn't a local. He'd gone off to college and law school right after, and he had barely set foot in Watford proper, despite being an elected member of the town council. There was some weird loophole about owning property in the jurisdiction but not having to live there, written long ago by people exactly like Trent.

"Why are you telling me about this directly, Trent?"

"Because we want you to be the organizer," Trent said.

If my jaw could drop even lower, it did.

"I run a store. By myself," I added. "The only general store in town. Why on earth would you think I have time for this?"

"For one, you're the one business owner that stands to gain the most from such a robust endeavor. Think of all the supplies that will need to be ordered in order to accommodate special requests, vendor booths, and everything else that comes with putting on a festival. All those orders, funneled through Watford General."

I couldn't deny that we needed the business. Even though only Imogen knew about the IRS breathing down my neck, I had no intention of making that public knowledge. Nor was I interested in losing the store—and my family's legacy—entirely.

"Which parts of this festival would I be organizing?"

I can only imagine Trent's grin at my request for more information.

"We'll provide you with the financial resources and some basic guidelines for activities and events we'd like to see at the festival, but mostly, you'd have creative freedom over how those things get done."

In other words, I was expected to do all of this on my own. "Creative freedom" was a bureaucratic cop-out when it came to actually helping instead of talking.

I pinched the bridge of my nose.

"And you seriously want to put on the festival in October?"

"Yep," Trent answered, far too cheerily.

"I want to be paid for my efforts," I said. "I'm not working for free. I love Watford, and I'll do everything in my power to see it thrive, but this is a lot on my plate."

I held my breath for a moment before releasing it. My old therapist would be proud of me for asking for what I need.

"Of course!" Trent chirped. "We wouldn't dream of asking you to work for free."

A shuffle of papers and murmured voices in the background told me they would indeed dream of asking me to work for free.

"We will pay you a baseline salary of ten thousand dollars for your planning work, and you can expense anything related to the festival, including hiring employees at Watford General to fill in the gaps."

I blinked slowly. "You're going to pay me ten grand for three months' worth of work?"

For some people, ten thousand dollars was a drop in the bucket. But for me, and the lake of debt that I'd accrued in the last few years keeping Watford General alive, that ten thousand dollars would allow me to get back on my feet.

"As I mentioned earlier, we've been approved for a rather sizable revitalization grant. We also had a sponsor for the festival come forward. He's the owner of an up-and-coming local farm, and he wants to be the front-running sponsor for the festival to get his name out there. What better way to invest in our local economy than to hire one of our own to help us put on an amazing event?"

If it sounds too good to be true, it probably is.

"We'll send the contract your way. Take as long as you need to review it," Trent said. "I'll be your liaison for the council. If you need anything, I'm your guy."

"When do you need my decision?"

"By close of business Friday," Trent said. I glanced at the calendar pinned to aisle three. Friday was four days away.

That was plenty of time for me to mull things over if I needed to.

"I'll call you," I said, and after a few closing niceties, I ended the phone call.

Kevin immediately popped out from aisle one, apron tied haphazardly around his waist. His hair was disheveled and greasy. I didn't want to consider the reasons for his appearance. I shook my head and pulled my tablet from my bag.

Teenagers, man.

"Sorry I was late to work again," Kevin said quickly, stopping a few feet from the checkout counter. "I was—"

"Romancing Kyrie and lost track of time?" I said, not looking up from the tablet, where I was already outlining ideas about the festival.

Kevin spluttered, and I could practically feel how red his face was getting. I smiled, finally looking up at him.

"It's fine, Kevin," I assured him, and the boy's shoulders visibly relaxed. "I was eighteen once too, you know. Constantly skipping out on work to hang out with my boyfriend."

I didn't know why I said it. Not only had I surprised Kev by sharing something so personal about myself, but I'd surprised myself by acknowledging that part of my life. I'd worked so hard to compartmentalize my memories of him in recent years. Thinking back on the good times, even briefly, actually brought me a sense of comfort, instead of dread.

"So, since you're the best boss ever, does that mean I can skip my shift on Friday so I can take Kyrie dancing?"

I shot him a look, and at least he had the wherewithal to scram and get back to work.

I laughed as I glanced down at my phone. There was a text from Imogen asking how my day was going. She was the person who always remembered to check in on people, even when those people weren't always the greatest at responding in a timely fashion.

I messaged her back and said that yes; I was having a good day. A surprisingly okay one.

And for the first time in what felt like months, I meant that.

Within the hour, I had an email from Trent with the contract. The salary money alone would wipe out most of Watford General's debt—possibly even some of my own. I also couldn't shake the idea that this would do good things for Watford. I didn't want to make this decision simply based on my business's needs.

There were so many small businesses in Watford that had suffered in recent years. The effects of the pandemic had hit the homesteads and farms first, but when they went under, so did places like the Roadhouse and Watley's Diner. Many of the businesses on Main Street had stayed afloat, but many local farms didn't survive.

This festival was an opportunity to put ourselves back on the map. Physically, yes, but also mentally. People would start thinking of Watford as a tourist destination worth visiting. As much as I hated to admit Trent was right, he was correct about one thing: Watford needed this festival. We needed this opportunity.

I busied myself with store maintenance, updating spreadsheets, and checking my business bank account—lots of minuses for expenses, and one measly deposit representing last week's sales—before I allowed myself to pull out my tablet and electronically sign the contract.

I had nothing left to lose.

Trent,

Thank you for the opportunity. I'm excited to partner together on the Watford Founder's Festival. Let me know when you have time this week to further discuss the council's vision for this event.

Sincerely,

Abbie Collins

Owner of Watford General Store

Chapter 4
Connor

Kameron buzzed with excitement beside me as we stood at the entrance to Winding Road. We waited on a shipment of equipment, tools, and supplies necessary to begin work on the venue.

"You really didn't have to do any of this," Kameron said, rocking back and forth on his feet. "Just having you here and willing to help is more than enough."

For what felt like the millionth time, I gave him a small smile.

"You've done more for me than I can ever repay you for, Kam. Investing in your mission is the best way I can think of to say thank you. You'll be able to reach so many more people who need this program and need this place."

I gestured behind us, to the sprawling farm fields, the cows and horses grazing in the pastures beyond. Behind the last field was the faint horizon line, dotted with the Washington mountains and a dense forest full of possibilities. If heaven on Earth was a place, I was pretty damn convinced it'd be here, at Winding Road.

This is why I'd had no issue calling Amelia back the next day, asking her to help me set up a wire transfer straight to Winding Road's bank account. She understandably felt disappointed that I didn't need to sit down with her wealth management banker, but she also felt relieved to see that I no longer had six figures sitting in my checking account. She'd joked that I was practically begging for someone to hack my online banking and rob me blind. The minute I got the notification that the money had left my account and gone into Kameron's, I felt like the weight of the world had lifted from my shoulders.

I swore Kameron's cheeks flushed pink under the calm morning sun.

"Your investment is going toward expanding operations on the for-profit side of things so that I can expand the nonprofit recovery program. Every penny."

"And my paycheck," I shot back.

Kameron laughed, clutching his torso as he shook. "Good point, Harvey. That too."

It always took me by surprise how much better I felt when I let go of things associated with my uncle. Anna and I had talked at length in the last few weeks about how I kept holding onto things out of a misplaced sense of guilt. My childhood had mostly sucked. But I wasn't that kid anymore. I hadn't been for a long time.

It was okay for me to let go of the things that didn't belong in the new life I was creating for myself.

I turned my head at the sound of panting and footprints coming from the road behind us. Lucas Morales came running up, jogging in place as he stood beside me. Lucas glanced down at his watch, giving me a thumbs up and a grin.

"I still run a five-minute mile," Lucas panted. His shoes kicked up dust from where he was still running in place. *Insufferable bastard.*

I rolled my eyes.

"We can't all have a perfect PFT score, Morales."

"My therapist says it's good for me to have an outlet," Lucas replied.

"Every active duty Marine uses fitness as an outlet."

Lucas's mouth dropped open.

"That's *not* true. And frankly, offensive. Take it back."

My grumpy facade cracked, and I smiled. "No."

"All right, gents, there's the first truck," Kameron said, practically beside himself with glee as the first dump truck turned onto the gravel road. "I'll stay here to direct traffic. Harvey, you'll stand about 300 yards behind me here. Since the road is still unmarked, I don't want anyone getting lost on the way to the barn and accidentally running over a chicken."

I grimaced.

"That's morbid."

"Morales," Kameron continued, ignoring me, "can you jog the half mile back to the barn and point out the loading zone? I also don't want these guys dumping landscaping rocks in the paddock."

Lucas looked delighted at the idea of running back. He was probably the only person who would feel positively thrilled at being told he needed to run back to the place he'd just come from. We all had our vices and crutches we used to deal with the things we'd been through in our lives, but Lucas seems to have taken that to another level.

At some point, we needed to talk to him about finding an outlet other than fitness, but Lucas was only three months out of the service. He barely had his civilian legs about him. The man could keep running.

"Aye aye, cap'n," Morales said, and with a mock salute, he was off, jamming his earphones back into his ears and fist-pumping as he ran down the driveway toward the main house.

I couldn't help but admire the dedication. It had been a long time since I'd been half as dedicated to anything as Lucas was to staying in shape. I was still lifting, but running was a different story. A man had his limits.

I did as Kameron had instructed, walking the 300 yards back down the gravel road. I flagged the dump truck drivers to continue down the road, all of whom gave me a small wave of thanks. There were only three trucks of supplies in this run—namely, gravel and landscaping rocks. Kameron was already in contact with some local lumber farmers and millers to locate locally sourced supplies for the rebuilding, but they wouldn't have those supplies to us for at least a few weeks.

Kameron had spruced up the back area of the barn, including the gazebo, which was barely standing. The massive project of renovating the barn intimidated Kam, but repairing and landscaping the outside of the venue seemed like a logical first step.

Lucas helped the trucks dump their loads in the designated areas, and once they'd made their way back down the gravel road and out of Winding Road Farms, I started back toward the farmhouse.

The farmhouse was the hub of Winding Road. Not only did it boast four bedrooms—what Lucas had taken to fondly calling the "barracks"—and three full bathrooms (a luxury the Marine Corps would have never granted us), but the dining and living rooms had become communal working spaces. We were all invested in Kameron's vision, and as much as the three of us liked to joke around with each other, we could be serious when we needed to be. Kameron's work was saving lives. Hell, it had saved ours. And knowing the full story behind why Kameron had begun this work made me even more proud to be part of it.

I put on a pot of coffee for all of us to have a late-morning pick-me-up. I kicked my alcoholic tendencies with the help of Winding Road, but caffeine was the one addiction I knew would follow me until the end of my days. Four years in the military—most of which were spent actively trying to avoid dealing with any of my issues—lent itself to a caffeine addiction of the highest order.

I'd kick the habit one day. Probably.

Kameron burst through the front door with Lucas hot on his heels.

"I made coffee," I said, nodding my head toward the kitchen as I took a seat at the dining room table, which was currently covered in paperwork. We had an unofficial tradition of a morning meeting every day, so we would all be on the same page about what needed to be done.

"Thanks, but no thanks. Can't mess with my gains," Lucas said as he finished chugging his water bottle. I blinked at him.

"If caffeine messed with gym gains, the American military would be in serious trouble."

Lucas waved me off, and I shrugged. Lucas and I weren't close, not in the way Kameron and I had become. We butted heads more often than not. Kam joked it was because our personalities were too similar, but I disagreed.

I knew that people who didn't know me thought I was a grumpy millennial trapped in a young adult's body. Growing up the way I had didn't make me particularly keen on getting to know people or letting them get close to me. That Kameron knew me as well as he did had more to do with his persistence than my willingness to open up.

I barely knew anything about Lucas other than that he loved the gym and his transition out of the military had been abrupt. I had the feeling Lucas kept his true personality hidden behind jokes and deflections, and dealing with that kind of personality kept me on edge.

Kameron hadn't planned on taking in any more strays outside of a professional capacity with Winding Road. But Kameron also wasn't the guy to say no when one of his Marines called him and said he was in trouble. Lucas had never elaborated in front of me on what exactly that trouble was, and I knew better than to ask Kameron. He carried my secrets; it was only right for me to respect that he did the same for others.

So, we cleared the third bedroom, which we had used as our gym, moved the equipment into one of the farmhouse outbuildings, and welcomed Lucas into our ragtag family.

"You're going to want to sit down for this," Kameron said, pressing his tongue into his cheek to hold back a smile.

"We're sitting," I replied, smirking behind my coffee mug as Lucas sat across from me, a white Gatorade in his hand. What kind of person willingly drank *white* Gatorade when there were at least four other color options? A psychopath, I quickly decided.

"What's up?"

"We're going to sponsor a local festival," Kameron said, a broad smile brazen across his face as he looked to both of us for our reactions.

I returned the smile. Kameron's excitement about his work, and Winding Road's mission, was infectious. One couldn't help being drawn into his energy.

"That sounds epic," I said honestly. "Where's the festival being held?"

Kameron's smile faltered for the briefest of moments, and my eyebrows raised. It wasn't like Kameron to be unsure of something he was this excited about. His excitement meant he was confident enough in whatever the thing was to even get excited about it.

"The festival is being put on by a neighboring county, and they're looking for local businesses to be sponsors. Because we've had a recent influx of income, we were able to secure the top sponsorship spot. We'll have a table at the vendor fair and the opportunity to partner with other small businesses in the host town. It's the ideal way to put Winding Road on the map for people who don't already know we're here," Kameron gushed. "It's a big undertaking, and I know it's not the best timing with the barn renovations, but I really think this could be a game changer for us. The organizers seemed confident that it'll draw an enormous crowd, considering the tourism wave that happens around here in the fall months."

"It's a brilliant idea, Kam," Lucas said, and his earnest tone surprised me. I didn't think Lucas was an airhead, but he was often flippant in a way that got under my skin. And yet, every once in a while, his ability to peel back those ditzy outer layers impressed me.

"So, when's the festival happening?" I asked.

Kam shifted in his seat. My eyes tracked the movement as unease slithered up my spine.

"Mid-October. I've got a contact in town."

The vague answer, coupled with Kam's awkward movements, set me even further on edge.

"Which town, Kam?" I asked.

Kam blew out a breath and gave me a weak smile. My chest tightened painfully. Laketon County was fairly rural, and there was only one neighboring county that had a small town large enough to host a festival like this.

"Before you freak out, I didn't know it was going to be held there when I said yes to the sponsorship opportunity, and we're already locked into a contract."

My hands shook. There were only a handful of places within two hours of us big enough to host something like this. My mind ran through all of them in rapid succession. Laketon was far too small. Westport was far too rural. And the last I'd heard about North Crest, the place was practically a ghost town. The pandemic and severe restrictions that impacted tours a few years back had done them in.

Which meant there was one town on this side of the county left to consider.

"What's the name?" I asked, grinding my teeth together, hard, as if that would somehow stop this from happening.

"Watford," Kameron said, looking me in the eye. "The festival will be in Watford."

I closed my eyes, grappling in the dark for the regulation tactics I'd walked through a thousand times.

"I wouldn't have said yes if I'd known," Kameron said. I met his eyes through my hazy vision. I hadn't registered that he was reaching out for me, but the touch was grounding.

"It's fine," I said, shaking my head. Kam grimaced. "It *will* be fine," I quickly amended. "It's just been a long time since I've been back."

Over five years.

"Of course," Kameron said earnestly, taking a long sip from his mug. "Whatever you need."

I nodded, and the conversation moved on from the festival sponsorship to other administrative tasks. Kameron gave us an update on the lumber sourcing, and Lucas gave his morning update on the livestock. I'd visited the far fields to investigate the corn and wheat growing there.

"The crops are doing all right, as far as I can tell," I said with a shrug. "Since it's the first year trying to grow anything out there, it'll be a few weeks before we can estimate how much our potential yield will be."

Kameron scribbled something on his notepad as he nodded.

"Sounds good. Lucas, would you be willing to take on communicating with the organizer? Her name is Abbie

Collins. I'll send you her contact info. We'll also be working with—"

The floor dropped out from under me as I stumbled, whirling around to face Kameron.

"What did you just say?"

Blood roared in my ears; Kameron's response was barely audible as my heart lodged up in my throat.

"Abbie Collins is our contact in Watford?" Kameron repeated, tone inquisitive. "She's planning the festival."

My mouth went dry at the sound of her name. I hadn't dared to say it aloud in the five years since I'd left Watford. Saying her name made it real. Saying her name was a painful reminder of what I'd done to her. Of how I'd thrown away my one chance at true happiness.

You left her.

It was the one sin I could never atone for, and at the mention of her name, it was suddenly the only thing I could think about.

"Wait," Lucas said, looking from Kameron's confused expression to my pale face. He let out a disbelieving laugh. "Don't tell me she's your ex or something."

"Don't," I warned, my tone sharper than I intended. "Don't say another word."

Lucas frowned but pressed his lips together in a fine line.

Kameron no longer looked confused. Instead, the guilt of this decision etched deep lines into Kameron's face, and I hated it. He opened his mouth to speak, but after taking another deep look at me, he closed it once more.

I hated that I was making my best friend, the man who had saved my life in every meaning of the word, feel guilty for making the best decision for himself and his business. I was the problem in this situation. Me and my trauma, me and my stupidly complicated feelings about Watford and *her*—

I was the one who needed to get my shit together, so I didn't ruin this incredible opportunity for Kameron.

"I just need some time," I forced out, my voice rough. I swallowed back the lump that had lodged itself in my throat. "I—I'm going to take a walk. Please don't call."

Kameron nodded slowly. Lucas was still frowning, the gears turning in his head as he fought to put the pieces together.

I would tell them. I had to, especially now that we would work with her in the coming weeks. I would have to tell them about my history with her. Maybe my entire life story. All the raw, ugly, disgusting pieces I preferred to keep to myself and in my conversations with Anna.

I stepped outside, letting the screen door slam behind me. I barely heard the loud smack as I set off down the dirt path that would take me away from the farmhouse and toward the back pasture, where the horses were grazing.

As I ventured farther down the path, the familiar scent of hay and fresh grass filled the air. The wind rustling through the trees provided a white noise background to my thoughts. The vibrant green of the surrounding meadows contrasted beautifully against the clear blue sky above. With every step, the distant figures of the horses grazing in the back pasture became clearer.

As I approached the pasture gate, some of the lingering tension eased. The horses, sensing my presence, raised their heads and turned toward me, their curious eyes meeting mine.

Carefully unlatching the gate, I stepped into the pasture, surrounded by the comforting presence of these magnificent creatures. The soft grass beneath my feet provided a cushioned pathway as I made my way toward them. I reached out my hand, feeling the warmth of one's velvety nose against my skin.

I was tunneling down into the darkness, barely cognizant of where I was walking.

I'd gotten damn good at managing my triggers. I rarely felt the urge to drink, or punch walls, or do any of the many of the unhealthy coping mechanisms I used to have. I wasn't a sunshiny person, but I'd learned how to control my temper.

But Abbie . . . Abbie was my biggest trigger. The only part of my past that I hadn't reconciled.

Because what I'd done to her—to *us* and the future we would have had together—was unforgivable.

Chapter 5
Abbie

There was something about balancing the till that calmed me.

Imogen said it was my one truly obsessive trait—I was the chick that wanted all the bills facing the same way in the drawer, neatly organized.

I also gave out the nasty bills as change before digging into the small collection of crisp new bills I'd collected over my years.

It was rare that I needed to make any cash deposits these days, but on this day, my drawer was a whole twenty dollars over my baseline. I was grateful that the Roadhouse had installed an ATM, which meant I didn't have to keep excess cash on hand until I had time to drive all the way to Laketon to deposit it at the credit union.

The sharp crash of a bottle splintering against the outside of the store broke me out of my reverie.

"Fuck's sake," I said, shoving the cash and coins into the lock bag and fumbling for the key. *Guess the deposit would have to wait.*

Kevin left over an hour ago, so I was alone in the store. Because I wasn't a completely terrible boss, and he had a date with Kyrie tonight, I'd taken the closing responsibilities on myself. I quickly locked the deposit bag and shoved it into my purse, grabbing my keys.

Another crash of a glass bottle erupted in front of the store. My body flashed hot with rage.

"What the f—"

I opened the door, frantically following the sound, fully expecting to see some rowdy teenagers in town for the weekend having a little too much fun. Instead, my eyes landed on one man, with shaggy black hair, already clutching a fresh bottle in his hand.

My heart sank, and my jaw fell open in utter disbelief.

"Tilly," the man moaned, and my calm facade cracked.

No, not in public. Please, God, no—

"Where's my wife? Have you seen my wife?"

Anything but this, Lord, please—

"Dad," I called, forcing myself to stay out of my head. I rushed over to him.

A small crowd had gathered across the street at the laundromat and past the crossroads near the Roadhouse. Malcolm Collins had been enough of a recluse these last few years that this outburst would no doubt make us the talk of the town. And knowing people were talking about us—more than they already did—was a distraction I didn't need.

"Dad, it's me. Can we please go inside?"

"Tilly?" he whirled towards me, still clutching the half-broken bottle he'd smashed against the brick wall. "Tilly, my love, is that you?"

Breathe, Abbie. Breathe.

"No, Dad, it's me. It's Abbie."

"Son of a bitch," he roared, chucking the broken bottle at my head. I ducked, so the bottle missed hitting me square in the forehead, but it still nicked my cheek. I barely felt the sting, my mouth open in horror and embarrassment as the world around me slowed.

The other shoe always dropped. I knew that, and I'd still let myself get wrapped up in the way things were finally turning around. With the new job opportunity, I'd allowed myself grand visions of fixing everything that was wrong with Watford General, and my life.

"Dad, please," I whispered, throwing my hands up in a peaceful gesture, trying my hardest to placate him without drawing further attention from whoever might be watching. "Let's just go inside, okay? You need to sleep this off."

"Where is she?" my father roared once more, this time turning away from me and gesturing to the gathering crowd across the street. "You're all just going to stand there? Start looking! Where's my wife? Where's my wife?"

His voice broke on the last syllable, and he paced on the sidewalk, spiraling down into his panic and distress. My mind went fuzzy around the edges, and I found myself unable to think of my next move.

What do I do, Mom? What should I do?

I didn't think of her often. I couldn't think of her without getting swept up in the many emotions her death brought up for me.

A shout rose above my father's tirade.

"Abbie!"

"John," I whispered, and my knees nearly gave out with relief. Officer John Ludgate, one of the two deputies who lived in Watford, barreled toward us through the crowd gathered outside the Roadhouse.

"I'm sorry, Officer Ludgate. Normally, I can settle him. He seems—"

Another yell from my father cut off my words. This time, he directed it at Officer Ludgate's new partner, who also made the sprint from the Roadhouse to Watford General. His partner was a stick-skinny, baby-faced teenager, who looked like he'd never hiked as a kid. My drunk, large, rather imposing father was now pressing him against the brick wall of the store and threatening all manner of violence against him.

"Fuck," I swore as Ludgate leaped toward the wall to pull him off. No mantra or breathing exercise was going to bring me out of this.

"Collins, chill the fuck out," Ludgate said, pulling my father off the other cop and shoving him away from the wall. "Let's not do this here."

My father rattled off a string of profane curses that had me wanting to melt into the sidewalk. There was no coming back from this. The entire town of Watford would soon know that my father wasn't just a social recluse who didn't trust people, but that he had turned into a vile, violent drunkard who held all matters of ill will against his own daughter. Once, these people would have been his friends.

This was exactly why I desperately tried to avoid it.

I could handle the shame on my own, because I could tuck it away inside, along with all the other dark parts of me I didn't like on display. I could handle my father's ugly comments and the way he treated the people closest to him. I could bear the weight of two people's grief. I could take it. I was a master at compartmentalizing.

But having his struggles—and by extension, my own—out in the open like this, had nausea churning in my gut.

"Have you considered putting him somewhere, Ms. Collins?"

Ludgate's partner, who I was now realizing was probably close to my age, turned to face me as Ludgate continued trying to calm my father down, this time with his handcuffs in hand, waiting for his opportunity to cuff him and sit him down on the curb.

"No, no—Tilly! Tilly, where are you? Where'd you go?"

I closed my eyes at the wail that had returned to my father's voice, trying to return to a calm place where I could take my emotions out of this situation.

I'd accepted a long time ago that my father would probably never recover, but that small, girlish part of me still hoped. I'd grown up fast in the time between my high school graduation, my mother's death a week later, and my father's nosedive into his addiction.

I tried to think of a logical and realistic way to explain my father's grief to the officers, somehow making them see he wasn't a bad man. He didn't want to hurt anyone. There was so much anger inside him, at himself and at God, for taking my mother from him.

The alcohol gave his grief teeth and claws, determined to shred through all the good things still left in his life.

All the trauma and guilt he bore was given life inside of a bottle. Inside the bottle, he didn't have to feel. He didn't have to look at me, his only child, and feel the weight of losing his life partner.

My father wasn't an evil man. No matter how bad things got, I couldn't see him in that light. This was my *dad*. The man who came to all of my soccer games, who brought Imogen and me lemonade in the evenings when we spent summer nights scouring the backyard for fireflies. The man who held me against his chest while I cried at my mother's funeral, who let me sleep with her shirt, who didn't always know how to comfort me but still showed up for me.

He wasn't a dangerous man.

"Tonight's just a bad night."

"Seems to have a lot of those, recently," Ludgate said, and I didn't know how to reply. My father sat on the sidewalk, hands cuffed behind his back, still whimpering quietly to himself as he rocked back and forth. The whispers from the crowd gathered across the street seemed incredibly loud in the night's silence.

There was nothing I could say or do to get us out of the situation. The damage had been done.

"Do you need us to take him for the night?"

Officer Ludgate's voice pulled me from my thoughts. I tried to quell my shaking hands by pressing them into the pockets of my hoodie. My father was still moaning, his head forced between his knees, although he still couldn't regain his bearings.

"What?"

My voice sounded distant, dazed.

"Do you want us to take him in for the night? We can book him for drunk and disorderly and property destruction. Even if it is *his* property."

"I . . ."

My head spun. The world around me was slipping through my fingers. For the first time in years, I realized there was no escape hatch. There was nowhere else to run.

"It's okay, Abbie. We've got him. Let him sober up in the office tonight," Ludgate said, squeezing my shoulder. "We'll make sure he's safe."

There were many promises unspoken in Ludgate's words. Malcolm needed to be taken back to the station because he was a danger to the store. To Watford. To *me.*

My mother's words from a lifetime ago rang through my head.

It wasn't supposed to be like this.

A sound that felt embarrassingly like a sob climbed up my throat.

"I'll walk you home," Ludgate's partner said. I finally looked down at his nametape. *Officer Waller.*

"I'm okay," I replied, though the words sounded robotic even to my own ears. How many times had I said that over the years and truly meant it?

"At the very least, let me call someone for you," Waller said. "You don't look well."

"Abbie!"

Imogen's voice rang out loudly in the overcrowded streets. My head snapped up to see her shoving through the crowd, cursing at someone who had their phone out, no doubt recording the popular gossip of Malcolm Collins losing his mind in the middle of the street. I couldn't hear Imogen's words to the man, but her furious eyes revealed her anger.

On my behalf. On *our* behalf. Imogen had always been my protector; it had been her and me against the world for so long. After her divorce, I stepped up to be that person for her. I walked with her through those long months of healing from the mental and physical abuse her husband had inflicted on her.

Now, I was barely conscious, drifting in a terrifying cloud of grief, rage, and unending pain. Imogen had tried her hardest to pull me out of it, and in some ways, she had. But from the way her eyes locked with mine, I could tell she knew the truth. All the downplaying I'd done in recent months couldn't stop this from happening.

I wanted to call him. I always did, especially on the bad nights.

I wanted to talk to someone who knew me better than I knew myself. Hell, I didn't even want to talk. I wanted to be held, to feel him rub my back, to wake up to sheets that smelled like him and find a note that said, *ran out for eggs, be back soon, love you.*

I needed to be with someone who knew me better than I knew myself. And my heart splintered anew when I remembered I didn't have someone like that. Not anymore.

"Let's go home, yeah?"

Imogen didn't wait for a response to her question before she slung her arm around my shoulder, tilting me away from the small crowd. The spectators hesitated, torn between leaving or continuing their gossip at the Roadhouse, perhaps waiting a few more minutes to see if something even crazier occurred.

I looked over my free shoulder to see my father shove his face into John's chest, sobbing against the older man. John wrapped his arms around my father, gesturing to Officer Waller to disperse the crowd while he helped my stumbling father down the street to their forgotten police vehicle.

"It's for the best," Imogen whispered, squeezing my shoulders tightly. "He'll sleep this off and you will, too. I'll stay with you tonight."

Imogen walked me down Main Street, past the Roadhouse and its shining neon lights, past the old bank and post office, all the way toward the two-story Watford Lofts building that had become my sanctuary. Imogen fished my apartment key from my purse and gently guided me toward the bedroom.

She pulled a sweatshirt and jogging pants from my drawer, leaving me to change while she brewed us both a cup of hot tea.

"Thank you," I croaked. "I-I don't deserve you."

Imogen gave me a soft, sad smile. "Alcoholic fathers are a special breed. They take and take and take. Only they never get better, no matter how much they siphon from the surrounding people, and you somehow wind up being his caregiver. You are not your father, Abs. His actions don't define your life, nor who you are."

"I miss him, Im," I whispered, squeezing my eyes shut against the hot well of tears that threatened to spill over. Based on the small sigh that slipped from her lips, she knew I wasn't talking about my father.

Imogen sat beside me on the bed, taking my now-empty teacup from my hands.

"You probably always will, Abbie, especially on the bad nights. But Connor left Watford. He left *you*."

Pain wrapped like a vise around my chest, threatening to squeeze the air from my lungs. I avoided saying his name aloud, because even after four years, it felt like a fresh wound opened whenever I did.

He left you.

Imogen's words sobered me, dragged me back from the dark place I'd been right after Connor had left Watford, when I'd searched hell and high water trying to find him. He hadn't left a trace—he was just *gone*.

"First loves are never easy to let go of," Imogen said quietly, and I swallowed tightly. "But you will find peace, eventually. Promise."

I knew she spoke the truth. Imogen, of all people, would know that time heals all wounds. I'd repeated those words to her over and over upon her return from Camp Pendleton.

I heard Imogen place the cups in the sink and turn off the lights in my apartment, coming by to press a quick kiss to my forehead.

"Get some sleep, Abs. I'll be in the living room if you need me. See you in the morning."

I lied awake, staring at the ceiling, listening to the distant thunder roll over the mountain hills, only closing my eyes to sink into the memory of quiet mountain nights spent with Connor in the back of his truck, where we traded love confessions and dreams, and swore to always hold on to each other.

He left you.

He left you.

He left you.

Chapter 6

Connor

A few days after Kameron broke the news that we'd be sponsoring the Founder's Festival, we decided it would be best if we went to Watford in person. Kameron wanted to scope out the physical specs of the festival space so we could start designing signage and pamphlets to promote the festival. We also wanted to create graphics we could share on social media, to encourage people to book their cabins early, if they wanted to stay at the new campsite. Lucas wanted to create the festival playlist of all things, as well as scope out the "vibes" of the place. His words, not mine.

I asked my therapist if we could meet earlier in the week compared to our usual time on Fridays, and the appointment with Anna had been interesting, to say the least.

"So, how are you feeling about the festival?" she'd asked me on our Zoom call, adjusting her notebook in her lap and giving me her full attention.

"It's complicated."

"I can imagine. What feelings should we discuss first?"

I shrugged. My therapist knew me far too well. Anna knew how to phrase questions in a way that helped me move forward, rather than keeping everything inside.

"I guess I'm feeling anxious."

She nodded, waiting for me to continue. I took a deep breath, rubbing my sweaty palms against my jeans.

"When I left Watford, I swore I would never go back. The minute I saw that place in my rearview mirror, I vowed to myself that those chapters of my life were closed."

"Because of your uncle?"

My chest tightened. "Yeah."

"Just your uncle?"

I paused. I hadn't brought up Abbie in therapy yet. I'd been so focused on working through my childhood that I hadn't caught up to my teenage years.

"And because when I left Watford, I also left behind someone I really cared for."

"Watford brings up memories of this person for you."

I let out a small laugh, running a still sweaty hand through my blond hair, shaking my head. I crossed my arms over my chest reflexively.

"That person is still there, apparently. She's actually the festival organizer."

Anna hummed, leaning back in her chair. "So, presumably, you'll have to interact with this person a lot in the coming weeks."

"I'd like to avoid that as much as possible."

Liar.

Despite everything, I wanted to be close to her. I simply hadn't allowed myself that kind of daydreaming in recent years, because there was no way in hell she would ever look at me with those kind blue eyes ever again—not after everything I'd put her through.

"Something tells me that might not be the full truth," Anna said with a small smile.

I shrugged and pressed my arms tighter against my chest.

"I can't get involved with this festival on an emotional level. I finally feel like I'm headed in a good direction. I've got a good job doing work that matters. Kameron and Lucas are counting on me. Getting this close to Watford, and to Abbie . . ." I swallowed hard, avoiding eye contact with the webcam as I looked toward the ceiling.

"It's threatening to unravel so much of the work I've done," I said. "It feels like a cruel, cosmic joke that I finally put my uncle's money to good use—the money I didn't even want in the first place—and instead of keeping me away from Watford, it's dragging me back there."

Anna considered this for a moment. "Do you think it's possible to view this from a different perspective?"

I gave her a wary glance, finally meeting her eyes.

"In what way?"

"How would it feel to view this from the perspective of gaining closure, and making amends, rather than something that's being forced upon you?"

"I left the girl I loved because I couldn't face my crap," I muttered. "There is no atoning for that. She's spent the last five years wondering what the hell happened."

"Did she tell you that?"

"What?" I asked, rubbing my temples. I knew today's session was going to be grueling, but I didn't expect it to hit me this hard.

"You seem confident about her feelings," Anna said. "Did she tell you she felt that way, or are you assuming it?"

I paused. She had me there.

"I used to know her better than I knew myself. If she'd left me in the same manner, I . . . I don't know that I'd be here today. How screwed up is that?"

Anna shrugged her shoulders, her kind eyes meeting mine. "It's not screwed up. It's life. You were eighteen when you left Watford?"

I nodded my head.

"Despite what most eighteen-year-olds like to think, eighteen is still young. You were a teenager. Watford was a place where you had to endure horrible things, leaving you with terrible memories and feelings. You signed a contract with the Marine Corps because you wanted to do something good in your life, and for the first time, you had a way to escape your abuser. Your actions are not unreasonable."

"It doesn't make it okay."

"I didn't say it made it okay," Anna said, leaning forward and placing her notebook on the table beside her. "I said it's not unreasonable for your brain to have been so panicked and desperate to get away that you made a decision you now regret as an adult with actual life experience. You have more perspective now, an understanding of why what you did wasn't acceptable."

I considered this for a moment.

"You're saying it's possible for her to forgive me?"

Anna gave me a small smile and shook her head.

"I'm saying it's possible for you to forgive yourself, Connor."

That last statement from Anna had burrowed under my skin. I merely went through the motions the rest of the day, sending a few logistical emails and following up with vendors we had contracts with for the barn renovations. By the end of the morning, I'd been staring at a screen for over four hours straight, and I was itching to get my hands dirty. I closed my laptop and grabbed an apple from the kitchen before climbing the stairs to the "communal chill out" loft space and flopping down on the couch across from Kameron's desk.

"Put me in, coach."

"Hm?" Kameron said, not breaking eye contact with his screen.

"I've been staring at my email inbox all morning. The blue light is melting my eyeballs. I need to do something else with my day," I said.

Kameron swiveled toward me, taking a slurp of what looked to be a green protein smoothie. I grimaced.

"What *is* that?"

"Fruit smoothie."

"Yuck."

Kameron rolled his eyes. "Eventually, you'll have to grow up."

I slung my arm over my face, shielding my eyes.

"But adulthood sucks."

Kameron chuckled and took another loud slurp. "That it does."

"Do you have any farm work that needs tending? I'm itching to get out of this freaking house."

"Sure I do. On one condition."

"What's that?"

"Tell me about Abbie."

All the air seemed to vanish from the room. I removed my arm from my eyes and stared up at the ceiling before meeting Kameron's eyes.

"What do you want to know?"

"Whatever you're willing to tell me. And let's skip the bullshitting. I saw how you reacted when I said her name. It was a combination of terror and relief."

My throat was sandpaper as I opened my mouth to speak.

"Abbie was my girlfriend when I lived in Watford."

How were you supposed to describe your first love? The person who was light incarnate? A person who always stood tall in the face of life's many distractions and downs? Girlfriend was too pallid a word to describe who Abbie was to me. Who she *is* to me, even all these years later. The woman who saw me as more than the sum of my past and my introverted tendencies.

Kameron said nothing, simply fixed his eyes on me and leaned back in his gaming chair. Whatever email he'd been drafting was long forgotten.

"Her family owned the town's general store. We met in our freshman year of high school, when my uncle moved us to Watford. She was the first person to say hi to me on my first day."

I smiled at the memory of Abbie's brown curls bouncing toward me, a genuine smile plastered on her face as she stuck her right hand out in greeting, offering to give me a tour.

"Watford High wasn't a big place, but something about her energy was infectious. She felt . . . safe. On some level, I knew she wouldn't hurt me or poke fun at me. So, I let her walk me through my schedule, introduce me to a few of my teachers, and show me where the cafeteria and bathrooms were. After that, we started hanging out more. It turned out that I excelled in math while she had exceptional talent in English, so we would exchange tutoring sessions in the evenings."

I paused, taking in Kameron's smile. "What?"

"You realize this is something out of a small-town romance book, right? High school sweethearts who tutor each other? Who are opposites on paper, but they just seem to work?"

I shifted uncomfortably in my seat.

"That's how it began. I haven't told you how it ends."

Kameron silently waved a hand for me to continue.

"We would always go to her house, because my Uncle Ellis was abusive, and I didn't want Abbie anywhere near him. Ellis was a social recluse anyway, and really only came into town to buy beer and the occasional bag of groceries, but the fewer opportunities they had to meet, the better. By the end of our freshman year, we were dating. And by the time we'd hit the end of our junior year, we were inseparable. She was . . . She was everything. My world revolved around her."

I took in a shaky breath, adjusting myself on the couch so that I could stare up at the ceiling for the next part of this story.

"At the beginning of our senior year, we were in her kitchen, drinking chai tea and eating freshly baked cookies. It was the beginning of fall, and fall was Abbie's favorite season, so we'd made everything from scratch. When her parents came in and sat opposite us at the dining room table, I thought for sure they were about to have the *what are your intentions with our daughter* talk. Instead, her mother, Tilly, reached across the table for Abbie's hand and told us about her cancer diagnosis. It was late-stage breast cancer. Incurable."

I exhaled shakily, my skin crawling with the memory of Abbie's smile faltering as she fought to comprehend her mother's words.

"The doctors had given her a year, but based on her recent scans, Tilly was certain she had less. Abbie was beside herself. She didn't understand why her mother wasn't planning to fight it. Even after she saw the scans herself, talked with her mom's doctors, and saw the reality of how bad it was with her own eyes, she couldn't accept it.

"Tilly passed in June, the week after we graduated, a few months shy of a year after she'd received her formal diagnosis. I always thought of that as poetic in the most tragic way—that Tilly could hold on long enough to watch her only daughter walk across the stage, make that monumental transition. Her mom's death destroyed Abbie. I assume anyone who was close with their parents would be."

"And how do you play into all of this?"

I sat up then, letting my feet ground me into the floor.

"Abbie and I were pretty serious. We'd been dating for over two years at that point. Toward the end of senior year, I found myself overwhelmed. As much as I tried to be there for Abbie, my mind was elsewhere. My uncle wasn't a great guy. I've never told you why because, frankly, I don't talk about it. He was abusive in every way you can think of."

Kameron's face sank. "God, Connor, I didn't know."

I held up a hand, fighting to calm my racing heart. I don't know what possessed me to share that part with Kameron, and I didn't want to dwell on it.

"I didn't tell you for pity, or because I want you to look at me differently. But going back to Watford is going to be really hard for me, and I want you to know why. So, if I'm extra grumpy, or need more alone time than usual, don't push me."

Kameron nodded. "Of course. Thank you for trusting me with this. I can't imagine how much of a burden that's been to shoulder."

I let out a shaky laugh. "You have no idea."

"I'm really proud of you, Connor. You've accomplished so much since you got out. And I hope that this festival, and the work we're doing at Winding Road, will help you make peace with your past, and with Watford."

"Thank you," I said earnestly, meeting Kameron's soft expression. "I wouldn't have been able to do any of this without you. And I hope you know that I'll do my best work at the festival, regardless of my personal feelings. I know how to compartmentalize."

"You don't have to remind me." Kameron chuckled, taking the last swig of his protein shake. "You always were the best at that, even among a squad of traumatized assholes."

I snorted before I could stop myself. "Thanks, I guess?"

At that moment, Lucas Morales graced us with his presence, making a cacophonous racket as he took the rickety farmhouse stairs two at a time to meet us in the loft.

"Are you running *from* something?"

"He has to be, with the level of obsession he has," Kameron said, wiggling his eyebrows in Lucas's direction.

"My worthless ex-wife, obviously," Lucas replied, reaching up to pull his earbuds out and stick them back in their case.

Kameron and I shared a quick *is he serious* glance and quickly decided that yes, Lucas had finally shared something personal about himself, completely out of the blue.

"I'm kidding," Lucas said, waving a hand toward Kameron.

Neither of us responded. Kameron slunk back in his chair, and I rubbed the back of my neck. I didn't have a knack for this kind of intense conversation the way Kameron did. When someone shared personal traumas or experiences, it made me lock up, whereas Kam could jump into action.

This time, though, he left that where it was, and didn't pursue any lines of questioning. Interesting.

"What's up?" Kameron asked.

"I heard from the campsite in Watford. Turns out they just finished a massive renovation project—ten cabins, newly remodeled and updated within the last two years."

My eyebrows shot up. Where the hell would the owner have gotten that kind of capital?

"They'd be happy to host us for the weekend. The town council will cover the cost of our stay with the grant money they received for the festival, and we'd be on our own for meals, transportation, and incidentals. Are we in?"

A heavy weight lodged itself in my stomach, but I kept an encouraging smile on my face for Kameron's benefit. I'd spent five years of my life tucking my crap out of sight so I could do my job. I could handle a weekend in Watford.

"Hell yeah," Kameron said, that familiar smile gracing his features.

"Sweet. I'll call him and let him know the three of us will be there Friday afternoon."

Friday afternoon. A little over a day and a half away.

While Kameron and Lucas began discussing travel plans, I slipped quietly downstairs to pour myself a glass of water. I stood at the farmhouse sink, looking through the window with red plaid curtains tied neatly at the sides, focusing on the horses in the pasture and the chickens squawking in the yard. I took a deep breath, held it for several seconds, and released it, slowing my breathing.

I could do this. I *would* do this. For Kameron, and Winding Road, and all the men and women out there who needed this place to recover and find themselves again.

·❤·❤·❤·❤·❤·

"Got your ID? Winding Road's nonprofit paperwork? Extra pairs of socks and underwear?"

I rolled my eyes, tossing my duffle bag into the passenger seat before slamming the driver's side door of my Chevy. I turned to face Kam, leaning against the side of the car.

"Yes, Mom, I packed extra underwear."

Kameron was beaming. "Good lad."

I laughed, which helped uncoil some of the tightness in my chest.

"You're sure you don't want to blow that guy off and come to Watford with Lucas and me instead?"

Kameron's smile was strained, and I could only imagine why. Yesterday evening, Kam got a phone call from someone who seemed to shake him to his core. I couldn't remember ever seeing Kam so rattled. He told me that someone he knew long ago needed his help and would arrive at Winding Road later.

I knew better than to ask too many questions, but I could sense Kam's unease. I'd offered to call off the entire Watford trip to stay here and help him through whatever craziness might unfold, but he'd waved off my concerns and told me there was no way in hell I was getting out of it.

"I'm sorry," he said, and I gave his shoulder a reassuring squeeze.

"Don't worry about it," a chipper voice said from behind me, and I barely held back an eye roll. "I'll keep Harvey company. We'll have good times."

Kameron was clearly biting back a laugh.

I pressed my lips together in a thin line. "The *best*."

Lucas threw his weekend bag in the cab of my truck, and I gave Kameron one more pleading glare, which he answered with a smirk of his own.

"You boys have fun. But not too much fun. You're there to work."

"Will do, Dad," Lucas said airily, then hopped in the passenger seat, letting the door of my truck—my *baby* —slam shut. I winced.

"Be careful this weekend, and call me if you need anything," I said to Kam, who nodded his thanks.

"I will. And Connor?"

I looked over my shoulder to meet his eyes.

"Thank you," Kameron said quietly. He didn't need to specify.

I slipped into the front seat of Lucy, my '87 blue Chevrolet, and some of the tightness in my shoulders eased.

"This is a nice truck," Lucas said almost reverently. "Like . . . really nice."

As I cranked the engine to life, I took a deep breath.

"She's been with me through some crazy adventures. Treat her nicely, Morales, or I'll wring your neck myself."

Lucas rolled his eyes. "Bit melodramatic, don't you think?"

"I don't screw around when it comes to my truck," I warned. "If you put your boots—or worse, your *bare feet*—on the dashboard, I'll have no choice but to kill you and dump your body somewhere in the valley where they'll never find your remains."

Lucas blinked, trying to determine whether I was joking. I kept up what I hoped was a neutral expression. Lucas buckled his seatbelt without saying another word.

Watford was nestled deep into the mountains with a few stops once you crested the first peaks. Winding Road was in one of the valleys en route to Watford, leaving my hometown less than two hours away.

I still didn't know what I'd do when I got there.

Lucas flashed me a thumbs-up, letting me know he was ready to roll. I plugged my phone into the cassette-to-aux contraption so I could play my music without having to sift through the radio stations. It was helpful in this stretch of mountains, where good radio service was scarce.

I gripped the steering wheel tighter, trying to control my breathing.

Zach Bryan's voice lulled me to that zoned out place where I could imagine she was with me, riding in the passenger seat, the dogs we'd always wanted to adopt running across the backseat, their faces against the wind. In these moments, it was the sound of her sweet laughter and the smell of the highway wildflowers that gave me peace.

For just a heartbeat, I closed my eyes, and I imagined I could take it all back.

That I'd never left Watford. That I was the same person I'd been. That my uncle wasn't a terrible human being. That we could have made a life for ourselves in Watford. That I'd given Abbie everything she'd dreamed of. That she was mine in the same way I was hers.

The last part had been true for longer than I dared to admit aloud.

A heartbeat later, I focused my eyes on the road ahead. I turned the volume dial up to the max and let my mind become white space.

I wasn't that person anymore. I knew I would never be the object of Abbie's innermost desires ever again. The dreams we shared and promises we made to one another had gone up in smoke the moment I left her behind. No matter how much I wanted to believe she could love me again, I wouldn't allow myself to bask in her glow. I was a coward before. I let my emotions and feelings control me in a way that destroyed the people I cared for the most.

I'd make my peace with that one day. But I knew, as I turned off the dirt road and onto the main highway leading me deeper into the mountains, that day was nowhere in sight.

I spent the entire two-hour drive struggling to ease the tightness gathering in my chest. My unease peaked as I passed the worn-down sign advertising that I entered Watford County. Lucas was knocked out in the seat beside me; he didn't snore or seem bothered by the volume of my music, both of which I was grateful for.

My grip on the steering wheel slipped slightly as sweat gathered in my palms. I cranked the air conditioning up. Lucy shuddered with effort, and I rubbed my thumb over the top of the steering wheel. If I'd been alone, I would have given her some words of encouragement. The rational side of me knew I was pushing my old girl to her limits, but the stubborn part of me had faith that she wouldn't give out on me.

Not when we were this close to home. To Abbie.

I fought to keep my breathing even, turning onto the gravel path that would take us directly to the campsite off the back roads into Watford. I'd once joked with my friends that the only way into Watford was through back roads because this was the most remote place I'd ever lived, but there was still one main road that cut right through the center of town that most people rode in and out.

I wasn't ready to face the masses in Watford. I wasn't arrogant enough to think that my old blue Chevy was still a recognizable landmark in Watford the way it had been five years ago, but small-town folk had excellent memories.

I was barely ready to face Noah Wilkinson, the owner of the Watford Campsite.

I rumbled down the gravel road, passing the broken barbed wire fence. I rolled my eyes. It didn't exactly sur-prise me to see they hadn't fixed it, but part of me wanted confirmation that this place had changed like I had. That it hadn't been stagnant these last few years. It was a constant war in my mind, whether I wanted things to change or stay the same.

I didn't know which would bring me more comfort.

Craggy rocks and dry wood lined the two-lane road, and as I drove further into Watford, the arid wilderness of the mountain desert faded into dense trees and lush pinewood forest, in classic Pacific Northwest fashion. The gravel back road became a dirt one, leading us to the campsite.

When we cleared the last curve, the cabins came into view. I let out a low whistle as I pulled into the unpaved space next to the first cabin. The dust from my tires was settling as I shook Lucas awake.

They'd taken the word renovation to heart. When I left Watford, only two one-bedroom cabins existed, both originally decorated in the early seventies. Now there were ten cabins, all of which were larger and modernized. They were mostly uniform in color and shape, with gorgeous stained pine logs stacked high, and tall windows framing the rustic French door entrance. They'd even added a small balcony awning with a rocking chair on the second story, where people could gaze out at the forest and the desert beyond as they sipped their morning coffee.

My heart twisted at the sight of the beautiful cabins. How many times had Abbie and I talked about wanting a house that looked just like this?

"We're here already?" Lucas groaned, trying to wipe the sleep from his eyes.

"We're here," I answered, willing my heart to slow. "Did you talk to Noah on the phone?"

"Yeah, says here we're in cabin two," Lucas said, sliding his phone out of his back pocket and swiftly tapping at it. "Just gotta pull up our key."

My eyebrows shot up. "They have electronic entry now?"

Lucas gave me a *yes, old man* look before going back to flipping through his email. I cranked off the ignition and swung my door open wide, jumping down to the forest floor and gazing up at the trees.

The ground didn't shudder beneath my feet, and the songbirds still sang in the forest, so I at least had that going for me.

My heart skipped as I glanced to my left, catching a view of the newly installed campsite map. There, in the middle, marked with a bright yellow star, was Watford town center—less than a mile west of the campsite.

"Christ," I muttered. The familiar creak of Lucy's passenger door opening boomed loudly in the quiet clearing.

"Got the key. Grab your bag and let's get settled. We're supposed to meet with Noah here in about an hour to talk about the festival. I think he's interested in helping us out with a giveaway."

I did as I was told, gazing at the forest beyond. Even with my complicated feelings about what was to come, being back in this forest still felt like coming home.

Chapter 7

Abbie

"**Y**ou can do this."

I bit my bottom lip as I gently coaxed the tall glass flour jar off the very top shelf of the storeroom.

Refilling the newly milled flour Imogen brought from her homestead once a week had to be my least favorite restocking activity. Namely, because I apparently hated myself and decided the most convenient place to store the insanely large bulk jars was on the tallest shelf. It required me to give myself a pep talk every time I had to retrieve a new jar.

I paused as the metal shelf beneath me wobbled. I desperately needed to invest in a new ladder that was tall enough to reach the top shelf, but that was neither here nor there.

"Come to Mama," I said, grunting with the effort of extending my arm farther back. I wiggled the jar another inch forward, and then another, finally pulling it far enough to the front that I could grab it with one hand. Using my left arm to balance myself against the shelf, I pulled the jar into my right, making the final leap back down to the ground.

I grinned, looking at the jar as I strolled back to the front of the store.

While flour filled the glass jar through a large funnel, I let my thoughts wander to the flower farm I dreamed I'd have one day. I grunted with the effort of moving the burlap sack of flour to the floor behind the counter. Imogen was endearingly hopeful about how many people in Watford were actually coming here to buy flour in bulk. Kelly would be in for her weekly sourdough refill, and someone from the Roadhouse or the diner almost always needed a last-minute refill during the week, but other than that, the only person who'd be using this flour was me.

If I'd had the chance to cultivate my flower farm, I could have been dealing with a very different flour—one that would excite me far more than this. I could have spent today lounging in a field of lush mountain wildflowers that I tended myself, curled up with a new release from one of my favorite authors. I slid the now-full jar of flour toward me and latched the lid.

"God, you're heavy," I sighed, pushing it down the wooden counter as far as it would go. I looked at aisle two, where most of the bulk goods were located, and let out a moan.

I finagled the jar into my hands by carefully pressing it against my chest, using my core to brace against the weight.

The front doorbell rang, announcing someone had entered the building, and my eyes widened.

"Crap," I breathed, my grip on the incredibly heavy jar slipping. I shuffled my way forward, poking my head around the end cap, searching for the individual who'd just walked in.

"Hello! I'm so sorry to whoever just walked in, we're actually closing now. Sorry for the confusion, haven't updated the hours sign—"

"Abbie?"

Everything in my body went rigid at the sound of that voice.

His voice.

It couldn't be him.

It'd been a rough few weeks, and my mind had officially started playing tricks on me. It was the only logical explanation for why that man—*boy*, the last time I saw him—would be in my store and talking to me right now.

Between managing the store and fending off the IRS lady who is hellbent on nailing my father for tax evasion, I was at my limit every hour of every day. The universe wouldn't fuck me like this.

"Abbie Collins," the man spoke again, more sure of himself this time.

The jar of flour slipped from my hands.

"Shit," I swore, and then flushed with embarrassment at having cursed in front of a customer. In the same breath, I wanted to sprint away because the man in front of me wasn't a stranger passing through on their way to bigger cities.

It was Connor Harvey.

He rounded the corner, and I staggered back a step. My mind raced to reconcile the image of Connor now with what he looked like on the day he left. He'd grown his dirty blond hair out, so much so that it was almost shoulder length. He was all long lines and hard muscles, and as he kneeled to assess the flour disaster at my feet, I couldn't ignore the way his biceps flexed and strained against his cotton shirt.

I was gawking and helpless to stop myself from doing so.

"Let me help," Connor said, giving me a small smile. His brown eyes met mine, and I was helpless to do anything but stare. "Got a dust pan so we can sweep up the glass?"

"Behind the counter. Should be beneath the cash register," I said quickly, unable to do anything but stare at the man in front of me.

Connor nodded, heading in that direction. I wiped my damp palms on my jeans and willed my sweaty fingers to keep from shaking. I suddenly wished I'd at least put on lip gloss or something this morning. How many times had I dreamed of running into the guy who broke my heart while looking drop-dead gorgeous and making him wish he'd stayed?

Was this my life now? I'd always imagined I would be the image of calm if I ever ran into Connor again. I wanted to be the chill ex-girlfriend who was unflappable. *You completely abandoned me? Whatever.*

In reality, I looked more like a fish stunned into silence from utter shock, outfitted in stained work jeans and a classic dark pink button up.

"I didn't mean to sneak up on you like that," Connor said, reappearing in front of me, unclipping the broom handle from the cheap plastic dust pan. "I wasn't expecting to see you here."

I swallowed, averting my gaze to the freshly ground flour that now covered the wooden floor. Something ugly and raw cut through me at how casual he was. I snapped back to reality, giving my head a small shake.

"Where else would I have been?"

It was Connor's turn to look uncomfortable as he returned his gaze to the floor, instead choosing to focus on sweeping up every small piece of glass rather than answer my question. Anger flared alongside my pounding heart.

My head and heart were both trying to catch up to the sight in front of me. Connor Harvey was in Watford. In *my* store. Connor was the opposite of the scrawny kid he'd been when he left. Connor was conversing with me as if nothing had ever happened between us. Connor was *here*.

"For a long time, I guessed you'd made it out of here by now. Even with what happened—"

I inhaled sharply, the noise cacophonous in the quiet space between us.

"You did enough leaving for the both of us, I'd say."

Connor's eyes flashed with a darkness I'd never seen in him before. That dark, twisted place in me felt a flash of satisfaction. That ugly part of me wanted him to hurt. I wanted him to feel the faintest sliver of what I felt all those years ago. I wanted him to know that I sat there, at the edge of town, waiting to see his familiar truck cresting the horizon.

I waited for him to come back to me. For months, I'd waited, until John Ludgate had finally had the decency to tell me he wasn't coming back. That he was gone for good.

Connor Harvey, once a beloved athlete on Watford High's football team, deemed "most likely to inspire you to greatness" by the senior yearbook staff.

The man who left me behind mere weeks after my mother died of cancer. The man who stole the future I would have had. Deep down, I knew it wasn't fair to blame him for everything that came after my mother died.

Connor said nothing, only offered a tight-lipped smile as he dumped the shattered glass and ruined flour into the nearby trash can. I'd cry over how much money my clumsiness had just wasted later—I refused to give him the satisfaction. I walked back over to the checkout counter. Connor stood there awkwardly, shifting his weight from one foot to the other.

"Spit it out," I said, grinding my teeth together. My emotions were a tidal wave that threatened to pull me under.

"I'm not here to fight," Connor said, setting his jaw forward.

"Then what the hell are you doing here?" I yelled, slamming my palms down on the table. I couldn't deny that it felt good to let my anger out. For so long, I had to be the one to keep it together. And I had kept it together. I had successfully kept my business and what remained of my family afloat.

But now, my heart was tearing in two all over again. I couldn't handle this.

Connor was the one thing I couldn't handle losing again.

"I'm here for business. I'm with Winding Road Farms. Kameron is my business partner. I'm here with Lucas Morales. We're here to get some preliminary information about the festival and how we can help as the main sponsors."

"Oh, great." I laughed, unable to stop the hysterical tone from slipping into my voice. "Of course it's your farm that's sponsoring the festival I got roped into organizing."

Connor's jaw twitched. "I didn't come here to—"

"Oh, I know you didn't," I muttered, the hysterical laugh dying in my throat. "Did you know I was the coordinator?"

Connor swallowed, but he held my gaze. Damn him.

"Abbie—"

"Don't—" I took a sharp breath, trying to rein in my temper. I needed to let sleeping dogs lie, and I knew—God, help me, I *knew*—fighting with Connor now wouldn't change the past, but the ugly, dark part of me wanted to see him wounded. I wanted him to leave the store with his tail tucked between his legs.

I wanted him to bleed like I had.

"Don't say my name."

Connor pressed his lips into a thin line, and my skin flushed hot as I watched his eyes scan me. I could imagine what he was seeing—no doubt noticing the weight gain, the new acne scars, the long brown hair that desperately needed a cut. I shifted my weight from one foot to the other, uncomfortable under his unabashed stare.

And because I wasn't in the mood to let him win at anything, I decided that I'd look until I had my fill too, since he clearly had no problem doing so.

God, he *had* changed. The rational side of my brain knew that it had been over five years since I'd last seen him.

But this . . . this was a far more incredible sight than my brain could process. Gone was the childlike roundness of his face. He stood taller, more confident. Gone was the boyish grin and slight awkwardness. The man that stood in front of me knew who he was, and what he wanted.

And yet, he was still the same grumpy, scowling boy I once befriended. I pictured those small smiles reserved only for me, the delicate moments in between heartbeats where he looked at me as if I was the sun he revolved around.

My cheeks flushed as our gazes met, and I quickly averted my eyes. I really needed Kevin to check the A.C., because it was damned hot in here. The wave of nostalgia threatened to drown me.

"We're going to be working together for the next several weeks," Connor said. "It's going to get weird if I can't call you by your name."

I heaved out a frustrated sigh, putting my hands on my hips.

"It's already weird, Connor," I said. "But you have a point. I'll give you permission to use my name."

Way to take a weird situation and make it even worse, Abs!

I wanted to groan and possibly smash my face into a wall somewhere to hide from the feelings of this moment.

Connor's lip lifted in a small smile. "Bossy."

My jaw hinged open even as I felt my flush returning. Connor's eyes widened, as if even he couldn't believe he just said that.

I would not survive this.

I had half a mind to call Trent back and demand to know why in the hell he'd accepted sponsorship from anyone affiliated with Connor Harvey, but that idea quickly faded when I realized that doing so would mean I'd have to acknowledge that Connor's presence here was a problem for me.

And I was determined not to let it be a problem.

So, we were in love when we were seventeen. So, just three weeks after my mom's funeral, he left me. So, I had no idea where the hell he'd been the last five years, or who he'd been with.

None of that mattered. I needed the money the festival would pull in. Watford needed this opportunity to put ourselves back on the map. I could put my messy personal feelings in a trunk and lock it up for the next two months. Five years was a long time to be parted from someone. I certainly wasn't the same person I was at eighteen.

I had nothing further to say to him today. I didn't need anything from him. Period.

My brain was a swirling mess of emotions and thoughts. Imogen was going to have a fit when I told her about this.

Connor turned on his heel, regarded the barer-than-usual aisles of Watford General, and grabbed one of the wire baskets at the end cap of aisle two.

"Connor?" I called, pinching the bridge of my nose and scrunching my face up. I needed him to leave so that this choking tightness in my chest would ease.

"Yes?"

"What are you doing?"

"Buying groceries?" He shifted uncomfortably onto his right foot. "I know you mentioned you were closed, but we just got into town this afternoon, and . . . well, I know Lucas and I could eat at the diner, but I'm not ready to see anyone else. I was planning to cook at the cabin for the next few days."

I'm not ready to see anyone else.

His words ignited something in me. Anyone else . . . meaning he had come here first? To Watford General? Hoping I would be here?

I had to be reading into his words. I was twisting them to fit my heartache, to soothe the wounds that were clearly still open. My gut twisted with longing and dread as the reality of the situation sunk its claws into me.

My hands trembled as I gestured to the refrigerators lining the far wall.

"Of course," I said, my voice thick with unshed tears. "Grab whatever you need."

Connor nodded, disappearing behind aisle one. I heard the distinct squeak of the fridge opening and then closing. Connor reappeared, carrying with him a pack of ground beef, a carton of eggs, a small jar of milk, a block of cheese, and, to my eternal surprise, a bag of frozen broccoli. He laid them out gently on the counter as I logged back into my merchant system, booting up the scanner.

"Vegetables, huh?"

Connor's eyes shot to mine as I scanned the carton of eggs.

"All part of a balanced diet."

I couldn't stop the incredulous laugh that escaped me as I finished scanning the rest of his items. Things certainly were different.

I felt Connor's eyes on me as I began placing the food into a paper bag. I flipped the tablet around so he could scan his card, but Connor smiled and handed me two twenty-dollar bills. My chest seized as I met his gaze, unable to make my heart understand that things were not the same as they were.

Things could never be the same.

Connor saved me from making a fool of myself by putting the change I barely remember counting out into the small jar next to the register. He turned his back to me, heading for the front door.

"Connor?" I said, digging my nails into my palm as I fought to keep from screaming.

He hesitated, shifting the brown paper bag to his other arm as he looked over his shoulder.

"I don't know how long you'll be in town, but you should know that I don't talk about the past anymore." I took another deep breath, knowing that what I was going to say next would shatter both of us. But I also knew that if I didn't set this boundary now, I would never set it. And for my sanity—for my wellbeing—I had to.

"And you lost the right to ask me anything about my family when you left."

Connor went rigid with a precision I'd never seen from him.

"I'm happy to assist you in purchasing whatever resources you'll need for your stay in Watford," I said, fighting to keep my voice level, "and I'll assist you in whatever way I can for the festival, but I respectfully ask that you keep business between us strictly professional."

"Understood. You'll have no trouble with me."

I could have sworn the light faded from Connor's eyes as he nodded his agreement, tucking the paper bag beneath his arm and forcing the door open. The momentum from the door slamming flipped the door sign from 'open' to 'closed.' I dusted off the remaining flour from the front of my jeans and inhaled a shaky breath.

I slumped down against the back wall of the general store and focused on the sound of my breathing.

"I can't do this," I whispered to no one in particular. I still didn't know what I was going to do with my father. The store was drowning in debt and the IRS audit, and my heart . . . My heart kept breaking over and over and over again.

Because I *wanted* him. I had never stopped wanting him, even in the darkest weeks after the funeral. I wanted my person. I wanted to know that my life wasn't spinning out in front of me in some irrevocable way.

I had kept my eye on the door.

I had kept my eye on the horizon, waiting for Lucy to appear on Main Street, where Connor would be back at my side with a perfectly reasonable explanation for why he'd disappeared in the first place.

God, help me, I still wanted that. I wanted to deny it, but I couldn't.

How was I supposed to forget someone I knew so well? How was I supposed to ignore someone I once planned to spend forever with?

I had lost everything in the month after graduation. I'd lost my mom, and by extension, I lost my father. But I also lost *him*.

And now, Connor Harvey was back in Watford, and I couldn't fucking *breathe*.

Chapter 8

Connor

I let the front door of Watford General slam shut.

The ache in my chest turned to a blazing burn.

The dark and twisted part of me wanted to punch an inanimate object, but I knew better than to trust my emotions at this moment.

I placed both of my palms against the cool window of my truck, allowing my emotions to take the reins for one, two, three seconds, before I pulled back and calmed my breathing.

When I first joined the service, all I wanted was violence. I was angry. I wished for a war so I could prove to everyone—especially my uncle—that I wasn't weak-willed or weak-minded. I wanted to show that I could hold my own in the toughest military branch and could have a successful career far away from Watford. I wanted anyone and everyone to know I was capable.

I quickly discovered that the military would teach me many lessons about life. None of them were lessons I was expecting, and all of them were lessons I desperately needed to learn.

Most importantly, I understood that there was nothing in my life I could control. I'd been thirsty for control, desperate for it—even as I stood at Camp Pendleton's gate with a drill instructor screaming at me. When I stood at the phone booth where new recruits made phone calls to their families to let them know they'd arrived at boot camp safely, I knew damn well there was only one person I could dial, and she wouldn't pick up the phone.

I pretended to call home. I picked up the phone, read the script, and slammed the phone back down on the receiver. I vowed to leave Watford behind as I sat in the chair to have my head shaved.

I left it all behind. I was young and naive enough to think that I could simply erase all memories of her, of our time together, from my memory with enough willpower. I reasoned I could focus on my career hard enough that all memories of my past would fade. I convinced myself I could outrun the abuse, my developing addiction issues, and the gaping Abbie-sized hole in my chest.

It was a foolish hope even then.

"You all right?"

Lucas's voice shook me from my thoughts. I rubbed a dirty palm down my face, grateful for the dirt and sweat that covered my body. I'd always enjoyed working with my hands. Knowing that I was doing something that mattered, even if it was simply scouting out the Watford landscape, gave me a small dose of satisfaction.

"I'm all right. Got in touch with Abbie."

Lucas raised an eyebrow. When I didn't elaborate, he nodded. "Thanks for doing that. I grabbed you a burger and fries for dinner. Hope that's okay."

It was my turn to nod. I'd use the groceries I just bought to make dinner for the guys tomorrow when everyone was together again. Lucas grabbed my groceries while I slid into the driver's seat, cranking the engine to life.

I dared one last glance back at Watford General while Lucas was buckling his seatbelt. Abbie stood behind the counter, fiddling with the necklace in between her collarbones as she watched me.

My heart sped up. I hadn't even thought to look at the necklace.

I wasn't stupid enough to think it was the one I'd given her back in high school, but that silly, boyish part of me still roared to life at the idea that it was the silver daisy chain I'd bought her.

Abbie looked surprised as our eyes met, and she quickly averted her gaze, grabbing a clipboard and practically sprinting to the back of the store.

I shook my head, clearing all thoughts of Abbie.

Abbie had set a boundary. It was best we kept our distance from one another. It wouldn't do either of us any favors to open old wounds. Or, in my case, pour salt in the ones that still hadn't healed.

"I've got to stop by the sheriff's office on the way back. Got a text from Kameron about there being some permits and safety pamphlets for the festival there for us to pick up. That okay with you?"

"Sure," I said.

"Mind staying with the car?" Lucas asked as I parked along the curb outside the sheriff's office. "I'll just be a minute."

Something about Lucas's demeanor felt off to me, but I said nothing. I couldn't imagine he had personal business in Watford, but then again, the guy seemed to play his cards close to his chest.

"Not at all. Go ahead."

Lucas ducked inside the sheriff's office, and I shut off the car, hopping out and onto the curb. It was a mild day in Watford because autumn was approaching. A gentle breeze swept the sand and dirt around my boots as I leaned against the truck, looking down the street toward the majestic mountains beyond.

The Roadhouse still stood tall and proud on the north corner of the major intersection, which didn't surprise me. This entire town could crumble into dust, and the Road-house Bar would be the only establishment left standing.

I stuck my hands in my pockets, drawing random designs into the dust with the toe of my boot.

"Connor Harvey?"

My head snapped up at the sound of my name, and I searched for the person who'd called me.

"Sorry to spook you, son. I honestly wasn't certain it was you."

"Officer Ludgate," I said, straightening my back and extending my hand to him. "It *is* me."

Ludgate took my outstretched hand and shook it, more out of politeness than anything. He looked shell-shocked to see me standing on the curb outside of the sheriff's office.

"I gotta say, Harvey, I didn't expect to see you back here. Ever."

My jaw twitched as I pulled my hand back from his. *You and I both.*

"I was surprised to hear that my uncle left town a while back."

Ludgate's face revealed nothing as he tucked his hat further into the crook of his elbow, readjusting his shoulders.

"Not before he lifted cash from the Roadhouse's main till."

I let out a harsh laugh that held no humor. "Doesn't surprise me. He was never a stand-up guy."

"That's putting it generously."

"Well, in case you weren't aware, he died. About a year ago now."

Ludgate nodded. "Can't say I'm sad about that."

We stood there staring at each other. I was grateful Ludgate didn't offer his sympathies. Out of everyone in Watford, he was most likely to understand.

Ludgate had done what he could for me. As a kid, I hadn't been willing to formally come forward with abuse allegations against my uncle, and Ludgate's hands had been tied. I believed my uncle when he told me everyone hated me and no one would believe the word of some scrawny kid over a person they already feared.

"Have you seen her yet?" Ludgate finally asked, his voice barely above a whisper.

I inhaled deeply, fixing my vision on a point behind his head.

"Yeah, I've seen her. Lucas and I just left Watford General."

"Did she tell you what happened the other night?"

My gaze snapped back to his.

"What happened?" I demanded, my fingers twitching at my side. Though I knew I didn't have a right to ask anything about her life, it didn't stop me from wanting to defend her. Ludgate's mouth twitched, almost like he wanted to smile, but he schooled his expression back into neutrality before I fully deciphered it.

"Malcolm's not doing well, Connor. Hasn't been in his right mind since Tilly died. He finds solace at the bottom of a bottle more nights than not."

I closed my eyes as several emotions flooded me at once. A dagger in my chest would have hurt less than the knowledge that Abbie had most likely been doing everything on her own for years on end.

Alcoholism was a brutal beast that ravaged souls and tore families apart. I would know. I slipped my right hand into the pocket of my jeans, fiddling with my sobriety coin as I waited for Ludgate to continue.

"I'm probably not supposed to tell you this," Ludgate muttered, his eyes flickering to the office door. "But my retirement is only a year away, so screw it. Two nights ago, Malcolm lost it. Publicly. Most folks around here had assumed he'd turned into a recluse. But you know how people talk. Malcolm was throwing bottles, screaming at passersby, asking where his wife was. Turned his anger toward Abbie. My partner and I stepped in before it escalated, but . . ."

"Christ," I muttered, dragging a palm down the side of my face.

"We took him into custody that night, allowing Abbie a night of peace to get her bearings back. But it's getting worse by the day. He's in a bad way, Connor. I know it's none of my business, but I'm worried about her."

"She shouldn't have to deal with this on her own," I said.

Ludgate's eyes flashed with something that looked an awful lot like anger.

"No, Connor, she shouldn't have to. But she's done a mighty fine job of keeping the store afloat since Malcolm became indisposed."

"I don't doubt that."

Ludgate frowned. "I don't mean to pry, or to put more on your plate, but you should check on her. She's as stubborn as a bull, that girl of yours."

I forced a tight smile, even though something in my chest cracked right down the middle.

"She's not my girl anymore."

Ludgate let out a boisterous laugh. The sound shocked me.

"She's always been your girl, Harvey. Never stopped. Even when you left, she never stopped waiting for you."

My chest tightened painfully at Ludgate's words. The guilt and shame, the weight of the knowledge of what I'd done to the woman I'd loved with every part of my being, threatened to swallow me whole.

"Did you tell her?" I asked.

"No. I've wanted to punch you in the jaw more times than I can count over the last few years for putting me in that position and asking me to keep it quiet, but no. I never told her you joined the military. It wasn't my place."

I released a sigh of relief. Enlisting into the armed service in a small town proved to be tricky, because I didn't want anyone to know where I was headed. When I asked Ludgate to be a character witness, I also asked him not to tell anyone what I was doing. When I left Watford that night, I could only pray he'd keep my whereabouts a secret.

"Why are you here, Connor?" Ludgate asked. There was no judgment in his tone, but I knew he had to be suspicious.

I inhaled deeply.

"My best friend, Kameron, owns a nonprofit called Winding Road Recovery, about an hour and a half north of here. He's sponsoring the festival to help put his farm and nonprofit work on the map. Lucas and I are his associates; we help him carry out the day-to-day requirements of managing the farm, so he can focus on the nonprofit side. Winding Road changes lives. It changed mine. I promise you, John, I'm here to support the man who dragged me from my rock bottom, and nothing else."

That didn't feel like a lie. A stretch of the truth? Sure.

But the image of Abbie's gaze as Lucas and I drove away from Watford General would be etched in my mind forever.

"You're going to put the woman you love through this again?" Ludgate asked, his gaze sharpening.

"Loved," I corrected, straightening my stance. "And it's not peace if she has no closure about the way things ended."

Ludgate's gaze sharpened as he continued to stare at me.

"You already left her once," Ludgate said. "You already broke her down. One of your coworkers couldn't handle the front-end operations for this festival?"

"It's not about what it can do for me," I said, and that was the truth. "I left Watford a broken boy who couldn't handle his crap. I joined up, did my time, and now I'm back. I'm a man who can own my past mistakes. I screwed up when I left. But if there's a chance that I can help repair some of the broken parts of this town, then I want to do it."

Ludgate continued to stare at me, stroking his neatly trimmed gray beard with his thumb and forefinger.

"All right," he said, glancing at the ground beneath his boots before looking back at me. "Promise me you'll check in on her."

My brows knitted together. "John, I—"

"Look, Connor, I get it. There's a lot of time and space between the two of you. You've both been through a lot of shit." Ludgate absentmindedly twisted the wedding band he still wore on his left hand, although he hadn't been married in over two decades. "But you're both here. God put you two back in the same town. That's no coincidence."

"With all due respect, Officer Ludgate, I'm not religious."

Ludgate gave me a small smile. "You don't have to be. Call it a gift, call it fate, call it whatever you want. But don't be an idiot and squander the opportunity."

I didn't know how to respond, so I followed my grandmother's advice about not saying anything.

"I should warn you, Connor, that Ellis's actions—especially after you skipped town—caused a lot of rifts. I know you want to do your best to repair things, but there's a chance the townsfolk won't receive it well. People associate you with Ellis, and that's unfair, but doesn't change the way things are."

I gave a small shrug.

"They've never *received* me well. They can add my presence here during the festival to the list."

Ludgate's brow raised, and he shook his head.

"Even if I hadn't known you were a Marine, I'd have guessed by this conversation. I'd know that arrogance and self-confidence anywhere."

I smiled then. "It was good to see you, John."

"You too, kid."

Ludgate paused before pointing a finger in my face and said, "Don't squander what is freely given," before he turned to enter the sheriff's office.

I didn't have time to ponder the full meaning of his statement before Lucas stepped through the door just seconds later, opening a manila folder and sliding a thick stack of documents inside.

"Everything all right?" Lucas asked.

"Yes," I replied as the two of us returned to the cab of the truck, ready to head back to the cabin.

I needed space to think. To remember. To prepare myself for what was to come.

I'd made so many promises in my life. I'd broken many of them.

But this time, I'd keep my promise to Abbie Collins like an oath.

Chapter 9
Abbie

After Connor left the store, I called Imogen to tell her I was closing up early, asking if she would bring her produce the next day. She was understanding of my need for space. She always had been. I'd checked in with Dad, who passed out on the bed in his loft. I verified he was still breathing, removed the half-finished bottle from his hand, put a fresh water bottle and a bag of chips on his nightstand, and dumped the remaining liquor down the drain before heading back to my apartment.

I spent the night in the bath, drinking sparkling water out of a wine glass, and scrolling through pictures from high school. I'm not sure why I tortured myself in that way. Seeing Connor's boyish face was a sharp contrast to the man who had walked into Watford General earlier today.

I frowned when I looked at my teenage self. The girl in those pictures was so innocent. She had the American dream: loving parents, a gorgeous best friend, and a boyfriend who loved her and swore he'd marry her. She had everything in these moments, and she didn't even know it.

I shut the photo app after scrolling for an hour, when the bubbles had disappeared and the water had grown cold.

I chose not to cry, even though I knew it was probably necessary. I didn't want to give those memories that kind of power over me.

I didn't want to give *him* that kind of power over me. I couldn't do that to myself again. I had known love with Connor—full body, cosmic love, the kind I had once believed only existed in movies and novels. I was still angry about not having gained more life experience first.

I wish I had known what I do now.

The next day, I texted Imogen, asking if she'd grab coffee with me before we headed to the store. She accepted.

As I drove to her homestead, my mind drifted to everything we'd been through over the last few years. Even with her return to Watford and my father's struggles, we still made time for each other. I was grateful to have such a loyal friend.

I let Imogen out at the street corner in front of Blackbeard's Coffee before I pulled up on the curb next to Watford General so we could unload the produce. I had only hauled a few boxes inside before Imogen walked up to the store, two coffees in hand.

"Who is that?" Imogen asked, gesturing to a black-haired, bearded man with a backward baseball cap, loading supplies into the back end of Lucy. I didn't know his name, but after a little, an all too familiar blond-haired, brown-eyed man got out of the driver's seat.

I swallowed.

"I don't know who the first guy is, but that second one *might* be Connor Harvey."

Imogen did a spit take right in the middle of the sidewalk. One passerby jumped back and grimaced. My cheeks flamed red hot as I grabbed her arm.

"Jesus Christ," I hissed, pulling her into the store. "I told you I had something important to tell you."

"Nowhere in that text did you suggest that what you needed to tell me involved Connor freaking *Harvey*," Imogen screeched. "I can't believe I didn't recognize that damn truck."

The front door slammed shut behind her, the sound rattling in the previously quiet space. I put my head in my hands and groaned loudly.

"Now, do you understand why we needed fancy coffee? What the hell am I supposed to do, Imogen?"

Imogen's face softened.

"I'll kill him if he comes near you."

"I appreciate that, but it's unnecessary. We already talked yesterday."

"How are you feeling about that?"

My laugh bordered on hysterical.

"I'm trying not to feel anything," I answered honestly. I pulled one box of produce down from the counter and strode toward the refrigerators and freezers.

"That's never worked out for you before."

I shrugged and pulled the fridge door open.

"Doesn't mean I can't try."

The alternative was allowing myself to feel it all, and with things the way they were with my father, I didn't have the emotional capacity to allow myself to be hurt by him again.

As I poured my coffee the next morning, I tried to outline my day in my head. I'd tossed and turned the entire night, unable to settle my thoughts or racing heart. The knowledge that the many parts of my past were converging at the same moment, with Connor's return and my father's addiction turning a sharp, dangerous corner, had me on edge in a way that I hadn't been in years.

I realized, as I locked the door to my apartment and tucked my key into my purse, that the last time I had been this anxious had been in the days after my mother's death. In those days, I could barely get out of bed.

As I walked to the store, I nodded politely at the passers-by, but I mostly kept my gaze fixed on the ground at my feet. I didn't know how long Connor could fly under the radar. In a small town like this, word traveled fast. And given that the word on the street was that Connor Harvey was back in town . . .

I sighed heavily as I unlocked Watford General's door and flipped on the overhead lights. The minute the townsfolk found out that he was back in town, they would hit me with a million questions. I would return to that dark place, where everyone bombarded me with questions, and I had no answers to give them.

I could only pray that Connor would hold his own against the tirade this time.

I set my bag on the shelf beneath the cash register and grabbed my clipboard. I walked past the door, changing the sign to 'open' and texting Imogen to let her know she was good to bring the produce.

Inventory had already been done recently, but it was monotonous enough that the actions of counting and tallying helped calm my racing mind. I barely heard the overhead bell chime to alert me to a customer. I tucked the clipboard under my arm and the pencil behind my ear—so I didn't lose yet another one to my clumsiness. I adjusted my denim overalls and rounded the corner so I could greet them.

"Hi, welcome to—oh."

Connor Harvey stood in the doorway to Watford General in all his glory. My throat tightened, my gaze briefly sweeping down his body. He wore a fresh set of jeans, the same brown boots from the day before, and a plaid shirt rolled up to his elbows. He smelled like pine and leather and spice. I stopped in my tracks, not daring to take a step closer. I trusted my judgment very little these days, and Connor's closeness was a distraction I couldn't afford.

"Hey," he said.

"Hey yourself."

Connor gave me a friendly smile, and I was grateful for his willingness to forget my inability to speak like a normal human being.

"I'm here on official business, I promise. Kameron just sent me the graphics for Winding Road. Things like the logo and some copy text. Could you help me get the signage ordered?"

My heart sped up at the asinine request. Connor was more than capable of pulling up many signage vendors on the internet and placing the order himself. Asking me to place a special order was deliberate. Was it because he wanted to support the store? To support me? Or was it because he was still as ridiculously inept with technology as he'd been as a teenager? My gut told me it was a mix of all three.

"Yeah, of course," I said, gesturing for him to follow me over to the counter. "Let me get my laptop out and we can get things ordered."

I headed to the right of the counter while Connor came up to the opposite side. I pulled my tablet out from my laptop bag and set it up so we could both see the screen.

"What's first?"

"Kam wants a huge banner that we can hang between buildings in the square on the weekend of the festival. What's a good email to forward the graphics to?"

I rattled off the store email address. My personal email address was still the same one I had as a teenager, and I didn't need to level up my embarrassment.

"Okay," I said, biting on my bottom lip. I pulled up the same signage supplier I'd used for Watford General's rebranding a few months earlier, logged in, and fiddled around with the banner settings until it looked right.

"How does this look?" I asked, flipping my tablet toward Connor so he could critique the mockup.

Connor squinted at the screen. I bit down on my bottom lip to keep my smile at bay and rocked forward on my heels.

"Looks good," he said. I added the main banner to my cart. A flush broke out across my skin. Had Kevin messed with the air conditioning again, or was I simply unable to hold my own where Connor Harvey was involved?

I cleared my throat, pulling my shirt collar away from my skin so a sweet kiss of air-conditioned breeze would caress the flushed skin there.

"What else?"

"Kameron mentioned wanting some literature he could pass out at our booth. He's designed a brochure that talks about the nonprofit side of Winding Road. Could we add two hundred printed copies of those?"

I lifted an eyebrow.

"Do you think that'll be enough?"

I admired Connor's optimism for the event's turnout, and was about to tell him as much, when the bell above the door rang again and took my attention.

Imogen's gorgeous black curls bounced with every step as she practically ran over to me, grabbing both of my hands in hers.

"Betty had her calf this morning!" she gushed. My face lit up with excitement.

"Congratulations, Im! Mama and baby both doing okay?"

"Yes, everyone's doing amazing. It was so incredible, Abs, I wish you could've been there! I would have called you, but I didn't think Betty would give birth today."

Imogen released my hands, a cool distaste slipping over her features as she saw who was on the other side of the counter.

"I heard you were back," Imogen stated. Connor didn't so much as blink as he held Imogen's stare.

"I am," he said.

"Why?"

"Long story."

Imogen snorted, crossing her arms over her chest as the two of them continued their stare down.

"No, why are you *here*, in this store? I don't recall anyone informing you that you would be welcome back here after what you did."

"Good to know the two of you can still have a grump-off even at twenty-three," I mumbled.

Connor leaned against the counter, gripping the lip of the wood tightly with his palms. He shook his head slightly, briefly closing his eyes before he looked back at Imogen.

"Look, I'm just here to help, okay? My business partner is the main festival sponsor. I'm in town this weekend to get the ball rolling on plans. That's it."

Imogen didn't look convinced, but she gave an imperceptible nod of acquiescence and headed out the door to grab the produce to restock the shelves.

"I think two hundred brochures are ambitious," I admitted, biting my cheek. "I think we need to be on the same page with expectations for this festival, especially since your partner is bankrolling part of this operation. He sounds like a great guy, and I don't want to waste a penny of his funds."

Connor tilted his head, considering this.

"Fancy taking a walk with me? We can head to Watley's for an early lunch. I'm buying."

"Connor, really, let's—"

"I'm not asking you to marry me, Abbie, Jesus. It's just a walk and a meal."

I bit down on my lip, rocking back on my heels. My heart jumped at the turn of phrase, and for a moment, I swore I could see it, all the plans we used to have together, before it all went up in smoke. Even Imogen's head snapped up from where she was placing the beans and broccoli into the fridge, no doubt ready to cuss Connor out nine ways from Sunday for having the audacity.

To my eternal surprise, I barely held my smile at bay. For a moment, it felt like we were all in high school again.

"I can watch the store while you're gone," Imogen called. "And before you argue, it's no trouble. I'd literally just be watching grass grow at the homestead. This is far more entertaining."

Connor's eyes met mine, and my heart skipped yet another beat. His expression wasn't pleading or trying to sway me one way or the other.

He was simply looking at me. At *me*, rather than *at* me, like so many other folks in town have since my father's outburst.

Connor always just saw *me*.

"Okay," I said quietly. "Let me grab my purse from the stockroom, and I'll be ready."

I knew I would regret this. God help me, I knew this was just about the worst decision I could make for myself right now, but deep down I knew it didn't matter.

I needed this. Even if there was no spark between us anymore, even if we were both changed people, I could no longer deny the part of myself that screamed to be near him.

Connor's smile threatened to break me down to my seventeen-year-old self, exposing all the raw nerves I'd worked so hard to cover up in the years since his departure.

Chapter 10
Connor

Abbie stepped to the backroom to retrieve her purse, while Imogen slinked further back into the aisles, restocking various items from her homestead goods and rearranging some of the more disorganized shelves.

At that moment, someone came sprinting down the stairs from the loft, making a beeline for the cash register, when he realized Abbie wasn't behind it.

It took me several moments to understand that the man was Malcolm Collins. He looked like he'd been to the deepest part of hell and back, which I supposed was true. His long black beard was unkempt, and his hair was an oily, greasy, and matted mess.

"Connor?" he spat, and I squared my shoulders. This would not be a fun conversation. "What the hell are you doing back here? Did you bring that no-good uncle with you?"

My jaw twitched. Of course, he would be less worried about my presence in Watford, and more about where Ellis had run off to. Abbie's parents never liked Ellis. While they never said so directly, I always suspected that they were worried about Ellis's potential presence in their daughter's life.

As if I ever allowed Ellis within three hundred feet of Abbie.

"Ellis is dead," I stated bluntly.

"Good riddance," Malcolm grumbled, grabbing a wad of cash from the register and shoving it inside his chest pocket. I frowned.

"Seriously, Malcolm?"

"You better shut the hell up, Harvey," he growled, wagging a finger in my face. "This is none of your—"

"Connor. Dad," Abbie's voice rang out in the tense silence as she appeared from the stockroom, clutching her purse with both hands. "I didn't hear the doorbell. What are you doing?"

"He was rifling through the cash register," I said before Malcolm could deny anything, and Abbie's face crumpled.

The utter defeat and embarrassment on her face ignited a rage in me I hadn't felt since I left Watford the first time.

Malcolm Collins had been through something unimaginable to most—no husband should have to bury their wife so early. But seeing him actively undermining Abbie, actively ruining her life and her self-esteem, made me want to grab him by the collar and shove him against the wall.

If he wanted to act like that toward his daughter, I'd make sure he could go toe-to-toe with someone who wouldn't put up with his crap.

"Come on, Dad, let's go upstairs."

"I need to get some liquor from the Roadhouse," he spat, shoving her hand away. "You already poured the last of my beer down the drain, you absolute—"

Abbie inhaled sharply, and the edges of my vision tinged red. I stepped forward, gently grabbing her shoulders and pushing her behind me. I snatched his wrist and gripped it tightly, walking him backward a step. Malcolm winced, meeting my eyes as I towered over him.

"I wouldn't finish that sentence. Touch her like that again," I warned, "and I will snap your wrist."

"What a respectful man you've grown into, Harvey," Malcolm snapped, and I gripped tighter.

"It has nothing to do with respect, Malcolm. I simply won't let you touch her like that. Are we clear?"

Malcolm sneered up at me, attempting to jerk his wrist from my grip. I smiled darkly. It was a feeble, drunken attempt that didn't so much as budge my fingers.

"You Harvey men are all the same. Mean sons of bitches."

I laughed, and it was a dark, hollow sound.

"Try me, and you'll find out exactly how mean I can be."

"Connor, stop," Abbie said, pushing past me to her father. "You already went once this week, Dad. Willie won't give you more until your clock resets."

"To hell with the clock," Malcom shouted. "I need it, and I need it now."

The anger in my chest tempered slightly at the sheer desperation in Malcolm's voice. It reminded me of how it hadn't been that long since I'd been in this same spot, begging Kameron to let us go to one more bar, swearing up and down how I was fine and could handle it, that I didn't have a problem. I would never stop being grateful that Kameron never let me get to this point.

"You need to eat something, Dad," Abbie said, fetching an apple and a bag of beef jerky for him. "Please. Let's get you back upstairs."

Malcolm took the food from Abbie, not abandoning the fight completely, but based on the way he kept glancing back at me, he wasn't keen.

Good. Hopefully, he understood I would cross that line if I had to.

"Sorry about that," Abbie said when she returned downstairs. Her eyes were red, and my chest tightened at the realization that she was most likely holding back tears.

"He's got an . . . arrangement with Willie from the Roadhouse. It's really expensive importing liquor this far into the mountains, but we go half in on orders with them. Willie and I are trying to limit his access to the bottle, but—"

"It's hard," I finished for her. "I get it. I really do. You don't have to explain yourself to me, Abbie."

I knew enough about alcoholism to know that Malcolm really believed he'd never be able to function without. That he had completely ruined his life, wrecked his close relationships, and that the only way to survive in this new world was to tunnel deeper into his depression and addiction. I prayed there would be an opportunity to change that perspective, but until we could get him away from the bottle long enough to realize it, it was more a matter of keeping him, and the people around him, safe from harm.

A small light returned to Abbie's eyes as I extended a hand toward the door, all too eager to get her away from this situation.

"Shall we?"

As I opened the front door of Watford General for Abbie, her hair shifted over her shoulder with the small jump down onto the sidewalk and my stomach went taut with the all too familiar feeling of butterflies.

I knew somewhere in the mountains, Kameron was laughing at my sheer inability to talk to women in anything other than a professional capacity. I hadn't told any of my close friends in the service about Abbie, but being around other young men, that often meant that most of them had figured out my inability to hold a conversation early on.

"Which way are you parked?"

I nodded my head toward the Roadhouse and the sheriff's office on the far side of the road.

"I parked in the north lot."

Abbie nodded, pulling her brown satchel farther up her shoulder.

"Lead the way," she said as she tucked one of her curls behind her ear.

I realized then that I was staring. I awkwardly cleared my throat, slipping my hands into my front pockets before turning on my left heel and walking down the sidewalk. Abbie fell into step beside me. The silence between us wasn't uncomfortable, but it was a stark reminder of how much had changed.

And despite it all, walking with Abbie felt as familiar as breathing. The desire to wrap my arm around her shoulders and bring her close to me, to whisper some stupid joke in her ear just to make her stumble and laugh in a way that meant I could catch her and kiss her, threatened to consume me.

"Watford hasn't changed much," I said, inclining my head toward the small laundromat on the crossroads corner, just one storefront down from Watford General. "I always imagined they'd rebrand at some point."

Abbie shrugged. A sudden gust of wind tousled her hair, and she reached up once more to tuck it behind her ear.

"Well, Paula died at the beginning of last year. Heart attack," Abbie said, frowning as she updated me about the owners. "Safe to say Bobby's not doing well."

I sighed, a heavy ache settling in my gut. "That freaking sucks."

Abbie gave me a small smile, though it looked like she was fighting it.

"You still don't curse?"

"Only for dramatic effect, or when it feels necessary."

"I have to say, I'm impressed," Abbie said, waving to a young woman in the laundromat who was folding freshly dried clothes into her hamper. The woman smiled and returned her wave. "I kind of assumed that was a phase you'd grow out of. You know me and my potty mouth."

A pause stretched between us as I began walking once more.

"Where did you end up?" Abbie finally asked. Her voice was hesitant and soft, no doubt preparing herself for my answer.

My heart hammered in my chest. The truth of where I'd been in the last few years was the first of many truths I would share with Abbie over the next few days. I inhaled deeply, lifting my eyes to the back of her head.

"I learned how to play the guitar," I blurted.

She turned back to face me, her mouth falling open slightly. Whether in shock at the entire conversation, or the fact that I had the audacity to make a small joke, I couldn't tell.

"Jesus Christ," was all she said. She knew there was more, but for whatever reason, she sensed my hesitance to share and backed off. It was an allowance I didn't deserve, especially from her.

I smoothed my hair back and returned my hands to my pockets. Abbie and I both remained silent as the Washington sun climbed the horizon.

It was better this way. Abbie had asked to keep things strictly professional, and while I didn't think either of us had crossed that line yet, revealing too much of our recent histories would forge a kind of intimacy I didn't think either of us could handle.

I could still see the wheels turning in her head, though.

I paused at the Roadhouse bar, unable to stop myself. I was surprised that my fingerprints weren't permanently etched into the glass, considering how much time I used to spend there, pressing my nose and palms against the window, scanning the crowd for my uncle.

My gaze moved beyond the Roadhouse logo decal and into the beer hall. A laugh escaped me when I saw the pool table that was still front and center in the parlor.

I was reminded of all those late nights hustling pool for my uncle, who always took things too far. The pool table where it all happened was still there. Someone replaced the carpet beneath the table. They stripped away the evidence of all of those fights I had been caught in the middle of. I took my hands out of my pockets and flexed them, balling them into a tight fist before releasing them.

I'd had the steadiest hand at boot camp. My grip on my rifle never faltered. I wasn't some scared kid anymore, tired and exhausted, and begging my uncle to let me do something other kids my age were doing, like playing sports or learning to care for livestock. Even when I was falling asleep with the pool stick in my hand, clearly exhausted after a long day at school, Ellis would slap me on the back of the head before returning to his corner booth, telling me to get myself together and win.

"Connor?" Abbie said, her warm voice pulling me from the cold recesses of my mind. "What's wrong?"

"I'm fine."

"You don't look fine," she whispered, raising a hand to my face and running her fingers down the side of my cheek. The touch of her fingers against my skin shocked me. I felt that delicate touch everywhere. My focus narrowed on the brief touch of her fingers, and my eyes widened at the same moment hers did.

"I'm so sorry," she said quickly, jerking her hand back as if she'd been burned.

"It's okay," I replied, my voice rough. I closed my eyes for a moment. "It's fine."

She nodded, her cheeks flaming with embarrassment. Abbie turned away from me, shoving that darn strap over her shoulder again, setting a brutal pace down the sidewalk, and it took every decent bone in my body not to grab her by the arm and kiss her until we were both breathless and panting.

That touch had been instinctual. She'd touched me not because she'd really thought about it, but because she'd done it so many times before. How many times had I stared off into space with Abbie on the couch next to me, or in the cab of Lucy, and a simple touch of her fingers had brought me back?

I rubbed a hand down my face. I *had* to get it together. I wasn't willing to jeopardize the delicate peace Abbie and I had brokered.

God help me, I needed her. That touch of her fingers, however brief it was, had awakened something in me.

I shook my head, clearing that line of thought as quickly as it had entered my mind. I didn't understand how it was so easy for me to forget.

Because you're selfish.

That voice in my head—my *uncle's* voice—was something I could never outrun. I'd been to a desert thousands of miles away, I'd become a leader and a fighter, and none of it mattered. I'd become a man who fought desperately to be good, to be a man and leader worth respecting and following, and it didn't matter.

Being back in Watford, and looking into that bar, had transformed me back into that scared ten-year-old kid, whose parents loved drugs more than their own child, and whose uncle was a cruel, mean old bastard who could never make something of himself, and instead took from everyone else.

I jerked my head up to where Abbie was still rushing down the street, her head turned down toward the pavement.

I wasn't that scared, weak kid anymore. I'd worked myself to the bone to make sure of that. Those horrible, cruel parts of my past were just that: they were in the past.

As the sun crested over the eastern buildings of town, Abbie's brown hair let up with a golden hue that took my breath away. She looked back at me, and I could have sworn she smiled softly in the early morning sun.

My future was still being written.

Our future—whatever that looked like—was being written at this moment.

Despite it all, I had hope.

Chapter 11

Abbie

I didn't know what on God's green earth had possessed me to touch Connor's face. To make matters worse, I didn't just touch it, I practically *stroked* it.

My cheeks flushed again as Connor jogged to catch up to me. I didn't realize how much space I'd put between us until I'd remembered to look back. He'd still been standing outside the Roadhouse, retreating into himself in that familiar way. His eyes had glazed over, his chest rapidly rising and falling with the rising panic I recognized all too easily.

I couldn't stand seeing him hurt when we were younger, and apparently, I still couldn't.

I had no right to touch him like that, but I couldn't resist the instinct to reach out and comfort him, to pull him back to the present moment even though I had nothing to offer him.

I wanted to smack myself in the face. I was an idiot. I'd always been a bumbling idiot around Connor. I was bold to assume that awkwardness would fade over time. Evidently, neither time nor space could make me get that part of my shit together.

Connor and I walked the two blocks of Main Street to Watley's in silence. We opened the door, and I mentally and emotionally braced myself for whatever—and whoever—lay beyond the threshold.

Connor's sudden return to Watford had brought up more than a few questioning stares from the townsfolk. No one, save for Imogen, had dared to ask me how I was feeling directly, or if I knew anything about Connor's return. I took my silver linings wherever I could find them these days.

We sat down in a corner booth, and a red-haired waitress came up to us shortly after, welcoming us to the diner and taking our drink orders.

"I'll have water and a cup of coffee, please, Stacey, thank you," I said, taking the menu from the waitress.

"Just a cup of coffee for me, please," Connor replied. Stacey nodded and scampered off back to the kitchen.

While Connor looked over the menu, I looked around the diner. Watley's had been in operation for as long as Watford and had remained unchanged. It was the epitome of a 1950s diner, right down to the stereotypical red and white theme and a jukebox in the corner. The booths hadn't changed, and neither had the many, *many* pictures of Marilyn Monroe hung equidistantly between booths on the far wall. The waffle iron and milkshake machine lined the back wall behind the checkout counter.

Stacey returned with our drinks. I ordered chicken and waffles, while Connor ordered chocolate chip pancakes with an extra side of bacon. I smiled as I took a sip of my coffee. Some things really stayed the same.

"So," Connor said as he set his coffee down on the table, unable to find another, less awkward, way to break the tension.

"So," I replied, a coy smile playing on my lips. "Let's talk about the festival."

"Kameron was sad not to be here in person, but something came up at the last minute. I'm sure you know about Winding Road's mission?"

To my surprise, a small blush crept into my cheeks.

"I'm not going to lie, Connor. I have about as much guidance about this festival as you three probably do. That said, I know little about Winding Road other than that it's a nonprofit."

"Winding Road is a recovery program and regenerative farm, about an hour and a half east of here. We raise cattle and other livestock, and we grow a small variety of crops as part of the for-profit side, but the nonprofit program of Winding Road is where our mission really shines through. Winding Road is a place where veterans and first responders can come to receive true support for processing their traumas—including those they might have endured before their service."

Connor took a small sip of his coffee. His chest heaved with the effort of taking a single, controlled breath. Something about the motion had my heart squeezing painfully.

"I was part of Winding Road's first recovery cohort, and it changed my life. The work that Kameron does is nothing short of life changing. The men and women that come through each cohort show up at the farm hopelessly lost, many of them struggling with alcoholism or drug addiction, and they leave with new tools to cope with the stresses of life. More importantly, they reconnect with the world around them, with their spouses, kids, friends. It's incredible to see. A large majority of Winding Road's graduates transfer directly to addiction recovery programs willingly and stay there for the duration of the entire program."

I stared into Connor's eyes while the full impact of his words sunk into me.

"You were part of the first . . . wait," I said, blinking several times. Connor's expression was pained, but to his credit, he didn't pull away from my gaze. "Connor, you went into the military?"

Connor swallowed thickly.

"I joined the Marine Corps. When I left Watford, it was on a bus to Camp Pendleton for boot camp."

The world tilted on its axis. I fixed my gaze on the foam bubbles forming around the rim of my coffee cup. My brain was jumping from thought to thought, unable to make the connections it needed to understand.

"You joined the military," I repeated. A swarm of emotions crashed through me at once. Admiration for his sacrifice. Anger at his inability to leave a note or a voicemail. A bone-deep hurt that he'd kept this from me when I'd sworn that I would follow him anywhere.

More alarmingly, I felt grief for the life we might have had together, if he'd only taken me with him.

I stopped the selfish train of thoughts that threatened to derail my grip on reality. Since he left me behind, there had to be a reason. Despite everything that had happened between us, I still believed Connor was an honest man. A broken, beautiful, honest man.

"Abbie, I need you to know that I decided to leave Watford long before it happened, and it had nothing to do with you."

My gaze snapped back to his. My brain finally caught up to speed, and I let out a small, disbelieving sigh.

"I'm not sure that does anything to soothe the hurt you left in your wake, *sunshine*."

Connor's face twisted into a painful grimace at my sarcastic usage of the nickname I'd coined for him. "Crap, that came out wrong."

I held up a hand, shaking my head.

"Connor, really, we don't need to do this. Truthfully, I'm not sure I could handle that conversation right now. I'm glad you're safe, and that you're doing better. Maybe we'll . . ." I swallowed the lump forming in my throat. "Maybe we'll get to where we can talk about the past."

"What about trading truths?"

"Trading truths?"

"Abbie, I don't pretend to know anything about your life now. Five years is practically a lifetime. We were just kids when I left."

I was grateful for his unabashed ownership of the situation, even after what he revealed to me. He wasn't trying to gaslight me into thinking it wasn't as serious as it was, or that my hurt feelings and emotions surrounding the situation weren't valid.

"But I want to tell you these things, including the reasons I was so desperate to leave Watford. The things that wounded me so deeply I would leave the only ray of sunshine in my life behind."

My chest tightened at the small nod of his nickname for me. Sunnie, he'd called me. My boyfriend giving me a nickname had fulfilled one of my top girlish dreams. It seemed foolish to have such a visceral reaction to it now, but I swore butterflies took flight in my stomach as my eyes locked onto his.

"So I propose we trade truths. A one-for-one model. I'll tell you something honest and vulnerable about the last few years, and you'll return the favor."

Stacey returned with our meals, and I was grateful for the distraction. Connor's proposal felt like slippery territory. One mistake, one misstep, and I'd be sliding headfirst toward getting my heart broken once again.

"Can we table that conversation for another day? I need to think about it."

To my continued surprise, Connor's gaze held steady, and his lips curved into a small, grateful smile.

"That sounds good to me."

I sighed a deep breath of relief, picking up my fork and knife as I cut into my chicken.

"So, you've told me a bit about Winding Road. Their sponsorship is a big part of why this festival is happening, so I'm grateful to your leader. Kameron, right?"

Connor nodded, taking a bite of his pancake. "Yeah, Kameron's the executive director. Our ringleader, as Lucas and I often call him. He was sad not to be here this weekend, but something came up last minute. You can give me any relevant information, and I'll make sure it gets back to him."

I nodded, swallowing my bite of food alongside another swig of coffee. I leaned back in the booth and met Connor's eyes.

"The Watford town council approached me to put this event on. The last few years have been really hard between the pandemic and subsequent economic downturn. Trent and the other council members got a rural development grant, and that money, coupled with the sponsorship from Winding Road, has provided a sizable financial basis for us to work with."

Connor raised his eyebrows. "Trent . . . Surely you don't mean Trent Kaser?"

I snorted, trying to cover my face with a greasy hand. "The very one."

Connor's jaw hinged open.

"That snot-nosed kid is a *councilman*?"

"He's a lawyer now too," I added, poking my fork in Connor's direction. "Left for law school around the same time as Cassie did. Better put some respect on his name."

Connor let out a grunt of disgust.

"That kid gets no respect from me until he's earned it."

I wiped my mouth with a napkin to hide my smile.

"Anyway, I have a few ideas for the festival. We've received a basic structure from the council, mainly because the event needs to hit a few criteria so we can use the grant money. Namely, there needs to be a lot of local businesses involved. Every business owner in Watford needs to be made aware of the festival, and anything we can source locally, we need to take that route."

Connor shrugged, crossing his arms over his chest after setting his fork down against an empty plate. I couldn't help but gape. Hadn't we just sat down? How was this man already finished with his meal?

"Locally sourced sounds good to me. What else did you have in mind?"

"Phillipa from Blackbeard Coffee is also a sponsor, so there will be a coffee cart the day of. I'm already planning on asking the sheriff's department if they'd be willing to call in some favors and get a firetruck or ambulance to come hang out for a few hours in the name of promoting public safety." I took another bite of my food, suddenly eager to keep talking about the festival. It was nice to have someone to share my ideas with. It was good to know that we'd be on the same page about everything that needed to be done, especially given that Connor would be heavily involved with the festival over the next few weeks.

"I've been planning for lots of food vendors—between Watley's, the Roadhouse, Blackbeard Coffee, and other local restaurants from within the county, I think we'll have it covered there. There also needs to be a fireworks show at the end. I've already had multiple seven-year-olds demand this, so it's nonnegotiable."

"Of course," Connor said, smirking. "Can't disappoint the kids."

"One last thing," I said, my heart thumping erratically. "I know this would take a lot of legwork, but given that it's a festival designed to help put Watford back on the map, I want there to be a vendor fair. I plan to encourage Watford businesses to take part, but I also want to bring in local businesses from the county proper. Who knows what connections we could make? Owning a small business in a remote area is difficult, and making more connections might save people money in the long run."

Connor's smile reflected my excitement back to me, and my chest squeezed painfully. I couldn't hold back my answering smile.

"It's a great idea, Abs. I'm happy to help with whatever you need. Just say the word and I'm there."

"Thank you," I said, returning my gaze to my plate. Connor asked to see the rest of my documents, including some of the initial brainstorming pages, my cheeks heating as I handed them over. He flipped through the folder while I finished my waffle and downed the rest of my coffee.

"I'm in," I whispered.

"Hm?" Connor questioned, the noise a low rumble in his throat. I bit my lip.

"Your proposal of a truth for a truth. I think it would help me."

Connor gave me a small smile. "Yeah. I think it would help me too. There's a lot I want to tell you, Abbie, but I won't dump my crap on you. We're partners."

My jaw twitched, and Connor grimaced.

"The words just aren't flowing for me today. Not romantically speaking. For the festival."

"Right," I agreed, my throat suddenly dry. I sipped my water. "Of course. For the festival."

"So, first things first. I'll let Kameron know we've got the Winding Road literature ordered. That's a big item on my to-do list checked off. What's next for yours?"

I sat back, tapping a finger on my cheek as I considered. This whole endeavor felt overwhelming to me. I needed the money too badly to say no to Trent's offer to become the festival coordinator, but I'd never done something like this, outside of being the yearbook editor my senior year of high school. Watford needed this festival. I needed this festival.

"I think I'd like to reach out to potential vendors," I said. "Given that we're on such a tight deadline, I want to make sure the businesses and nonprofits that might organize a booth have ample time to do so. Trent gave me a list of some up-and-coming small businesses in Watford County that might be interested."

"Sounds good to me," Connor said, removing his credit card from his wallet and sliding it toward the edge of the table.

"We talked about festival business. I'm sure the grant would cover it."

Connor flashed me a grin. "It's no problem."

He meant for it to be cocky and self-assured, but a familiar pang of inadequacy shot through me. Connor had been in Watford General enough over the last few days to observe our stunning lack of customers. I was barely keeping my business afloat, and every time I checked my personal bank account, I wanted to cry. There was almost always less than a hundred dollars in there at any point.

I wanted to believe he meant nothing by covering the bill so nonchalantly, but I couldn't ignore that sharp, slicing pain of feeling that struck me.

"Truth?" I asked quietly, and Connor met my eyes, something unfamiliar and unrecognized simmering in his gaze.

"Truth," he replied.

"Watford General isn't doing well," I admitted. Though my voice was barely above a whisper, it felt as though my admission boomed through the small diner, as if my words echoed off the walls back to me, driving me deeper into my shame.

"The pandemic really took a toll on our customer base. Fewer people could tend to their farms past the basics of keeping their families and livelihoods afloat. I didn't realize we'd become so dependent on our customers needing the latest and greatest. And before you ask, Malcolm isn't entirely to blame. Tilly did most of the administrative work to keep the store running, and my dad focused more on the financial and business side of things. That's just how they divided tasks. Unfortunately, when my mom died, and my dad went off the deep end, so did the organization of important documents. Tax documents, to be exact."

Connor raised a brow, but thankfully, said nothing.

"So, I now have the IRS breathing down my back, asking for documents from several years ago that I'm pretty sure we don't have." I pressed two fingers into my temple to rub away the dull ache forming there. "All that to say, I need the money from this job. The rural development grant has allowed Trent and the council to offer me a very generous salary, and I need to do a good job. I can't afford to screw this up. Literally."

I inhaled, finally lifting my gaze from our cleared table to meet Connor's eyes. His gaze was soft, his chest inclined toward me.

It had been so long since I'd been able to offload my feelings without fear of judgment. A warm feeling filled my body at the knowledge that he was listening. He wasn't trying to solve my life problems, as Imogen often did. Connor was simply listening to me. Hearing me. Offering encouragement and support in the way only he could.

I tucked a piece of my brown hair behind my ear and gestured for him to speak.

"Truth: I always felt awful when Tilly and Malcolm paid for me when we went places," Connor began, sitting back and throwing his right arm over the side of the booth. His gaze wandered to the door as he drummed his fingers on his empty coffee cup.

"I was your boyfriend. I should have been the one taking you out, and instead, I couldn't even rub two pennies together to get my girl an ice cream cone. Even worse, your parents were amazing people, who never blinked an eye when they said 'all together' at the cash register whenever we went out to eat." Connor shook his head, cracking his neck to the side to dispel some of the tension bracing his body. "I worked so hard when I was a teenager. I did everything my uncle ever asked of me, and by the time I left Watford, I didn't have a cent to my name. When I got my cammies at boot camp, that was the first time in over three years that I'd received brand new clothes."

I inhaled sharply, unable to look away, even though a raw aching pain shot through me. I wasn't naive enough to think that Connor's life had been sunshine and rainbows since he left. I wasn't stupid enough to think that I was the only person in this world capable of hurting.

But in that moment, I realized I had gravely underestimated who Connor had been. I'd been so in love with this boy, infatuated with him in what was a borderline unhealthy way, and now that I was sitting across from him, four years of real-life experience between us, I suddenly realized that maybe we never knew each other at all.

"All that to say, I understand that money comes and goes, and I am more than happy to pay for this meal. And it's not because I feel like I'm repaying a debt. It's because I want to. You're not a burden, Abbie, financially or otherwise," he finished.

"Neither are you," I whispered, my hand reaching for his out of pure instinct. His warm, calloused hand enveloped mine, and something loud and damning locked into place inside my heart. "You have never been a burden, Connor."

Connor's gaze locked with mine as he squeezed my fingers tightly. My eyes fluttered shut. There were so many questions I needed to ask. So much I needed to say. But I couldn't bring myself to open my mouth.

I would let myself have this moment. My brain screamed at me to pull back, knowing that all of this—Connor's presence in my life, his closeness—would be restricted to a small sliver of time that would be gone in a flash. I'd be left picking up the pieces of my life all over again.

But as the comforting sound of eggs frying on cast-iron pans surrounded us, with the familiar scent of chicken and waffles wafting through the space, and the feeling of Connor's calloused hands holding mine, I couldn't pull away.

Chapter 12

Connor

The next morning, Kameron arrived at our cabin. Kam and Lucas were both hunched over their laptops at the dining room table, sipping their respective beverages—coffee for Lucas and that God-awful green smoothie Kameron seemed to like so much. I poured myself a mug of coffee and opened the screened door to allow some of the fresh mountain air to circulate the cabin. I inhaled deeply, letting the familiar scent of evergreen pine and black coffee settle over my bones, and sat down at the table across from Kameron.

"How was your drive?"

Kameron shrugged, running a hand through his hair. He looked tired in a way I hadn't seen from him in months.

"The drive was fine. I'm sorry again that I couldn't be here earlier in the week. The guy that showed up was in a bad way. Ended up checking out of the program early, despite my efforts to get him to stay." Kameron blew out a breath. "I contacted the local precinct according to the address he gave us, but I'm worried about him."

I pressed my lips together. This was perhaps one of Kameron's only personality flaws, if one could call it that.

He was so passionate about his work that he sometimes got too close to the people who came through. Kameron knew he couldn't save every struggling soul, but that didn't stop him from trying like hell to do just that.

"It'll be alright, Kam," Lucas chimed in. "You've done more for him in three days than most would do in a lifetime. It's ultimately up to him whether he takes those resources and uses them."

I nodded. "Lucas is right. You've done what you can."

Kameron laughed. "I'm not sure that will ever be enough."

"For you, my perfectionist? It will never be enough."

Kameron smiled, jerking his chin in my direction.

"Lucas gave me the rundown on the work he's done this week. Making some good connections with the locals?"

Lucas sniggered into his coffee, and I shot him a death glare.

"Something like that," I said, rubbing my chin. My stubble was getting long, and I knew I needed to shave, but part of me wanted to see how long I could grow my beard out, now that I wasn't required to shave every day. "I've had several discussions with Abbie. She's looking forward to working with us for the festival, and she's got some great ideas about how to bring local businesses and resources together to make the event a success."

"She sounds amazing," Kameron said, a small smile playing on his lips.

Instead of gushing about Abbie and putting up with that ridicule for the rest of my days, I launched into an explanation about the vendor fair, and Abbie's plans to involve local businesses for sourcing. Lucas shared an idea he had about setting up a designated kids' section at the festival, so there would be a safe space for families to enjoy their food while their kids explored. Kameron was a huge fan and gave Lucas the lead on that effort. To my surprise, Lucas seemed genuinely interested in assisting with the project. I was learning more about him with every passing day.

"I'll be working on some more marketing graphics today. Since we've got a decent social media following, I figured we could use that to our advantage, to see if we can't drum up some online hype for the upcoming festival. Could you ask Abbie to send over whatever Founder's Day graphics the council has provided for her? Since this is a joint effort, after all."

"Sure," I said. "I was planning to head into town here shortly, if either of you wants to join me."

Lucas waved a hand in dismissal while Kam shook his head.

"I've got a few meetings this morning, so I'm unfortunately glued to my laptop," Kam said.

"And I'm planning to go for a hike. It's been ages since I've been on a good hike."

"Killer's Ridge is good, if you're looking for something more challenging."

Kameron and Lucas both looked at me with blank expressions.

"The name makes it sound like some serial killer funhouse," I acknowledged quickly, "but it's not. It's named after one of the most prominent founding families in Watford, whose surname was, unfortunately, Killer."

Kameron let out a low whistle. "Told you these small towns give me the creeps."

Lucas shook his head.

"I don't know what you're talking about. That sounds cool."

I smiled as Kameron barked out a laugh. I rinsed out my coffee mug and set it off to the side.

"See you losers later."

I headed toward Watford General with two of Blackbeard's lattes in hand. I tried to tell myself that the coffee wasn't a peace offering, but there was no escaping the fact that it definitely was. It was also helpful to focus on something other than the way the teenage girl working at the coffee bar had been furiously texting her friends as soon as I picked up the coffees and turned to leave.

"Hello?" I called as I pushed the door to the store open. I put my latte behind the checkout counter to grab later. It was still piping hot, and unlike Abbie Collins, I wasn't a fan of having my taste buds burned off while drinking my coffee.

"Back here!" Abbie's voice was muffled by the aisles and pillars between us. I shook my head, a smile appearing on my face subconsciously.

"Where is—"

I almost dropped the latte in my hand as I came face-to-face with Abbie's backside. Abbie Collins in jeans was a sight to behold, the denim fabric hugging her hips and curves in a way that had me clenching my free hand into a fist to keep from grabbing and pulling them against me.

"Sorry," Abbie said, grunting with the effort of pulling something to the front of the shelf. "A certain someone decided all the spare nails needed to be kept in the most difficult place to reach." Another grunt of effort as she stood on her tiptoes. "That someone being me."

The movement stretched the fabric even more, and I barely stifled a groan.

"Can I help you?"

"I can do it."

"I don't doubt that," I replied, my voice rough around the edges, "but Kameron arrived in town this morning. He hired some extra hands and paused programming this week in order to focus on the festival. I'm staying for the foreseeable future."

That statement caused Abbie to momentarily forget she was precariously perched on top of a seven-foot ladder and whip her head toward me. Her foot slipped from the top rung, and she wobbled unsteadily for exactly three seconds before that gorgeous backside made a beeline for the floor. I shoved her latte on the nearest shelf and caught her.

"Did you just catch me?" she asked, and I could feel her heart pounding against her rib cage.

I gently set her down on the floor. She swayed slightly and used my forearms as a balancing agent, her wide eyes meeting mine.

"*Without* spilling the coffee?" she added.

"Is that a serious question?" I asked. "Of course I caught you. I wouldn't let you crack your skull open on the linoleum floor."

Abbie frowned as she looked at the floor between us, holding my arms tighter.

"I guess that would be hard to clean."

I laughed incredulously. "There is something wrong with you."

Abbie shrugged. "Maybe it's best that you get the nails. I should probably keep my feet on the ground."

I nodded once, and she finally released my arms. The fact she did it slowly, as if savoring the feeling of my muscles, had me smirking. I glanced behind me to make sure she was clear of the ladder before grabbing the box with ease, tucking it beneath my left arm.

"So, can I assume these nails are for the new stalls that need to be built?"

Abbie nodded, taking the box of nails from my outstretched hands. I climbed down and returned the ladder to its storage corner.

"The council gave us blueprints, measurements, and the money to buy supplies, but as you can probably tell, I'm not gifted in the building department."

I shook my head, gesturing for us to head back onto the sales floor.

"Lucky for you, I'm a master builder."

"I doubt that."

"Ouch," I said, smiling.

Abbie returned my smile, setting the large box of nails down on the checkout counter while waving to Kevin, who was restocking the chip bags.

"Imogen's been storing most of the wooden planks on her homestead, and I've got the blueprints here."

Abbie reached beneath the cash register and pulled out a manila folder. She briefly leafed through the paperwork until she found the stall blueprint. I glanced over it and shrugged. The stalls would be fairly simple to construct based on the schematic, but it had been a while since I'd built something. I had a feeling it would be time consuming.

"How many of these do you need?"

"Ten," she answered, a light blush heating her cheeks. "I know, I know. I completely dropped the ball on this. I kept saying I'd find a contractor to come build them, but the council wanted them to be 'Watford made' or whatever, and I—"

"It's fine, Abs," I said, giving her a reassuring smile. "I bet Kevin and I can get these done by the end of the week."

"Hey!" Kevin shouted from behind me. "I did *not* volunteer for building duty."

"I wasn't asking," I said, still looking down at the blueprint. Abbie slapped a hand over her mouth to keep from laughing, and Kevin muttered what I could only assume was a string of cuss words and a comment about how Abbie doesn't pay him enough to deal with this.

"Thank you, Connor. Seriously. This takes a load of stress off my plate."

Against my better judgment, I reached a hand out to touch hers.

"I told you I'm here to help, Abbie. Whatever you need."

Abbie's lips parted slightly, as if she was thinking of saying something and then thought better of it. I remained silent, knowing that if I opened my mouth, I would tell Abbie everything about the last five years. Telling Abbie everything about that time would make me feel better, but it would also distract and confuse her just a few weeks before an important event. I wouldn't do that to her.

"If you two are done making cartoon heart eyes at each other, can I please take my lunch break?" Kevin's voice rang out in the silence, and Abbie jerked her hand out from under mine like she'd been burned.

Her furious blush as she muttered for Kevin to 'do whatever' made my heart soar.

Chapter 13

Abbie

Saturdays are for the girls.

Imogen and I had an informal tradition of stress-baking cookies, pies, cakes, and whatever other sweet treats piqued our interest, beginning back when we were in high school. After Imogen's divorce, and her subsequent move back to Watford, we started the tradition back up again. There's something cathartic about rolling, punching, and mixing your tribulations and sorrows away. And despite what my grandmother would say about imbuing one's emotions into one's cooking, the cookies have always been pretty damn sweet.

"So," Imogen said, pulling her stand mixer down from the cabinet. I stood a few feet away, sorting the freshly retrieved eggs and glass milk containers, labeling each one accordingly. "Let's talk about Connor Harvey."

I choked on my next inhale, almost dropping the egg I was holding.

"Going straight for the throat today, huh? I haven't even gotten the sugar and flour out yet."

Imogen pinned me with her stare as she tied the red and white plaid apron behind her back. I followed her lead and retrieved my matching, monogrammed, slightly ridiculous apron from the pantry. We got them back when Imogen had first inherited the homestead from her grandmother. They were a promise to one another to always remember that friends and family were the most important part of our lives. Everything else could come and go, but as long as we had each other, everything would turn out okay.

The first room Imogen renovated in this house was the kitchen. Never a fan of the sad beige style that plagues most ranch-style homes, Imogen envisioned something moodier. She replaced the white cabinets with deep blue ones with golden knobs and accents. Instead of granite, she opted for butcher block countertops, weaving wooden accents throughout the kitchen. She saved a ton of money by refinishing the existing hardwood floors rather than ripping them up and replacing them with laminate. The only traditional ranch kitchen element she kept was a giant farmhouse sink. The result was a moody and cozy kitchen that felt incredibly welcoming, despite the darker hues.

"There's no sense in beating around the bush, babe," Imogen said, a teasing lilt to her voice. "You and that boy of yours are the talk of the town yet again."

Pink tinted my cheeks as I gathered the milk and eggs and stuck them back in the fridge, leaving out only what we needed for today's baking. We'd decided on snickerdoodle cookies, per my suggestion. If Imogen remembered that those were Connor's favorite, she chose not to call me out on it.

"I don't see why," I mumbled. I could still feel Imogen's eyes on me as I gathered flour, sugar, and baking utensils, and I knew resisting this line of questioning would ultimately be futile.

"If you remember, Connor and his uncle used to drum up drama back when we were kids. Ellis wasn't exactly a great guy."

"And Connor unfairly withstood that reputation," I said, the metal measuring cup clanking too loudly on the ceramic bowl as I dumped the first cup of flour into it. "Connor was a freaking kid, just like we were. It was unfair of the townspeople to attach his uncle's reputation to his."

I always felt defensive about Connor. I never interacted with his uncle beyond awkward run-ins at various establishments in town. Connor had told me his uncle was an asshole and that he wanted nothing to do with him. I suspected there was more at play than just him hating his uncle, but I hadn't known how to handle it. After walking through Imogen's healing journey alongside her, I knew more about the warning signs of abuse.

Connor was deeply misunderstood, even by me. Everyone in town, myself included, saw what we wanted to see in him. I can blame it on being in love—the love you believe in at seventeen—but the more I thought about it, the more I realized that I had been part of the problem, too.

We often want people to fit neatly into the molds we create for them in our minds. But in Connor's case, he didn't fit into any of the boxes people tried to place him in. Some wanted to hate him because of Ellis's actions, while others wanted to protect him from the unfair judgment he weathered.

Imogen gave me a soft smile as she cracked the eggs into the bowl attached to her stand mixer. I continued to mix the dry ingredients together.

"I love you, Abbie. I will always try my damndest to support you in whatever way I can. But this new connection between you and Connor makes me nervous."

I huffed out a laugh, wiping my forehead with the back of my hand.

"I know why you would be nervous, Imogen, but it's not like that. He's not idiotic enough to win me over after everything he did."

I bit the inside of my cheek, sucking the flesh between my teeth as I chose my next words carefully.

"I think I just need closure," I said. Imogen flipped the stand mixer on to cream the eggs, butter, and sugar together. We stood together with the sound of the stand mixer whirring.

"My therapist would say I'm projecting, but I need to get this off my chest," Imogen said, unlocking the machine and lifting the dough hook clear of the mixing bowl so I could pour in half of the dry ingredients. "You will not get closure from him. There are some wounds that no amount of time or discussion can fix. He left you, Abbie. He abandoned you and disappeared without a trace. Years came and went, and he never once reached out to you. And now, he shows up back here in Watford, expecting us all to accept that it was some freak coincidence that his business partner sponsored the very festival you were asked to coordinate?"

Imogen had never been one to pull her punches, and most of the time, I appreciated that. This was not one of those times. She gave voice to many of the misgivings I had about this entire endeavor, and if she had doubts about whether Connor's interest in the festival—and by extension, me—was genuine, I knew others in town would be suspicious too.

Hot tears stung my eyes. Imogen wouldn't judge me for crying. Baking day was meant to be cathartic, after all.

I was tired. I didn't want to shed another fucking tear over Connor Harvey.

"When is it going to be enough?" I whispered, propping my elbows onto the flour-dusted countertop and dropping my head into my hands. "I feel like I've been carrying the weight of the freaking world, and I was so happy, Im. I was so happy to finally have someone back in my life who knew me, where things could be easy, where I could ask for something and know it would get done. And you're that person for me most of the time, but it's not fair to always be leaning on you, not when you've also been through so much in the last few years."

Imogen wrapped her arms around my waist, and I finally let the tears fall, the half-mixed snickerdoodle batter forgotten on the other end of the kitchen island.

"You aren't selfish for being caught up in your own crap, Abs," Imogen said. "We both have different ways of dealing with the men who broke our hearts."

A small cry escaped my lips as a new rush of pain washed over me. The memories of Imogen stumbling into my apartment, bruised and terrified. Memories of how she held me while I sat at the window table in Blackbeard's during the rainy season, waiting to see a blue truck on Main Street that never showed. I'd had a bad feeling about her ex-husband from the start, but Imogen had been so desperate to get away from her parents that I'd still gone with her to the courthouse that summer to support her. Later, I drove Imogen to physical therapy in Brighton and sat with her in the courtroom while she waited to see whether her abuser would be brought to justice.

"I'm so grateful for you," I said, pulling back from her embrace. "So grateful."

"I'm grateful for you too," she replied, her eyes shining with tears that mirrored mine. "Now, let's finish these cookies. My entire kitchen smells like cinnamon, and I want it to smell like baked goods, too."

I snort-laughed, getting in line behind her at the kitchen sink so I could wash my hands before returning to the stand mixer.

After our unexpectedly heavy discussion about Connor, we opted for lighter topics of conversation, dominated by the discussion of what we were currently reading on our Kindles (me, a fantasy romance by one of my favorite indie authors. Imogen, an insanely spicy dark stalker romance).

Imogen was right—we dealt with our past trauma in peculiar ways.

With the cookies in the oven, and a timer set, Imogen and I curled up on her sectional, Kindles in hand and glasses of non-alcoholic sangria on the coffee table. I cracked the windows that framed both sides of the fireplace so we could get some fresh air.

Saturdays were the best day of the week by far.

When the timer for the cookies went off, I jumped up to remove them from the oven as my phone rang on the way.

"Hello?" I answered, tucking my phone between my shoulder and ear as I shoved my hands into oven mitts.

"Hey," Connor's gruff voice crackled over the line, and I almost dropped the burning-hot pan of cookies. I caught myself and placed the pan on the stovetop, removing the oven mitts and turning off the oven.

"Got a proposition for you. Are you busy?"

"Saturdays are for the girls," I said simply.

"I don't know what that means," Connor said, and he sounded so serious that I let out a full-belly laugh, unable to stop myself. Imogen's head popped up over the couch in the living room, a *what the hell* expression on her face. I waved her off, swallowing deep gulps of air to calm myself down enough to speak.

"Imogen and I still bake on Saturdays," I explained, leaning against the countertop as I slid my phone into my hand. "But what did you have in mind?"

"My grand overlord, Kameron, showed up last night, and we wanted to ask if you and Imogen would come over to the cabin tonight for an informal get-together. I'm assuming we'd probably do some talking about the festival, but mostly, I figured it would be a good idea for everyone to get to know each other better, given that we'll be working so closely together the next few weeks."

"Let me ask Imogen," I said, putting my phone on mute. I threw myself over the back of the couch, landing with a plop mere inches from Imogen's feet. She had her tassel blanket pulled up to her chin and a hoodie over her head, obscuring her face.

"What?" she asked flatly, already suspecting something up my sleeve. I smiled sheepishly.

"So, I know Saturdays are normally our day, but how would you feel about going over to the boys' cabin for a small get-together later tonight?"

Imogen blinked, as if trying to comprehend my statement.

"Are we seriously calling them 'the boys' now?"

"I don't know what else to call them," I cried, immediately regretting this decision. "I think it would be good to meet Kameron in person. And Lucas! Have you met Lucas yet?"

Imogen raised an eyebrow as she shut her Kindle case.

"I haven't met him, no. Do I need to?"

"You're just as involved with this festival as I am," I said. "Okay, maybe not exactly, but—"

"Abbie," Imogen cut off my rambling with a smirk. "If you want to go, we'll go. It's just fun to torture you first."

I heaved a sigh of relief. This was the perfect opportunity for all of us to get to know one another. And the presence of people between us, acting as a natural buffer, made me feel better about going somewhere where Connor and I would be expected to interact.

I took my phone off mute and pressed the speaker button.

"Hey, are you still there?"

"Of course," Connor answered, and I bit back a smile. "What's the verdict?"

"We'll be there," I said. "How does six-thirty tonight sound?"

"Perfect," he said. "Kam's planning to grill some burgers. If y'all want anything to drink, feel free. Otherwise, we'll see you when you get here."

Chapter 14

Connor

I mogen and Abbie arrived at our cabin at six-thirty on the dot—though, with Abbie driving, that didn't surprise me in the slightest. Lucas opened the door, inviting the two of them into our space. They both wore gorgeous sun dresses, Imogen's pale blue, while Abbie had chosen a sunflower-printed one.

My heart skipped a beat as I looked at Abbie. She was beautiful all the time, but there was something about her in a dress that sent my brain into overdrive. Before I was truly cognizant of my actions, I walked over to her, taking the bottle from her hands and pulling her in for a side hug. She melted into me, letting her head rest on my shoulder for the briefest of moments before pulling back.

"Welcome to our humble abode," I said, and she gave me a soft smile.

"Thanks for inviting us," Abbie said. "We brought cookies. And some sparkling grape juice."

Her cheeks flushed as she quickly added, "I don't drink these days. Haven't for a while."

This beautiful, strong, brave woman.

"Me neither," I replied, feeling the comforting and familiar weight of my sobriety coin in my pocket. Abbie cocked her head slightly to the side, as if she'd just peeled back another layer of my unspoken history. Kameron stepped up behind us, and Abbie immediately turned to give him her full attention, extending a hand to greet him.

"It's wonderful to meet you, Kameron. I feel like we've heard so much about each other indirectly, but it's nice to formally put a face to the name."

Kameron chuckled as he shook her outstretched hand.

"Likewise, Abbie. I'm honored to be here working with you. Please, sit. I'll grab some glasses."

Kameron retreated into the kitchen while Abbie and Imogen exchanged pleasantries with Lucas, who waved them through the entry portico into the living room. High, vaulted ceilings towered above us, with recess lighting and two massive skylights offering us a view of the night sky settling overhead.

"Did I hear correctly—that you were part of the renovation team for the campsite?" Kameron asked, handing Abbie a glass as we all took seats around the sectional. I grabbed my glass of water, decided not to test my luck, and sat at the end of the couch to keep a respectful distance away from Abbie. Her dress barely covered her knees when she sat, and my jaw twitched.

Perhaps tonight would prove to be more difficult than I'd expected.

"I was," Abbie answered, that flush still riding high on her cheeks. "Noah approached me and said he was better with exterior design and renovations rather than interior design. He wanted me to help with redesigning the interiors and giving them a modern facelift. Have you enjoyed your stay? Only a few folks have stayed at the campsite since we finished the renovations."

Kameron nodded, taking a sip of his water. "It's been wonderful. Thanks for asking. I'm glad we're able to stay here until the festival. It's a welcomed break from the day-to-day operations of the farm, I've gotta say."

"I can imagine," Imogen said earnestly. "Abbie told me about some of the work you do, and it's amazing. Did all of you meet while on active duty?"

I tensed, though no one else seemed to notice. I doubt Kam or Lucas would've laid that information out, so I suspected Abbie had dropped that bomb during their baking earlier in the day.

"Kameron and I were in the same unit for most of our careers," I said. "Lucas and Kameron hit the fleet together before being separated. Lucas and I were never in the same unit, but he came to work for Kameron at Winding Road a few weeks after I did."

Imogen nodded. Abbie focused on her glass.

"Where were you stationed?" Imogen asked, still trying to make small talk despite the awkwardness creeping into the space.

"We were at Pendleton mostly, though we frequently flew across the country to Camp Lejeune for training."

Imogen let out a long breath. She took a sip of her water as a silence fell over the room. I winced internally. I didn't know the full reason for Imogen's return to Watford, but I knew her marriage to someone stationed at Camp Pendleton had ended.

Kameron shot me a *do something, you fool!* glare from across the sectional, but I was locked up, staring at Abbie's crestfallen expression. I wanted to tell her more about my time in the military, but I wasn't sure it'd do any good at this point. My military career had been a turning point in my life, for better and for worse, in some ways, but that chapter of my life meant the ultimate betrayal in Abbie's eyes.

"Alright, not that I don't enjoy talking to you guys, but I'm cranking up some music," Lucas said.

"Are we not discussing the festival?" I asked, raising an eyebrow in Lucas's direction as he strode for the kitchen island, connecting his phone to the gray Bluetooth speaker.

"You can discuss whatever you want, but we're listening to Tyler Childers in the background while it happens."

Imogen's face lit up, and Abbie smiled in her direction.

"Careful, Lucas, Imogen's going to get attached," Abbie joked, as Imogen began humming under her breath when "Shake the Frost" came rumbling over the speakers.

Kameron launched into a conversation with Abbie about the vendor festival, while Lucas returned to his seat next to Imogen. The two of them started talking about the state of modern country music, and as soon as I heard Imogen say she was sick of wannabe country boys making crappy pop-country, I rolled my eyes. I knew little about Lucas, but one thing I knew for certain was that he loved his country music, and it seemed he'd finally met someone who could hold an in-depth conversation about it with him.

I took my cue to head to the kitchen and pour myself another glass of water. I was grateful Imogen and Abbie hadn't brought alcohol over. Sobriety was a strange beast. I could go weeks without feeling the urge to drink, but social situations like this were one of my triggers. I used to panic in social situations without a drink in my hand until it became a part of my personality. I was 'Party Harvey' in the barracks. Everyone knew they could invite me to their room, and I'd crank the fun-level up to a hundred, even if I woke up the next morning feeling like my life was falling apart. I found myself in my fair share of bad situations with drinking at parties.

I didn't know how much of that history I would share with Abbie yet. This truth-sharing quest between us was still new and fragile. The last thing I wanted to do was rush into things and scare her off. My past was heavy. I was aware of that now more than ever. And Abbie? Abbie had taken on so much these last few years. The only thing I wanted to do now was to help her carry some of that weight.

I leaned back against the counter, cradling my glass of water to my chest as I watched my friends, old and new, talking and laughing with one another. Whatever strange energy had threatened to disrupt our night earlier had vanished.

"Good Luck, Babe!" by Chappell Roan came on, and Imogen let out a shriek of joy, immediately grabbing Abbie's hands and dragging her off the couch.

I thought belting bridges was reserved only for Taylor Swift songs, but as the two of them screamed out the lyrics, off-key, at the top of their lungs, I realized the error in my assumption.

Lucas joined in with fist pumps, and even Kameron nodded along to the beat as the two women danced around each other.

"My chaotic queer icon," Imogen said, both hands clasped over her heart as she heaved a heavy sigh.

"Mainly because she brings out *your* chaotic bisexual energy," Abbie responded, knocking Imogen's hip with hers before returning to the kitchen for another sparkling water.

"Damn right she does," Imogen said, strolling over to where Lucas's phone was propped against the speaker. "I gotta say, Morales, I respect the playlist. Running aux at a party is no small task, but you've done well."

Lucas gave an overdramatic bow, hinging at the waist and throwing his right arm out to the side. "I live to serve, m'lady."

Imogen let out a small giggle, and I raised an eyebrow at the two of them. Kameron was in the corner, his mouth forming a frown as he watched the two of them. Very interesting, indeed.

"Hey," Abbie said as she walked over to the fridge, grabbing another strawberry kiwi water from the fridge door.

"Hey, yourself," I teased. Abbie rolled her eyes.

"It's been a long week. My brain power isn't what it used to be."

She cracked the can open with her thumb and took a large sip.

"Truth?" she asked quietly as Lucas and Imogen continued their music discussion. Chappell Roan faded from the speakers and Zach Bryan's "Deep Satin" came on next.

"Truth," I said, giving her what I hoped was an encouraging smile.

She inhaled deeply. "I hate the taste of every sparkling water I've tried except strawberry kiwi."

A laugh escaped me at the honest confession.

"I know it sounds crazy, but when I decided not to drink anymore . . . Well, I didn't decide for me, if that makes sense. My dad's drinking is completely out of control. And giving up drinking felt like protecting what I had left. This isn't making any sense," Abbie said, pressing the cool can to the side of her face.

"I think I understand what you mean," I said, taking a step closer and setting my glass of water down on the island. "Your dad is out of control, and that's scary. It's hard to navigate a strained relationship with the person who was supposed to love and guide you. So you took control in a healthy way. You can't control what he does, how much he drinks, or spends on alcohol, but you can make a different choice for yourself."

Abbie met my eyes, her lips parted in a small 'o.'

"Yeah," she replied. "That's exactly it."

"I've been sober for a year," I admitted, sliding my hand into my right pocket and pulling out the small silver coin, placing it on the kitchen counter. "I became a raging alcoholic when I got to my first unit. I hadn't discovered therapy yet, and I came into the military with a lot of baggage from my childhood. That, coupled with my bank account being fatter than it had ever been, and being surrounded by grown men who also couldn't handle their crap, I dove headfirst into the addiction rabbit hole. That man over there?"

I inclined my head toward Kameron, who was scrolling through something on his phone with a furrowed brow.

"He saved my life. He was the first person to call me out on my self-destructive nonsense, and he was the one who helped pull my head out of my ass before I did something truly destructive, like wreck my career or seriously injure myself. I owe everything to him," I said honestly. "That's why I'm here. That's why I care so much about making this festival a success. If I can give to him and his mission of saving the people who need help most, even a fraction of what he's given to me, I'll die a happy man when the time comes."

Abbie said nothing, her eyes locked onto mine. I blinked once, briefly wondering if I'd exposed too much too fast, but in the next heartbeat, her arms were wrapped around my waist, her face pressed to my chest.

It took several seconds for my brain to process that Abbie was hugging me, but as soon as I wrapped my arms around her shoulders and brought her impossibly closer to me, my chest sagged with relief. I rested my cheek on top of her hair, letting my eyes close as her lavender and vanilla scent enveloped me. Of course, she used the same shampoo. I'd never forget this scent, this feeling, for as long as I freaking lived.

Nothing had ever felt as right as having Abbie in my arms like this. This was where I belonged. Embracing her like this, I felt like I could protect her from anything that sought to hurt her.

I wasn't her boyfriend. I knew she wasn't capable of looking at me like that ever again. But I was someone she cared about.

Not even the years between us could change that.

"I'm so proud of you," she whispered, her arms still locked around my waist. I was sure everyone else was gaping at us, but all I could see and feel was Abbie. People would have questions, and we'd answer them after we figured our own crap out, but right now, I reveled in the feeling of her body pressed against me.

"That means more to me than you'll ever know," I said, emotion choking my voice. Abbie was the only person on the planet, outside of my uncle, that I'd ever sought true validation from. And knowing that she could see the work I'd put in, and all the effort I'd used to turn my life around, even after everything I'd done to hurt her?

My chest tightened painfully.

I would never deserve this woman.

"I'm going to get some air," I said. It physically pained me to disentangle myself from Abbie, but the air in the cabin suddenly felt stifling. My skin was hot, as anxiety began creeping up my spine. I refused to glance back in Abbie's direction as I made a beeline for the door. I heard Kameron call out my name, but I was focused on getting out into the open air.

As soon as I stepped beyond the threshold and into the dark Washington night, the cool mountain air wrapped around me, and the tight ball of anxiety in my chest loosened. I inhaled deeply, held it for five seconds, and released it. I repeated that until my hands stopped shaking.

How many times would I leave her until I finally got a grip?

I was selfish for allowing myself to get this close to her. It didn't matter what I wanted. I was here to give back to Winding Road and to get her closure. I wanted to give Abbie the answers I hadn't been able to all those years ago. And instead, I was letting her get close to me again, not keeping her at bay. Because I was a selfish man who still wanted it to be the two of us in the end.

"Connor," a familiar voice called, full of concern. The screen door of the cabin slammed with a loud smack, and I whirled to face Abbie.

"I'm so sorry for ambushing you like that," she said, grimacing. "You told me something deeply personal about your past, and I didn't know what to say, so I hugged you instead, but now I'm realizing that was probably the wrong thing to do, especially in front of your friends . . ."

I took several steps toward her, wrapping my fingers around her upper arms and rubbing reassuring circles into her soft skin.

"You didn't ambush me," I said quietly, looking into her blue eyes. "I'm still working on controlling my anxiety. It tends to flare up in public spaces on a good day, and talking about my sobriety with people who aren't Kameron can be difficult for me. I'm honestly grateful you hugged me. And I meant what I said in the kitchen. That you seeing my sobriety and the work behind it means a lot."

Her eyes shone brightly in the moonlight, and a wave of déjà vu swept over me. We'd done this so many times as teenagers. Snuck off into the woods during bonfires to lie down in a clearing with one another, gazing up into the night sky, renaming constellations, and talking about the future we'd have together. The air surrounding us felt charged, and as she took a step closer to me, the invisible string between us lit up like a live wire.

"Truth," I murmured. "Seeing you with my friends tonight made me realize maybe it's possible for the past and future to coexist. Maybe the work I've done to break out of my negative thought patterns means that now I get to step into a new future."

Abbie took my hands in hers and gave them a reassuring squeeze.

"Truth. The more time I spend around you, the more I realize that I never truly knew you. We were kids, and we wanted to see the best in each other. And I sometimes wonder if it was real. Because seeing you now, as a man who has done the hard work to heal past wounds, I can't shake the feeling that we could have had more if we'd met at a different time."

My mouth parted on a sharp exhale. Without thinking, I raised my hands to cup her face, my thumbs sweeping over Abbie's cheekbones. I took the tiniest step closer, our chests brushing against each other.

"Connor," she sighed. Her eyes fluttered closed, and I pressed my forehead against hers.

"Abbie," I whispered, absorbing every ounce of this moment between us, unsure if I would ever get something like this again.

Right as I tilted her chin up to slant my lips over hers, the screened door banged open, and we jumped apart.

"Oy, assholes, Imogen requests your presence for a karaoke version of 'Cruel Summer,'" Lucas called. "Not yours, Harvey. We all know you can't sing for shit. This message is for Abbie Collins only."

"We'll be right there," I called, and Lucas retreated inside. Abbie had taken several steps away from me, her cheeks deeply flushed, and one arm crossed over her chest as she held her bicep.

"Duty calls," she said sheepishly, brushing past me as she ducked back into the cabin.

I lifted my face to the moonlit sky and allowed my eyes to shut. The image of Abbie's eyes fluttering closed as her face neared mine danced across my eyelids.

Chapter 15

Abbie

I made coffee in my condo the next morning, unable to shake the feeling of Connor wrapped around me from the previous night.

I was playing with fire. I wanted to believe I was ready to get burned. That I could handle him leaving me again. I could handle a casual summer fling, even if deep down, it felt like the opposite of a no-strings-attached flirtation game.

We'd retreated into the cabin, and after my intense "Cruel Summer" showdown with Imogen, we'd made more festival plans. Today, Lucas would take on the stall construction while Connor and I visited some of the local businesses who had asked about supporting the festival either as vendors or donating things to the charity raffle. Most businesses wouldn't be open until noon, so we decided we'd have a slow morning. Given that it was Sunday in a small town, almost everyone was at church. Connor planned to meet me outside my apartment a little past noon.

I drank my coffee on the couch while reading the final chapters of the fantasy romance. I gave it a quick four-star rating on Storygraph, writing my classic 'full review to come' for all three of my followers. I glanced at the clock on the stove. There were thirty minutes until Connor arrived, so I threw my ass into high gear to make myself vaguely presentable with some jeans, my favorite pair of boots, and one of the faded band t-shirts from my clean laundry pile. It had been a long few days, and my house was suffering for it. I needed a self-care day soon.

Connor knocked on my door at ten past noon, right on time. I grabbed my belt bag off the hook by the door, giving him a small smile as I stepped out of my apartment and locked the door behind me.

"Good morning," Connor said, and I returned the greeting while giving him a quick once over. His new style leaned toward lumberjack, with his classic plaid button down rolled at the sleeves. His top button remained undone, revealing a respectable amount of skin that made my brain enter squirrel mode.

Everything Connor did seemed to set my skin on fire these days. It was becoming harder to tell the difference between what was driven by nostalgia for the life we once had, and the excitement about this new connection sparking between us.

"Where to first?" Connor asked as I walked toward the front door of the apartment building.

"I don't know about you, but one cup of coffee was not nearly enough."

"Blackbeard's it is," Connor said with a smile, running ahead of me to open the door for me.

Ugh, I groaned internally. *Please don't start being a gentleman today.*

I was fairly certain I couldn't handle any more of Connor's antics. Why hadn't I suggested Kameron accompany me to pick up raffle prizes today?

Luckily, Blackbeard's was only a block away from my house. Even though the investors had eventually abandoned the idea of Watford Lofts, only finishing five units before abandoning the project altogether, they had the right idea. In a larger town, these modern lofts would have been a colossal hit with the influencer-type. Luckily for me, the developers wanted to cut their losses, and I ended up purchasing the condo for far cheaper than expected.

Connor held the door to Blackbeard's open, and I stepped inside, waving to Kyrie.

"Oh, hi, Abbie!" she said, her face lighting up with a genuine joy that only existed in teenagers. I returned her warm smile.

"Hey, Kyrie. Can I get a medium vanilla latte? And one of the blueberry scones, if you have them."

"Of course," she replied, grabbing a cup from the middle stack and writing my name on it. "And for you, sir?"

Connor choked on his spit at the 'sir,' and I barely stifled a laugh. We weren't much older than Kyrie, but there was nothing as devastating as being called old by someone only a few years your junior.

"He'll have a black coffee," I jumped in, saving Connor from himself. I pushed him toward the 'pick-up' sign at the other end of the sleek coffee bar, pulling out my card to pay.

"Nice try," Connor leaned down to whisper, handing Kyrie his card instead. "You're not as slick as you think you are."

"Evidently not," I said, smiling.

Once we had our coffees in hand, we took a seat in the window booth that overlooked the main street. Things picked up outside, with hungry churchgoers heading to grab lunch after service. We drank our coffees in a comfortable silence, waiting for some of the crowd that had trickled in behind us to disperse. When there was a lull in traffic, I jumped back in line to speak with Kyrie.

"Kyrie, do you know when Phillipa will be in? We're putting together the fifty-fifth anniversary Founder's Day festival, and we're trying to get some local businesses in Watford to take part, either as vendors or by donating a raffle prize or two."

Kyrie let out a squeak of excitement that had me jumping out of my skin in surprise.

"Oh. My. *God*," she crooned, vibrating with excitement. "I've heard rumors about the festival, but no one could confirm whether it was really happening."

I offered her a small smile. "The Watford Town Council will make their formal announcement by the end of this week."

"I'm sure Phillipa would love to take part however she can. This is so exciting, Abbie! I'll pass on the info to her when she comes in later."

"Amazing! Thanks, Kyrie. Could you have her shoot me an email or call me as soon as she can? We're on a ridiculously tight deadline for the festival, given some administrative hiccups that were out of our control. I'd love to have a definitive answer within the next week if she can manage it."

Kyrie nodded aggressively, and I made a mental note to personally follow up with Phillipa in the next two days if I didn't hear from her beforehand. Not that I didn't trust Kyrie to give her the message, but I wanted to be sure Phillipa had all the relevant information before she signed up either way. As much as I loved Kyrie, she was easily distracted—often because Kevin Phillips was always ready to whisk her away.

After exchanging a few more pleasantries, Connor and I left Blackbeard's and headed toward Forest Grove Books, a local staple that had been around just as long as Watford General—if not longer. The indie bookshop was owned by Mari Pearson, an elderly woman with a gentle spirit, kind demeanor, and a knack for giving the best book recommendations.

The bell above the door chimed as Connor and I walked in. Mari gave us a friendly wave from where she was hunched over the counter, stamping a pile of books. This was one of the many reasons I loved shopping locally—little touches of personality that went into everything a small business owner did for their customers. Mari pressed a 'From the Forest Grove Library' stamp into the inner cover of every book she sold—a lifetime marking of where this book had once lived before it found its way into homes across the world.

"Hello, lovebirds," Mari said, and I let out an awkward laugh that was far too harsh for the small space. Mari simply shook her head and waved me forward. "I heard you were back, Connor. It's good to see you, young man."

Connor gave her a warm nod. "Thank you, Mari. It's very good to see you as well. Mind if I look around?"

"By all means," Mari replied, and Connor turned on his heel, disappearing into the haphazardly organized and precariously stacked books.

"He turned out to be a hunk," Mari whispered conspiratorially to me as soon as Connor was out of earshot.

"Mari," I gasped in mock outrage, shaking my head. "I'll have you know he was *always* a hunk."

"That he was," Mari agreed, her eyes crinkling with amusement at the corners. "Too bad for the other girls that he only ever had eyes for you."

I flushed, waving her off with a dismissive hand.

"I've got a question for you. We're bringing back the Founder's Day festival this October."

Mari's eyebrows rose. "How wonderful! Why, it's been an age since we last had the festival."

"Yes, it has. That's why we want to make this festival the best it can be. We want to have a children's section where parents can let their littles ones play and explore in a safe environment, so they can enjoy their meal. Would you be willing to donate a few books so the younger kids can have something to take home with them? I figured it would be a great way to promote literacy, which I know is something that's important to you and the mission of Forest Grove."

Mari's eyes lit up.

"I'd love to, Abbie. What a wonderful idea! If you'd like, I can also plan to do a read along for the littlest ones. Maybe one geared toward preschoolers? They love picture books at that age."

"That would be wonderful, Mari. Thank you so much for offering. I'll put you in touch with Lucas Morales. He's part of the team at Winding Road Farm, the main sponsor for the festival. They're helping us put everything together. Lucas is going to coordinate the children's play area. If you could call him with the details, he'll make sure you have a designated space for your activities."

Connor returned with three books. A space western, a swash-buckling pirate fantasy, and a military narrative nonfiction. I raised my eyebrows in his direction.

"A man of varied taste, I see," Mari said with a smirk as she took the books from Connor's outstretched hands.

"I didn't get to read much on active duty, so I'm making up for lost time."

Mari's smile grew wider as Connor handed her a wrinkled twenty and told her to keep the change.

"I like him," the older woman declared, and I swore I saw Connor's chest puff out further with male pride.

"Thank you again, Mari," I said, giving the woman a small wave as we exited the bookshop. I glanced at my watch, and my eyes widened when I saw it was already two in the afternoon. Jesus, time really was a construct.

"One last stop," I said, turning toward Connor. "We need to talk to Willie at the Roadhouse."

Connor's eyes darkened. "I'm not sure it's a great idea for me to come with you for that one."

I reached out and squeezed his arm in a reassuring gesture, trying my best to ignore the feeling of his thick muscle beneath my fingers.

"It'll be okay," I assured him. "If you really don't want to, you can head back to Watford General and hang out with Imogen for a bit. I'm happy to talk to Willie alone, if that would make you more comfortable."

Connor was quiet for a long moment, as if warring with himself, unable to decide.

"No, I want to go with you. Lead the way."

Tension radiated from him in waves. I linked my arm with his. Consequences be damned.

I've got you, I thought, though I was too scared to speak it out loud into the delicate space that existed between our bodies.

I've got you.

Chapter 16

Connor

I knew coming here was a bad idea.

The Roadhouse hadn't changed in the slightest since the last time I'd been there. It was still the same rundown bar and grille. Abbie and I entered the building together, her hand sliding from my forearm to interlock our fingers.

I hoped she couldn't feel mine trembling.

Three pool tables that had seen better days took up most of the open space, except for the small open mic section in the back left corner. There were a few bar stools and high tops, but the heart of the Roadhouse was the solid wood bar top that took up most of the right wall. Neon signs for every kind of domestic and imported beer on the market lit the space, illuminating old license plates, band posters, and a few faded polaroids and historical prints of Watford that adorned the walls.

No one else was in the bar at this hour, and for that, I was grateful. I resolved to take my wins wherever I could get them.

"Connor Harvey?" Willie said, straightening. "Jesus Christ, what the hell are you doing back here?"

"Willie," Abbie said, affronted, but I expected this reaction.

"Is Ellis with you?" Willie demanded, pointing a finger in my face.

"Ellis is dead," I responded, with no hint of emotion in my tone.

Willie let out a dark chuckle. "Guess the bastard had it coming."

I shrugged, burrowing deeper into that thoughtless place inside of me. I didn't want to talk about Ellis, especially not with a man who had watched him hurt me, who knew what he was doing was wrong, and did nothing to stop it.

Anna would get an earful about this at our next session.

"We didn't come here to talk about Ellis, or me, for that matter. Abbie is coordinating the first Founder's Day festival in several years, and she'd like to discuss some things with you."

"Like hell we're going to gloss over this," Willie argued, and I instinctively stepped in front of Abbie, sensing that things were about to go sideways. "Your uncle stole from me. I want what I'm due."

I should have gone back to the store.

"Willie, Ellis skipped town years ago," Abbie interjected. I wanted to tell her there was no use, but she pressed a hand to my chest, as if sensing my impending objection. "Everyone in this town wants a scapegoat, but Connor was a kid, and Ellis was the adult. Connor didn't steal from you. Ellis did, and now he's dead. You don't get to pin Ellis's shit on him. It's not fair."

Willie's eyes simmered with rage. "Abbie, you know I love you like you're my own. We have business arrangements between us, but more than that, I consider you part of my family. And because I love you, I need you to stop talking like you understand this. This is between me and Connor."

Something in me snapped loose at the condescending note in his voice. If he wanted to berate me, fine. He could yell at me and hurl insults in my direction until he was blue in the face. But I was so tired of people taking their emotional immaturity out on my girl.

"I don't know how you sleep at night," I growled, banging my fist down on the bar top, "knowing that there was a kid in your bar—a hungry, exhausted, scared *kid*—getting the crap beat out of him every time he lost a game of pool, and you watched it happen. For years, you watched it happen, and you said *nothing*."

Willie's face crumpled.

"You don't understand, Connor. Your uncle was an *evil* man. There wasn't a person in this bar that didn't have some kind of screwed up deal with him."

"You think I don't know that?" I roared, and Abbie jumped. She flinched away from me, and oily, slick shame slithered its way up my spine. "You think I don't know he was a bad man? I lived with him, Willie. I dealt with him every day."

The words settled heavy in the space between Willie and me as I met the older man's eyes for the last time.

"I will help you with whatever you need in a business capacity, because I'm here for her."

I jerked my head in Abbie's direction, keeping my gaze fixed on Willie.

"I'm here to make sure this festival goes off without a hitch. I didn't come here to talk about the past, and I sure as hell don't have to justify my actions to someone who was too cowardly to stand up for a fucking *kid* who had no place being in his bar," I snarled.

I reached into my pocket and pulled out a crumpled fifty-dollar bill, slapping it on the bar top.

"I hope that covers my debt."

The words hung immobilized in the stale air of the bar. I grabbed my books from Forest Grove and stomped toward the door. I let it slam shut behind me, unable to quell the roaring in my ears. All the unspoken words that had simmered within me for years threatened to spill from my mouth, and I wasn't ready to deal with the fallout from that.

"Connor!" Abbie's voice was distant, and the last thing I wanted to do was stop walking. If I stopped walking, I would lose my shit for real, and that was the last thing I needed.

"Connor, baby, please wait," she called, and I stumbled at her words. I whirled to face her, my face red with anger.

"Let's go back to the cabin, okay?" she said, cradling my face in her hands. I wanted to flinch away from her touch. I'd revealed too much at the bar. The last thing I wanted was for her to be kept in the dark about something else, for her to feel like all I ever did was keep secrets from her, but this was something I barely had a handle on myself. I didn't know how to tell her these things. I didn't know how to tell her in a way that wouldn't be me dumping all of my crap into her lap.

I finally nodded my acquiescence, because I didn't have the strength to fight her.

I was so tired of fighting.

Chapter 17

Abbie

When we made it back to the cabin, it was blessedly empty. Everyone else was out running errands, so Connor was able to calm down in peace. He sat down on the brown leather couch with his elbows on his knees, eyes vacant as he stared off into space.

I didn't know what to say in this situation, but I knew that sometimes people simply needed to have someone sit with them while they sorted their crap out. I headed to the kitchen to pour us both a drink.

"I brought you some water, in case you were thirsty," I said a few moments later, setting the glass on the coffee table and taking a seat next to Connor. To my surprise, he scooted back on the couch so he could lay his head in my lap. I laid back on the cushions, my hands finding his head and threading my fingers through the soft blond locks.

"Thank you," Connor said, his breath hot against my thighs. I shivered at the nearness of him. "Thank you for not turning away from me."

I opened my eyes to meet his gaze, tracing the lines of his jaw with my fingertips. If we were going to blur the lines, I wanted it to be worthwhile.

"Truth?"

Connor nodded.

"I know that everyone in your life has left you. I know that it's really hard to trust that people have good intentions, and that you're always waiting for things to get bad again. I know you are, because I am too." I took a calming breath. "Things are unstable. They have been for years, and that scares the shit out of me. But I hate the idea of you pulling away from me because you think I can't handle hard things. I need you to promise me you will let me decide what hard things I can handle."

"Truth," Connor said. "I'm scared to tell you everything. I'm nervous about screwing up whatever new friendship is growing between us. Having you back in my life has been so nice, and I'm worried that if I dump all of my childhood issues on you, you'll get spooked."

The word 'friendship' was like a bucket of ice water dumped over me. My fingers hesitated briefly, but I contin-ued stroking his hair. Of course, we were friends. Of course, we couldn't have what we did before.

"With all that said—" he gave a breathy laugh "—I promise to let you decide what you can and can't handle. My only request is that you let me decide when I'm ready to share those things."

I smiled at the ceiling.

"Sounds like a plan to me."

Founder's Day was less than five days away, and I was drowning.

The last three weeks had been a flurry of Zoom meetings with the Watford Town Council (which had mostly been a conversation between Trent, Kameron, and me) and returning phone calls regarding the vendor fair. After Kameron and Lucas had posted about the Founder's Day festival on Winding Road's social media, the festival email blew up, with local influencers and businesses wanting to know how they could get involved.

We organized a considerable list of vendors, which included a handful of nonprofits, and also arranged for two influencers with sizable social media followings to take part. In exchange for a free cabin rental, they would promote the festival to their followers and shout out many of the small businesses at the vendor fair.

The store rarely saw such a large amount of activity, and I found myself overwhelmed with the workload. Kelly Sakis had called in with another bulk flour order on Monday. Sourcing everything locally sounded like an amazing opportunity until Kelly had stepped up three weeks ago to suggest everyone use her freshly made sourdough bread loaves for all the burgers and sandwiches.

Things had gone downhill since Kelly's announcement. It was as if a switch had flipped and everyone around me was in panic mode. I was now stationed in the back of the store, trying to figure out where in the hell I was going to find the space to put said flour until Kelly could come pick it up. Imogen had stepped in to assist Kelly with her other baking ingredient needs, namely eggs, but I handled the bulk of the dry goods.

I simply didn't have enough space. Between storing supplies and equipment for other Founder's Day projects, and back stock of goods we sold in the store, I was at my wit's end. I kept reminding myself to breathe, just like Imogen did, but I was already at the point of pulling my hair out.

To top everything off, I'd barely seen my father the last few days. He'd gone on a huge bender at the tail end of last week, and I only went upstairs a handful of times to check he hadn't choked to death on his own vomit. I told him about the festival, about how I'd been asked to coordinate, but he didn't care. Being the petty individual that I am, I took that as a signal that my father didn't need checking up on. I simply didn't have the time to handle his shit, too.

The front doorbell jingled, and I groaned.

"What else could you people need?" I whispered, wiping my hands on my apron as I practically sprinted to the storefront, grabbing my inventory clipboard from the shelf and kicking the storeroom door shut behind me.

"Hello," I called. I nearly went to my knees with relief when I saw it was just Imogen.

"I am drowning," Imogen said, wiping sweat from her brow. "Kelly Sakis is going to kill me."

"She's going to kill all of her yeast if she keeps running that thing like she is."

"Poor Stella, indeed," Imogen agreed, referencing Kelly's decade-old sourdough starter.

I grabbed an ice-cold water bottle from the refrigerator and handed it to Imogen, who nodded her gratitude.

We both took a seat with our backs against the checkout counter, legs outstretched on the floor as we took turns sipping the water.

"Why did we even have this celebration every year?" Imogen groaned. "And why, in God's name, did they decide to bring it back?"

I smiled. "So we can celebrate the incredibly upstanding men that established this fine town."

Imogen rolled her eyes. "Whatever. It's just more work for us women."

I laughed as the overhead bell rang again. Connor stepped through the threshold, and my mouth went dry, despite having just taken a sip of water. Sweat soaked through the front and back of his blue cotton shirt, leaving nothing to my imagination.

Imogen nudged my foot with hers, startling me from my ogling session. I smiled sheepishly, my cheeks flaming.

"Hi, Connor. Can we help you with something?"

"Water?" he asked, and I lifted my foot to gesture at the fridge.

"Grab whatever you need," I said as he pulled his shirt hem toward his face to wipe the sweat from his brow. Long, sharp lines of muscle flashed before me, and my breath hitched in my throat. "But turn that fan on before you come over here."

Connor grabbed a bottle of water from the fridge, switched the fan on, and joined us, sitting on Imogen's other side. She scooted closer to me, wrinkling her nose.

"You smell."

Connor stuck his tongue out at her before cracking the bottle open and taking a long swig.

"It's been *five years*," I said incredulously. "How can the two of you still be acting like this?"

"He has cooties," Imogen said, as if that were a perfectly reasonable explanation for why two twenty-somethings didn't want to sit next to one another. "And, he smells."

"You've established that," Connor said, smirking around the bottle. "Gotta come up with something original if you want to get under my skin, Phillips."

"Anyway," I said, trying to avert a crisis before it happened. "It's too hot for anything today, but I am really stressed about getting these stalls built for the market."

Imogen shook her head. "I don't understand why the council decided this year, of all the years, was the time to redo all the woodworking."

"I don't either," I groaned.

Imogen and Connor both looked at me.

"I'm on the verge of closing down the store and moving into a hobbit hole in the woods."

"Does the hobbit hole have Wi-Fi?" Imogen asked.

"And a bathroom?" Connor added.

"I'll move with you if it does," Imogen said.

I groaned, knocking my head back against the counter.

"I don't know where I'm going to find the time or labor to build ten more market stalls. We have over twenty businesses and nonprofits confirmed for the vendor fair, and I only ordered enough supplies for ten. I put in a rush order and paid extra to have the lumber delivered within a week, but I got a phone call this morning that there's been a delay, and I don't have time to waste. Oh, and Noah Wilkinson came by this morning to let me know the campsite is booked. All *ten* of the new cabins! Booked! For the *entire* festival weekend."

My voice reached a fever pitch, and Connor and Imogen averted their gazes to their feet. The whine of the small window air conditioning unit was the only sound in the store.

"It'll be alright," Connor assured me, reaching across Imogen's lap and giving my hand a squeeze. The touch of his hand on mine threatened to send me into a tailspin. At the same time, it helped me focus my breathing on something other than the panic swelling in my chest.

"Where do we start?"

I took a deep breath before rattling off all the random tasks that still needed doing. During my tirade, Imogen reached for a pencil and paper and started scribbling things down.

"I spoke with Trent on the phone yesterday and everything is in place with the permits," I said, my brain finally slowing down after spending the last two weeks in high-power mode. Being able to brain dump and get everything out of my head has been more helpful than I expected. Some of the tension drained from my shoulders, and my heartbeat slowed.

"Judging by this list, it seems like most of these tasks are just putting the finishing touches on things, and double checking that we have everything," Imogen stated. "I think we're perfectly on schedule."

"I agree," Connor said. "I'll get in touch with Kameron and Lucas to make sure we're still on track with the stall building, and that all the signage has arrived. Kameron had to drive back to Winding Road to check in on things at the farm, but he'll be here at week's end. He plans to stay through the end of the festival weekend. Lucas has been out of town, too, but he'll also be back by Friday, so you'll have all hands on deck to help with the finishing touches. You've done a great job, Abbie."

I let out a slightly hysterical laugh.

"I couldn't have done any of this without your help. This would have been a massive failure if I didn't have the two of you. Also, Kameron. And Lucas. And—"

"Abbie?"

"Yes, Imogen?"

"Let's get you home. You need a night off."

"She needs several nights off," Connor amended, and I was suddenly far too tired to argue with either of them. "Come on."

Connor hopped to his feet in a movement which was far too graceful for a man of his size. He extended a hand to me.

"We've got it from here, Abs. Take the rest of the day off."

Normally, I would push back and insist that I was fine, but the bone-deep exhaustion which had been lingering around me for weeks was finally setting in. I needed to be my best self the day of the festival, and at the rate I was going, I wasn't sure I'd be well by the end.

So, instead of opening my big mouth to say I was fine, I simply nodded and allowed Connor to hand me my purse and gently push me toward the door. He gave me a two-finger salute as I stepped onto the sidewalk.

I snuck a glance back toward the store, smiling when I saw Imogen and Connor bent over the counter, divvying out tasks from my brain dump.

When I made it back to my condo an hour later, the exhaustion and brain fog had set in. I kicked my boots off before I collapsed on the bed, darkness and something dangerously close to peace enveloping me as I drifted off for a nap.

Chapter 18

Abbie

By the time I woke up that evening, the sun was low in the sky, casting an orange haze through the large window overlooking my bedroom. It took a moment for the panic of having slept so late to hit. Once it did, I jumped out of bed to grab my phone, quickly dialing Imogen's number. To my surprise, she sent my call to voicemail, instead shooting me two quick texts:

bffl

> I closed the store. In a meeting right now. Talk later?

> Hope you got some sleep. :)

My brows furrowed. Imogen was never in meetings, at least not in the traditional sense. She was an entrepreneur who made her own schedule, and there was no way Imogen Phillips was signing up for a meeting that late in the evening. I would hound her about it later. Right now, I was hungry and needed food. I slid my phone into my back pocket and headed for the kitchen.

"Good, you're up."

The sight of Connor in my kitchen, zipping up a small cooler, brought me up short.

"I assumed you went home," I said. "You scared me."

"Sorry," Connor replied.

"It's alright," I said, rubbing the last remnants of sleep from my eyes. "I assume Imogen told you where the spare key was?"

"Yeah," Connor admitted sheepishly. "Were you able to get some sleep?"

"Yeah. I slept great, actually. I clearly needed it, since I slept the last half of the day away."

Connor smiled and checked his watch.

"I know it's getting late, but if you feel like taking a walk with me, I'd like to show you something."

I looked at him more closely, feeling my heartbeat kick up when I saw hope in his eyes. He wanted me to say yes. More than that, he looked nervous that I might decline his invitation. If I had a single self-preserving bone in my body, I might have said no, but I wanted to go with him.

"Should I change clothes?"

"Wear something comfortable. It's a warm night."

I bit my bottom lip and nodded once, turning back toward my bedroom. I was eager to get out of my jeans. It was a testament to how exhausted I was that I'd been able to fall asleep in them in the first place. I flipped through my dresses quickly, cursing myself for having put off laundry day for so long. I finally found one that was comfortable and flattering, because again, self-preservation had left the building a long time ago. If I was going on an evening stroll with my incredibly attractive ex-boyfriend, I had a right to do it while looking good.

I slipped the blue cotton t-shirt dress over my head and ran my hairbrush through my hair to tame down some of the frizz. The dress had a v-neck that dipped just low enough to reveal the silver daisy chain I still wore. I wondered if Connor noticed I still wore it. Truth be told, I wasn't ready to admit that I hadn't taken it off. I grabbed my sneakers and stepped back out into the kitchen.

Connor stopped in the middle of closing the fridge as he took in my outfit change. His eyes swept over me, lingering longer than I expected. I fought back a flush.

"Do I need to bring anything?"

"Just yourself," Connor said, and just like that, whatever spell had been cast over the moment had broken, though I could have sworn his voice was rougher than usual. Connor grabbed the cooler, and we headed out the door.

Once we hit the main street, I was grateful Connor had told me to change clothes. This was not jeans weather. It was unusually warm, considering we were just days away from the first week of October being over.

"Do you remember junior prom?"

I couldn't mask my shock, almost tripping over my feet as we crossed the street. I tried to pay attention to where we were going, but the streets were unseasonably busy with passersby heading toward Main Street for a dinner out. People crowded the sidewalks, their conversations mingling with the sounds of distant music.

"Are you talking about when Imogen accidentally spilled punch on Jacob's suit and he almost flipped the table? Or when you took me and Lucy out into the field where the old community garden used to be?"

"The latter," Connor answered. "Though, looking back, I really wish I'd punched that dude in the jaw when I had the chance."

"You and me both," I said, anger flickering in me at the mention of Imogen's ex-husband. "As far as the other thing goes . . . it's the best date I've ever been on."

Connor paused at my words as we approached the street corner.

"I have to admit, I've been nervous about this since I first had the idea. You've been so stressed recently, and I wanted to do something nice for you. So, I planned a little evening out for you."

My jaw dropped as we turned the final corner, and I saw what Connor had done.

We were back in the field that had once been used for a community garden and now laid fallow most of the year. Lucy's tailgate was down, and inside the truck bed were lush pillows and blankets. Connor had looped fairy lights around the metal frame, illuminating the space just enough to feel cozy and safe. There was a larger cooler underneath the tailgate, and Connor set the smaller cooler in his hand down beside it.

"There's food, but I didn't want to set it out until you got here," he said. "I know you just said you associate this with our date, but this is for you. I want you to have a night where you can relax."

I tried to find the words to express how much this meant to me, but all of them came up short. Connor turned his back to me and began filling a large platter with an assortment of cut meats, cheeses, olives, breads, strawberries, and other fruit.

"I also brought your tablet in case you wanted to cozy up and watch a movie," he said. "And there are bug repellent torches stationed around the truck."

He rubbed the back of his neck awkwardly, and my chest squeezed to the point of pain. He'd done this for *me*. I knew he'd be fine if I asked him to leave, but that was the last thing I wanted. Right now, I wanted him. I wanted to know more about this man I used to love.

"Will you stay?" I asked, reaching for his arm. Connor hesitated.

"Please. I want you to stay." I hoped I didn't sound too desperate.

His gaze softened, and some of the tension seeped from his shoulders.

"I'd like that."

I kicked off my sandals and hopped into Lucy's bed, careful not to dismantle the platter of delicious charcuterie that had my mouth watering. I settled into the back right corner, reaching for the first plate he'd prepared and shoving a massive bite of food into my mouth. Connor smirked.

"I was so hungry," I said around a mouthful of crackers and cheese. "You're my hero for this."

Connor let out a small chuckle and popped a grape into his mouth. "I live to serve."

He hopped into the truck bed alongside me, lying down on the opposite side. I laid back against the pillows, gazing up at the sky.

"It feels like a lifetime ago that we did this."

"Almost five years ago," Connor added, mirroring my movement and lying back against the pillow, his right arm propping his head up so he could look at me.

"So much was different then," I said, my voice barely above a whisper. "Imogen and my mom forced me to go prom dress shopping with them, even though I insisted I already had something."

"Oh, really?"

I smiled as the wave of memory washed over me.

"Yeah. My mom insisted I should get the exact dress I wanted, because there was no guarantee I'd go to senior prom too. I needed to live it up in case I never got the opportunity again. So we went shopping, and I picked out the navy blue dress."

"I loved that dress."

I smacked his arm and laughed. "I know you did."

We settled into a comfortable silence as we ate. Ambient noise and conversations from the buildings across the street filtered into the quiet space, but it wasn't annoying. The background noise was helpful to keep my anxiety at bay.

"Did your mom ever tell you about the conversation she had with me that night?"

I sat up straighter, looking at him.

"She talked to you before prom?"

"Your mom was an amazing woman," Connor said. "She treated me like one of her own. I don't know if it was because she suspected what my home life was like, or because she took pity on me. Your dad wasn't my biggest fan, but your mom . . . she always showed me kindness. That meant everything to me. The night of junior prom, Imogen had a last-minute hair fiasco..."

A loud laugh escaped me at the memory of Imogen's panicked face. "Oh yes, I remember it well."

"While the two of you ran upstairs to fix it, Tilly sat me down at the breakfast nook, took my hand in hers, and told me that people would try to tear us down. She told me that people in town would look at what you and I had and write it off as nothing more than teenage infatuation. People would think we'd never amount to anything serious. And she told me that was bullshit."

I choked on a laugh that sounded more like a sob, my hand flying up to cover my mouth. Connor never cursed, but my momma certainly had. This conversation gave me something I thought I'd never have again: a new piece of my mother. A new story unfolded; a memory I had never experienced. This differed from someone in town telling me about the random time my mother showed them kindness. That was who she was as a person.

This was *Connor*, the person I once swore to her I'd spend the rest of my life with, telling me she knew it, too.

"She told me that if I loved you and wanted us to succeed, we could do it. We were stubborn and in love, and that was the most powerful combination. She told me to always fight for you." He sighed. "My biggest regret in life is that I didn't."

My chest tightened.

"I could have done both," Connor said. "I could have fought for you, for us, and dealt with everything from my past." He waved a hand, trying to diffuse some of the tension and grief thickening the air. "Sorry to drop that on you. I just . . . really wanted you to know about that conversation."

"Thank you," I whispered. "Thank you for telling me."

Despite my better judgment, I moved the platter of food from between the two of us and scooted closer to Connor, resting my head on his shoulder.

"Tell me if this is crossing some kind of line," I said, even while silently begging him not to.

"Abbie."

The sound of my name on his lips sent a shiver down my spine, and I pressed my face into his neck.

"You don't have to ask for this," Connor said, wrapping his muscular arms around me. I exhaled a shaky breath, bunching my fingers into his shirt, as if worried he would disappear on me again. "You never have to ask if this is okay. I'm here for *you*."

Imogen would have a cow if she found out about this, but I didn't care. For the first time in five years, it felt like I was making a decision for *me*. Not for my mom because our time together was running out, not for my dad because I had to take care of him, not even for Imogen to whom I owed so much to.

And maybe it was selfish to want something just for me, but so much had been forced on me these last few years. I went from being a high school senior dreaming about getting a degree in business so I could start my flower farm, to being stuck in my hometown forever because my dad couldn't live in a world without my mom.

"Truth?" I asked. Connor hummed his approval.

"I missed you," I admitted, thankful that my face was against his chest, preventing me from looking into his eyes. "I missed you so damn much. Even though I was confused and hurt, I would have put it all aside if you'd come home. I was willing to forget all of it to have you back. I stopped thinking about you because it hurt too much to remember the way things used to be, and it didn't make anything better."

My words hung heavy between us, but I didn't regret them. Based on the way Connor pulled me closer, it seemed my words didn't offend him.

"Truth," Connor said. "I've thought about you every single day since I left. I tried to forget. I tried to put Watford and everything that happened here behind me. I truly thought if I could do that, I'd be happy. But I wasn't happy, because the one thing I'd ever wanted was still here."

I released a shaky sigh.

"What a sorry pair we are."

Connor chuckled, and some of the tension in my shoulders eased.

"Yeah," Connor agreed, pressing a gentle kiss to the top of my head. "What a mess."

I didn't want the moment to end, so I held on. Connor didn't seem keen on moving either, so we laid there in comfortable silence, limbs tangled together in the bed of his truck, just like we had all those years ago.

Being with Connor now ignited the same feelings it had then, and I knew in that moment, everything had changed.

Chapter 19

Connor

"Did we ever follow up with that nonprofit micro-brewery?"

Abbie continued to pace with her fingers pressed to her mouth. It had been three days since our date that was not a date underneath the stars. Every day since that night had been a flurry of last-minute phone calls, email chains, and administrative work, making sure that everything for the festival was in place.

I'd finally convinced her not to bite her nails down to the quick, but the pacing continued. It was the night before the festival, and Abbie's anxiety stood center stage.

"And what about the raffle donations? We have the physical prizes at the store, but what about the digital gift cards and rewards certificates?"

"Abbie," I tried, only to be interrupted once again.

"What if none of the vendors show up because I made an error in the reminder email and they actually think it's next week?"

I closed the distance between us, wrapping my fingers gently around her upper arms and pulling her close to me. We stood chest to chest, and her panicked gaze met what

I hope was a calm and reassuring smile from me. I watched her exhale, long and slow. My chest tightened as she leaned into my touch. I don't think she realized she was inclining her body toward mine, and the instinct of it, the rightness of this closeness between us, set my nerves alight.

"You have done everything you can," I said, rubbing my hands along her smooth skin. It took everything in me to keep my focus on her face, and not on the feeling of my hands on her. "You have worked nonstop the last two months to make sure this festival goes off without a hitch. If there is anything left—not that there is anything left," I amended quickly after panic sunk into her features again, "it's someone else's problem to deal with."

"I have control issues," she blurted, and I couldn't help the laugh that escaped me.

"I know," I said, patting the pillow next to me on the couch. "Now, what are we watching?"

"You're letting me pick?" Abbie asked, a hint of suspicion in her tone as she stalked to the kitchen to grab two sparkling waters and shove a bag of popcorn in the microwave.

"Yep," I said.

Abbie went silent for the next few minutes, no doubt considering her film choice.

"*One Direction: This Is Us.*"

I blinked rapidly, my jaw dropping open like a fish. Our gazes converged on the remote sitting on the coffee table, and in the next heartbeat, I launched into action, swiping the remote while Abbie howled in protest.

"No," I said, tucking the remote behind me and sliding backwards into a defensive position on the couch. "Absolutely not."

"You promised me I could pick whatever I wanted," Abbie whined, perched on the edge of the couch like a tiger ready to attack as soon as she had an opening.

I set my jaw forward. "Anything but that. I beg you."

The sudden weight of Abbie's body in between my legs was a shock to my system. I let out a small sound that sounded embarrassingly close to a gasp when she placed her palms on either side of my head, essentially straddling me on the couch.

God help me.

I knew I'd lost the remote somewhere in the shuffle, given that my fingers were now twitching around empty space, desperate to hold Abbie, and pull her closer.

Abbie leaned forward, so close that our noses were almost touching. My heart hammered wildly in my chest. If I tilted my head just a fraction to the side, our lips would meet.

"You promised," Abbie whispered, her eyes searching mine. My lips parted of their own accord. The words felt loaded somehow, and some small part of me knew this went deeper than just a movie, even while my brain was overloaded with sensory input.

I laid all my metaphorical cards out on the table and reached my hand up to cup her face. Abbie's breath hitched in her throat as my thumb traced the delicate curve of her neck.

"I promised," I repeated, sliding my hand up to her face once more. I stroked my thumb gently over her cheekbone and tilted my face up to meet hers. A loud, rhythmic beeping rang out in the silence, and Abbie jumped.

"Oh," she exclaimed, her cheeks flushed as she practically leapt to her feet. Cold air rushed between us, cooling my heated skin, and forced me back to reality. "Forgot about the popcorn."

I stared up at the ceiling, cursing every religious figure I could think of for breaking the moment as Abbie rushed to the kitchen to pour the popcorn into a bowl. Realistically, I knew there were several conversations we needed to have before we became . . . physically entangled. But my stupid monkey brain fixated on the small noises she made when she pressed up against me, so close, and yet still too far away.

Abbie grabbed the remote off the floor—neither one of us had seen it drop—and settled in a respectable distance away. I knew it was for the best, but the space between us felt miles long after the closeness of earlier.

I barely paid attention to the film. My focus was entirely on Abbie—the way her eyes lit up when her favorite band member was on screen, the nostalgic smile that graced her face when an inside joke was referenced, and even the tears that welled in her eyes when they performed her favorite song.

Over the course of an hour and forty-five minutes, we slowly drifted closer. It started with my petulant demand to have the popcorn bowl closer and ended with Abbie resting her head on my shoulder as she explained the lore behind 1D internet fan culture in between the band's performances. I tried to pay attention to her animated explanation of the band breakup timeline, wondering if she could hear how fast my heart beat in my chest. If I failed the pop quiz afterwards because I was too distracted by the feeling of her body pressed against mine, I'd deal with the consequences.

By the time the credits were rolling, Abbie's head was resting in my lap, and she was fast asleep. I drew in a deep breath, trying to slow down the thoughts racing through my mind. My thoughts stopped and started over the same line: Abbie felt *safe* with me. She felt safe enough that she fell asleep next to me, despite being anxious about the festival and everything on her plate.

I turned the TV off, reached for the blanket thrown haphazardly over the back of the couch, and draped it over her sleeping frame. Unable to stop myself, I ran my fingers through her hair, pulling the strands back from her face, and tucking them behind her ear.

My heart stuttered in my chest as a million questions raced through my mind. The lines between us were becoming increasingly blurred, but neither one of us seemed willing to pull back. If Abbie asked me to keep my distance again, I would. But she hadn't asked. If anything, she was toeing the line right alongside me, as if waiting for me to be the first to cross over into dangerous territory.

My thoughts spiraled, but one question remained at the forefront of my mind.

Could it be this easy for us to fall into each other again?

We were different people now, that much was obvious. But this new tether between us felt stronger somehow, as if the years and distance between us had fortified it. I felt more ready to fight for this than I ever had.

I shook my head, allowing those thoughts to fade away into the background. Tomorrow was about Abbie and Watford. Tomorrow was about celebrating all the incredible work everyone had put in to make the new and improved Founder's Day festival a success.

I would wait to ask my questions. I'd wait to cross the line. For Abbie, I realized, I'd wait forever.

I settled back into Abbie's insanely comfortable couch. I closed my eyes and let the soft sounds of Abbie's breathing lull me to sleep.

Chapter 20

Abbie

When I woke the next morning, I was in my bed, with only fuzzy memories of how I'd gotten there.

I turned off my blaring alarm, blinking to fight back the darkness, and turned on my lamp. There was a vanilla latte from Blackbeard's on my nightstand, smoke curling from the small hole in the lid.

I immediately relaxed, remembering that Connor had been here last night. Connor had brought me coffee. Connor had brought me to bed after we'd both drifted off, watched my favorite movie, and made sure I got a good night's sleep. And, to my eternal surprise, Connor had stayed the night, judging by the faint clanging of pans and kitchen utensils drifting in from the hall.

Anxiety immediately sank its claws into me. Today was the day. Everything I'd been working toward for the last six weeks would come to fruition today.

For better or for worse.

I could only hope I'd done enough.

I still had on the same clothes as yesterday. I took a moment to brush my teeth, wash my face, and put on a clean set of jeans and a blush pink lightweight flannel. I grabbed the coffee cup from my nightstand and walked toward the kitchen.

"Good morning." Connor's rough voice shook me out of my stupor. Heat rose in my cheeks as I raised the coffee cup to my lips. "I slept in your guest bedroom last night. Hope you don't mind."

"Good morning," I said. "I'm glad you did. It smells amazing in here."

Connor's grin widened. "I'm making omelets. Yours is next. Are vegetables and cheese still your favorite?"

I turned my attention to the sizzling cast iron pan and the various vegetables, cartons, and cheeses covering my countertop.

"Yes," I answered, still shocked that Connor Harvey was in my kitchen making me breakfast. It was so painfully domestic that my chest tightened with longing. It felt strange knowing that these small moments were what I dreamed about as a teenager, and yet, I couldn't go to him. I couldn't wrap my arms around his waist and press my cheek into the firm planes of his back. I couldn't smack a sticky kiss on his cheek as I grabbed my keys for work.

The sight of him in jeans and the same fitted t-shirt he'd been wearing yesterday did nothing to quell my racing mind. He was a sight to behold. He always had been, but now that he was more a man than a skinny teenager, I was having a really hard time keeping my shit together.

"Thank you for the coffee," I said, taking another sip. "It means a lot that you stayed with me last night. You didn't have to."

"There is nowhere else I'd rather be," Connor said gently. I lifted my gaze to his, and my heart rate sped up.

I could see the truth in his honest stare. He slid a plate in front of me, but my eyes never left his face. The evidence of his concern for me was all around, from the steaming veggie and cheese omelet on my plate to the delicious latte warming my hands.

I was in trouble. So much freaking trouble.

"So, now that breakfast is served, I am heading out to meet Kameron and Lucas at Watley's. Ludgate and the other deputies have already blocked off the roads. We're going to set up the vendor fair. I'll also check in with Mari and see if she needs any help with the kid's corner. You stay here and finish your breakfast. I'll know if you don't."

My eyes narrowed as he grabbed his keys from the bowl.

"How will you know?"

Connor shrugged, grabbing his coffee cup and flashing me a grin. "Superpowers."

I opened my mouth to respond, but Connor blew me a teasing kiss before sliding out the front door and locking it behind him.

My gaze lingered on the door for another moment before shifting to the living room window. Dawn was still an hour away, but there was plenty to do between now and ten a.m., when the Founder's Day festival kickoff began.

I ate my omelet and sipped my coffee, allowing myself to soak up this moment of peace. Connor's presence was a balm to my anxious heart. With him, Kameron, Lucas, Imogen, and all the other people who had worked to make this festival a success nearby, I knew it would be a good day.

After breakfast, I did a quick five-minute meditation before heading to the town square to join Connor and Kameron in setting up the festival structure. By the time I arrived, the morning sun was cresting over the mountains, casting the crossroads in an ethereal pink and orange glow.

"You finished them," I said, and then amended my statement. "I mean, I didn't doubt that you would, but they're beautiful, Connor. You weren't joking about being a master builder."

"Well," Connor said with a gentle smile, "I had some help from a master woodworker."

I furrowed my brows as he stepped to the side, revealing the hunched form of my father. My dad had gotten a haircut, trimmed his beard, and by the looks of it, he was sober. He was inspecting one of the vendor booths.

Tears welled in my eyes as he approached me, wiping sweat from his brow.

"Is this where you've been the last few days?" I choked out. My dad nodded somewhat bashfully as he scratched the back of his neck and gave me a small shrug.

"I'm so proud of you, honey. You've worked so hard."

"Thank you," I whispered.

I let out a shaky laugh as my dad squeezed my shoulder and went to inspect the next booth. I didn't have time to process the emotional implications of my dad being here.

Not only was he here, but he was *sober*. He had showered and trimmed his beard, and he was *here*. I wiped my eyes before continuing down Main Street to make sure everyone had what they needed to be successful today.

The next few hours sped past in a blur. Connor and I spent most of our time checking in vendors, answering their questions, getting extension cords, and easing any concerns as they came up. Lucas and Kevin headed up parking duty, helping people find their way to the gravel parking lots on the outskirts of town. Imogen took point on all the food vendors, ensuring that everyone had enough space, tables, and chairs to serve the surprisingly large crowds beginning to flood the streets. Kameron stood at the entrance to the festival beneath the Founder's Day banner in a Winding Road polo, welcoming the crowds to Watford and answering questions.

I stepped up to the microphone, welcoming everyone to the festival. There were more people here than I was expecting. At least several hundred, if not a thousand plus. I felt tears of joy and relief welling behind my eyes, but I refused to let them fall. I wanted to see everything in crystal clear vision.

I welcomed the first band to the Founder's Day festival stage, and as the crowds filtered through the vendor fair to sample local food, brews, and products, my heart swelled.

I stepped down from the stage as the band began their set, passing the clipboard off to Kevin, who had offered to be the stage manager. Imogen was there to greet me, helping me down from the stage and giving me an excited hug.

"Let's go check in with Kam. They set the Winding Road booth up near the festival entrance."

Imogen linked her arm with mine and we set off through the crowd. I shook a few hands, expressed my gratitude to everyone for showing up, knowing my cheeks would probably be permanently stained red after today with all the blushing.

"Kameron," Imogen said as we approached the boys' booth. There was a blue and white 'Winding Road Recovery' banner alongside the top of the wooden stand, with a 'Festival Sponsor' title underneath. Kameron stood there in a pressed blue button up, his black stubble trimmed neatly. It was the most formal I'd ever seen him dressed.

"Imogen," he said. The slight tilt to his lips made me smile, too. I crossed my arms over my chest and turned to Imogen.

"How are things going? Is there anything we can get for you? Water or food?" I asked.

"Things are great. We had some fantastic conversations with local businesses about potential sponsorship opportunities. And no need to grab me food: Connor will be here to relieve me in a few minutes, and I fully plan on checking out the selection when he gets back. He's helping dish out food."

Kameron gestured across the crowded street to the line outside of Watley's. When my eyes landed on Connor's familiar sandy blond hair, my heart threatened to burst out of my chest. He was there, right in the middle of the chaos, with a wide smile on his face. He was handing a small kid a freshly made corn dog, kneeling to his level, and giving the kid a high five.

My heart raced for an entirely different reason then.

"Hi there!"

A very cheery, distinctly male voice interrupted my thoughts before they could travel too far into the gutter. I turned to introduce myself and was stunned to find Councilman Trent Kaser standing there in all of his five-foot-seven glory, in a solid black suit and blue pinstripe tie.

"Trent," I said, utterly surprised to see him here. "You made it."

"I wouldn't miss it, not after all your hard work," Trent said, running a hand through his slicked-back hair. I fought back a grimace.

"I'm so glad you could make it," I lied.

Imogen barely stifled her snort-laugh beside me, and I elbowed her gently.

"You must be Lucas, right? Pleasure to meet you," Trent said, extending a hand toward Kameron, who Trent seemed to just now realize was standing there.

"Actually, I'm—"

"Look at the time," Trent said, pulling out his phone. "Pro Ranger is about to take the main stage. Gotta run."

Trent was gone as quickly as he had appeared. I rubbed a hand down my face as Imogen burst into laughter.

"Who wears a pressed suit to an outdoor festival?" Kameron asked, bewildered.

"Trent has always been like that," Imogen answered, shoulders still shaking with the force of her laughter. "Oh, my God."

"Aren't you going to tell Kameron how you kissed him?"

Imogen's jaw dropped and Kameron burst out laughing. He clapped both hands over his mouth to try and stop the sound, but the damage was done. His shoulders shook with the force of it.

"I was young and naive to the ways of men," Imogen said. "It happened once and *never* happened again."

"And you!" Imogen whirled around to face me, one hand on her hip and the other pointing a finger in my face. "You swore to never tell another living soul. You *pinky promised.*"

I threw my head back and laughed, my face turned toward the rising sun, the warmth of its rays wrapping me in a hopeful embrace.

"I'm so proud of you," Imogen said, grabbing me by the shoulders and pulling me in for a tight hug. The festival was nearing its end, and while it had been an incredible day, exhaustion seeped in. "You made this happen. Look at how happy everyone is. Even Willie is smiling."

I glanced over to the Roadhouse, where Willie and Gale were behind a foldout table, handing out glasses of beer and wine, laughing merrily as kids ran past with their kites and younger folks stopped by to ask about the local breweries they worked with.

"We really pulled this off," I said, somewhat unable to believe it.

"That you did," a voice agreed from behind me, and I whirled to face him.

Connor stood there, clad in a short sleeve plaid shirt cuffed around his biceps in a way that left nothing to the imagination. His tan jeans also clung to his muscular thighs in a way that made me swallow tightly. I was grateful I hadn't really had time to look my fill, because if I'd seen this man earlier in the day, I might have shirked all my responsibilities and begged him to come back to my condo with me, consequences be damned.

"You look gorgeous," Connor said, completely unashamed as he took another step toward me.

"I'm going to—uh, bye," Imogen said quickly, and I couldn't blame her. I hardly noticed her leave as Connor continued to stare at me, a small smile on his lips.

"So."

"So," I repeated, allowing myself to smile.

"I heard a rumor from Kevin Phillips that there's an after-party tonight at the Roadhouse."

I swallowed again as he stepped in, leaning his mouth down to whisper in my ear. "Is that true?"

I shivered. For once, I didn't care what this looked like to the people around us. Everyone was moseying their way toward the edge of town for the fireworks show, and most of the vendors were packing up to head home. Families with younger kids had already taken the shuttle back to the campsite, or were in the process of doing so. For once, I only focused on Connor and the lack of space between our bodies.

"Yeah—yes." I cleared my throat. "Willie offered a free round of drinks for anyone who helped put on the festival, and well, you know how things spread around the youngins. Now it's a full-on, invite-only, exclusive party."

"Will I see you there?"

"Yes," I said. "Just going to make my rounds with the vendors and make sure no one has any concerns, and then I'll be there."

Connor leaned back, smiling down at me. "I'll be waiting."

My mouth went dry as he turned toward the Roadhouse, waving to Willie and Gale. He grabbed a tray from underneath the foldout table and started collecting trash and recycling nearby while Gale gave him instructions on where they needed his help.

I shook my head, clutching my clipboard to my chest as I made my rounds. All the vendors thanked Watford for the opportunity to come to the festival, many of whom asked for my card so that I could be in touch with them about future events. My face ached from smiling so much in a way I hadn't in years.

Finally, once all the vendors were packed away, everyone gathered on the edge of town. The mayor made a speech about this incredible turning point in Watford's history that had most of us locals teary-eyed.

For the first time in a long time, we felt like we'd done something as a town. We'd put ourselves back on the map. All the investing in ourselves we had done in the years since the economic downturn was finally paying off. And we were all there to see it.

I turned my gaze back to the Roadhouse as the fireworks went off overhead, and I could have sworn Connor Harvey smiled back at me.

Chapter 21

Connor

The Roadhouse was suffocatingly full of sweaty bodies.

If I wasn't so desperate to see Abbie let herself enjoy her success, I wouldn't be here. Bars and my history don't go well together.

I pushed my way through the throng of people, most of whom were already on their second or third drink. I could tell by the way they leaned into the aisle, making it difficult for everyone to pass through. And by the way they laughed and talked too loudly. There was a difference between talking loud enough to compensate for the pop music blaring overhead, and drunken cackling.

Most were leaning toward the latter.

Finally, I noticed Kameron sipping on his sparkling water at the end of the bar. Some of the tension in my shoulders eased as I made my way over to him, ignoring the sticky substance that clung to my shoes as I walked. Kameron gestured for me to join him at the bar, but I didn't take the empty seat, opting instead to lean back against the bar with my arms crossed over my chest. I told myself I was keeping a lookout for Abbie, which was true.

I also wanted to keep my eyes on the exit, in case my anxiety about being in this stupid establishment overtook me.

"Can I get you water?"

I shook my head. The last thing I needed was to drink anything here, even if it was non-alcoholic. I was already on high alert.

"This place hasn't changed," I muttered.

"It's certainly got character," Kameron said with a small laugh.

A torrent of cheers rose from the crowd, and I stood up straighter, searching for the reason the crowd suddenly seemed to lean in toward the door.

And there she was. Abbie and Imogen had entered the bar, Imogen holding Abbie's hand up in the air as if she was announcing the latest WWE winner. Abbie's eyes scanned the bar, and when she found me, she grinned wildly.

My heart seized in my chest.

I would give this girl the world. I had always wanted to give her the world. Even when I was broken, bruised, and beaten, wondering if I could ever be normal, I saw a future when I looked at her. She was my sun, a guiding star whose presence may have faded in my life, but never completely disappeared.

Abbie made her way toward me, only to be swallowed up by some vendors and other patrons celebrating the festival's success. Abbie patiently accepted their praise, dishing out hugs and compliments, but every so often, her eyes met mine, sparkling with amusement and something I couldn't quite place.

All of it—her gaze, her outfit—threatened to send me into a spiral. She had changed from her festival organizer attire into a yellow sundress and short cowgirl boots.

I stepped forward before I was fully aware of my actions. I felt drawn to her, as if an invisible string was tying her to me. Her wild eyes met mine, and I couldn't stop the grin that spread on my face as I opened my arms for her. She practically sprinted over to me.

"Hello," she said, and leaned into my embrace. I wrapped my arms around her and kissed the top of her head, not giving a damn who saw. There would be whispers. But Abbie and I had never cared much about what others thought.

I pulled back and held her face in my hands.

"I am so proud of you, Abbie. You did it."

"We did it," she said, and I shook my head, unable to stop smiling.

"You were our fearless leader from the start. Take credit where credit is due."

Abbie's smile widened, and she stretched up to kiss my cheek. She was so close, her warm body pressed against mine, and I was fighting not to ask her to come back to the cabin with me. I would kick Lucas and Kameron out and do whatever she wanted.

"I want to dance," Abbie announced, gesturing to the dance floor. "Everyone else here is drunk and won't remember my inability to dance in the morning. Tomorrow, it's back to business as usual."

I nodded, pulling her into my side as a gaggle of drunken girls stumbled past us, heading for the bathroom. Imogen came up on my other side, practically clinging to

Kameron's arm. My eyebrows raised in a silent question, but Kameron's unusually stoic gaze warned me away from that line of questioning.

"Well, I must say, there are more people here than I was expecting," Kam said.

"Just a song or two," Abbie said, grabbing Imogen's arm and wrenching her away from Kam's side. A country song with a beat most girls in the bar seemed to recognize—given their hollers of excitement—blared over the speakers. Imogen and Abbie shared a glance that spelled trouble, and they moved onto the dance floor.

Kam and I turned our backs against the bar, as Abbie and Imogen found their place among the two lines of people gearing up for the song.

"Where I'm from, the local bar used to host line dancing every Friday night. It was the place to be the summer after high school," Kameron said, gesturing to where the two women moved in time to the beat. Abbie started to grapevine right instead of left, and slammed into Imogen, who cried out in mock outrage. Abbie tilted her head back and laughed. The sound traveled past the crowd to me.

I smiled. It had been far too long since she laughed like this, without thinking about her mile-long to-do list.

"Abbie would have loved something like that. She used to enjoy dancing. She's always loved music."

"What about you?" Kam asked, shoving my shoulder with his. "You never talked about this place. I know you have terrible memories here, but most of the people here . . . they don't seem too bad."

"No," I said, crossing my arms over my chest as I continued watching Abbie dance, spinning and clapping and stepping in tandem with the others. "Most of these people mean well. That's the thing about small towns. Everyone knows everyone. If you're the golden child who everyone loves—" I waved a hand toward Abbie "—they'd go to the ends of the earth to make sure you were successful. But if you don't fit into their mold of what you're supposed to do, then you're on the outskirts."

"Is that how it was for Imogen?"

I sucked in a breath. "That's her story to tell, not mine."

Kameron sighed deeply.

"Everyone keeps saying that, but Imogen is no closer to telling me anything about what happened before she came back here. All I know is that she was married for less than a year before she came back."

"Take as much history as Abbie and her family have in Watford and double it. Imogen's family practically built this town. Imogen has never fit the mold her parents wanted for her."

Kam looked back at the girls. The song was drawing to a close, the line dance finished, and others swooped in, congratulating Abbie and Imogen on such a successful event. Abbie's face was flushed, both from the dancing and the compliments, and I wanted nothing more than to kiss her until she was truly breathless.

"For a long time, I didn't fit that mold either. I guess we have something else in common."

That left no room for commentary. I knew Kam would come to me if and when he wanted to talk about it.

"Jesus Roosevelt Christ, it's way too crowded in here. I can't think," Imogen said after weaving her way through the crowd. Kameron placed his hand on her lower back to move her out of the way of a gentleman carrying a tray of shots.

"We made our official appearance," Abbie said, releasing Imogen's hand. "What if we snuck out and went back to the cabin or your place?"

"I'm good with either," Imogen replied, her face twisting into a grimace. "I'm pretty sure someone just spilled beer down my back, and I'm not keen to repeat that experience."

A chorus of drunken shouts rang out from the dance floor.

"Definitely time to go," Kameron agreed. Imogen walked toward the door, then hesitated, turning back to Abbie with a mischievous grin on her face.

"Why don't the two of you go back to your condo," Imogen said, gesturing to Abbie and me. "Kam can drive me back to the homestead. We'll meet you for breakfast at Watley's in the morning."

I held my breath as I waited for Abbie to decide.

"That sounds great," Abbie said, her voice unusually high-pitched, even as she leaned back against me. Kam met my eyes, and I was glad to see he seemed back to his usual self.

"Don't do anything I wouldn't do," he said, and clapped my back.

"There's not much you won't try at least once."

"Exactly," Kameron said, giving me a mock salute as he and Imogen stepped out into the cool autumn night.

"So . . . my place?" Abbie suggested, looking back over her shoulder as we stepped out onto the street.

God, I wanted her.

I always wanted her, but looking at her like this, under the pale moonlight, her bare skin covered in a light sheen of sweat from dancing with Imogen, her long brown hair tousled lightly from the gentle breeze, my heart ached with the weight of that desire.

"Your place," I said, and took her hand in mine. She shivered, and I smiled to myself, thinking it unlikely that reaction had anything to do with the autumn breeze drifting past us, and everything to do with the feeling of my hand against hers.

Chapter 22
Abbie

As the door to my condo closed behind us, I pressed my back to it, letting the cool wood soothe my scorching skin. I leaned my head back against the door, watching Connor grab two glasses from the cabinet. Seeing him in my kitchen had become a regular occurrence. It felt *right*.

Connor sensed how quickly my thoughts were spiraling, filling the glasses with ice and then strawberry kiwi sparkling water.

"We can just go to sleep, Abbie," Connor said, extending the glass to me. I walked forward to receive it. "Imogen kind of ambushed you back there. I'm not expecting anything."

I took a long sip of my water.

"I don't think I'm ready for that."

"Truthfully, I'm not either. As much as I enjoy spending time with you, and as attractive as you are, I'm exhausted."

I let out a small laugh.

"Me too."

I leaned against the counter; my eyes locked on the floor. A storm of emotions roiled inside me. The festival being an enormous success, having fun for the first time in years, all while being with Connor . . . overwhelmed me in the best possible way.

"Look at me."

Against my better judgment, I did. Connor's brown eyes met mine, and my world righted itself once more. He stepped closer to me, gripping either side of the counter-top, effectively boxing me in.

"Truth?" I asked, breathless.

"Truth."

"I'm scared," I whispered.

"Why?"

I inhaled deeply, taking this opportunity to step away and get some air. Connor gave me space as I walked around to the other side of the kitchen island and sat down on one of the bar stools.

"Things are too good right now," I said. "The festival went off without a hitch. Even Imogen is happy hanging out with you and Kameron and Lucas, and I've never seen her this happy around people she barely knows or used to hate. You're being kind and understanding and attentive, just like you always were, but this time it feels different. Better."

Connor smiled slightly at that.

"And my father was *sober* today," I added. "In the five years since my mom died, I can count on one hand the number of times I've seen him sober. Today was good. It was a *good* day."

"But you're scared," Connor said. "I get it. Life has taught you that when things are really good, they get bad soon after."

"Yes," I breathed, grateful that he understood.

"I get it," Connor said, shrugging. He pressed his palms to the countertop again, leaning over the island. I didn't miss the way his shoulders stretched at the seams of his shirt, or his chest muscles flexing and moving beneath the fabric. "But in my experience, if you don't acknowledge when things are good, you'll get trapped in a never-ending cycle of good and bad. Sometimes things just are what they are. It doesn't have to be good or bad all the time. Sometimes, life is just life."

I smiled at him.

"When did you get so poetic?"

Connor returned my smile. "When I got sober, I suddenly found myself with a lot of free time where I needed to not be inside my head. I started reading and researching. Hit the gym more often. Listened to inspirational podcasts, all that jazz. That's actually how I stumbled across this thing called therapy."

"I always assumed Kam was the one who made you go," I said.

"First, no one makes me do anything," he said, pointing an accusing finger jokingly in my direction. "Kam also knew that part of the power of therapy is choosing to be there. If I signed up to go, it would be more impactful, because I made that choice for myself. He encouraged me, but never forced me. He's good like that."

I spent another moment just looking at this man who had once been the center of my world. Who had once promised to give me the world, if only he could find a way to do it.

"Another truth?"

"Greedy," he said, still smiling.

"I realized something," I said, and slid off the bar stool, taking one small step, then another, in his direction.

"Oh, yeah?"

"Yeah," I replied, unable to stop myself from grinning as I rounded the island to face him. "I realized I loved you then, in the best way I knew how. You did the same."

Connor said nothing and kept his hands where they gripped the edge of the counter, but he inclined his head in my direction.

"But now, I want more."

I reached for his hand, and Connor's breath hitched in his chest at the touch.

"I want to know things, Connor. All the things you've kept buried. I want us to be all in together. No more secrets, no more hiding. What we have between us is real. It survived plenty of beatings. I want to do it justice by doing things the right way."

Connor released his grip on the counter, fully facing me as he searched my face. He lifted his hand to stroke my cheek with the back of his fingers, and I pressed my lips together to keep from smiling as I gazed back at him.

"I would really, really like to kiss you, Abbie Collins. May I?"

My heart thundered in my chest, and I let out a small sigh as he leaned his head down, allowing my eyes to close as I reached for his shoulders.

Connor pressed his lips to mine, and the world melted away at the soft warmth, the rightness of it all.

How many years spent waiting for this moment? This moment where my world was no longer off-kilter, where

I wasn't anyone's caretaker, and could focus solely on this kiss, the feeling of Connor's strong arms around my waist, the press of my chest against his, the hard lines of his body holding me steady in place.

Connor tilted his head to deepen the kiss, and on instinct, I reached up on my tiptoes to follow him. The movement shocked him enough that Connor's back hit the counter, forcing him to spread his legs out to steady himself.

I devoured the low, greedy sound that escaped him, raking my hands through the short strands of his hair. I'd expected a slow buildup of heat, but Connor was a wildfire, razing my world like a storm. It had always been like that between the two of us. Connor was biting his lip hard enough to draw blood, and his need only fueled my own.

"My room?" I panted, pulling back only long enough to see the desire in his eyes.

Connor's grip on my arms tightened.

"Let's go to the *couch*," he said, stealing another small kiss from me before continuing. "And let's talk. Cuddle. We already agreed."

I was vibrating with butterflies and an excitement I hadn't felt in years.

"If the next words out of your mouth are something about how we should get to know each other, I'm going to smack you."

"You said you want to do things the right way. This is us doing things the right way."

Connor's smile was blinding as he took my hand in his, tugging me toward the couch.

His fingers interlaced with mine, full of promise.

Chapter 23

Connor

I f heaven existed, it would look like this.

Abbie's arms tangled around me. The gentle glow of morning sun trickling in through the curtains bracketing the balcony door. The rhythmic cadence of her chest rising and falling.

I hesitated, scared my movements would break the spell that enveloped us. The two of us had talked late into the night, laughing and sharing snacks we stole from the fridge downstairs. We exchanged kisses, but nothing more. We'd passed out on the couch sometime around two in the morning.

We both held things back. There were some conversations that needed to be held in the light of day. In the darkness of night, it's easy to hide behind the walls we've constructed. It's easy to ignore those wounds and scars we'd rather not see. It's far harder to hide from the ugly truths in the morning sun.

Abbie stirred next to me, momentarily interrupting that train of thought. I reached for my phone, squinting as my eyes adjusted to the screen.

"Oh crap," I said. Abbie grumbled, blindly fumbling for my phone, trying to turn the brightness down. "Kameron and Imogen are already at Watley's."

That woke her up.

"Damn, I completely forgot to set an alarm," she exclaimed, scrambling off the couch and sprinting toward her bedroom. "Did you bring clothes?"

"Nope," I said. "What I wore yesterday will be fine."

"I appreciate how practical you are, but you smell like sweat, grease, and stale beer. I think I still have a pair of your sweatpants in here."

That got my attention. Abbie ducked into her bedroom. I heard the distant sounds of her sifting through her clothes. I was grinning like a madman at the idea that Abbie had kept something of mine. I sat up on the couch right as she hurled a pair of gray sweatpants and a plain white t-shirt in my direction.

"You kept these?"

Abbie didn't meet my eyes, but I caught a small smile on her face as she turned away from me once more, this time heading for the bathroom.

"There's no way this shirt still fits me."

"Make it work," Abbie called. "You have three minutes to get ready."

I leaped to my feet, still grinning, making a beeline for the guest bathroom.

♥ • ♥ • ♥ • ♥ • ♥

Ten minutes later, much to Abbie's chagrin, we were finally walking down the street toward Watley's. She blamed me for distracting her when I walked past her room wearing the outfit she'd chosen for me.

"Good morning," I said, sliding into the booth beside Kam. Imogen scooted closer to the window so Abbie could sit beside her, tucking a stray piece of hair behind her ear.

"Have a good night?" Imogen questioned sweetly, and I rolled my eyes.

"There was no virtue stealing, if that's what you're asking."

"Both of you quit," Abbie said, looking first at Imogen and then at me. I shrugged and reached for a menu, despite already knowing what I wanted to order. "We slept in because we were up late *talking*."

"What about your night?" I asked, turning slightly to face Kameron in the booth. He was suspiciously quiet.

"It was fine," Kameron answered. Imogen shifted in her seat. Abbie didn't seem to notice, but I looked between the two of them. I had too many questions and very few answers.

"Where's Lucas?"

"Right here," Lucas said, grabbing a chair from the table across from our booth and sliding it up to our table, effectively making all of us crowded. Everyone shuffled farther into the booth. "I know you were all patiently waiting for my arrival."

"So, when someone says we're meeting for breakfast at nine a.m., does that mean something different for military guys?" Imogen asked, handing Abbie her menu to add to the pile at the end of the table.

"I don't know who in their right mind expected everyone to show up for a Saturday morning formation after a night of heavy drinking," Lucas said, shaking his head.

"None of you drink," Imogen said, scowling. I bit the inside of my cheek to keep from laughing, nudging Kameron's foot under the table, urging him to jump into the conversation.

"I don't drink around the two of them," Lucas corrected. "And that doesn't mean I can't be tired from being up all night with the ladies," he added, yawning for effect. Imogen mockingly sneered in his direction. The gesture reminded me of a sister making fun of her brother for doing something ridiculous.

"If the children have finished arguing," Abbie said, her eyes darting between Imogen and Lucas, "we should discuss what comes next."

"It's just about time for us to head back to Winding Road," Kam said, handing Abbie his menu to add to the pile. "We have a new cohort starting at the end of next week."

We were all saved from responding when our waitress came by to get our orders. Almost everyone ordered coffee, except for Lucas, who ordered a soda. For someone obsessed with their *gains*, he sure enjoyed his daily soda.

"When are you leaving?" Imogen asked once we ordered.

"I have to head back today," Kam replied. "There's plenty of work to do."

"I'm heading back with you," Lucas said. "My *appointment* was rescheduled because the other party is unable to attend."

He uttered the words with such distaste that I was momentarily taken aback. I could only assume he was referring to his ex-wife.

Abbie looked at me, and I realized out of all the things we discussed in recent days, the one thing we hadn't talked about was what would happen after the festival. All the air seemed to vanish from the room at the knowledge that one way or another, this would end. It would either end with us finding a way to make things work going forward, or it would end for good this time.

I never saw myself staying in Watford. There were too many terrible memories of things that happened here. I didn't want to raise a family in the place that took so much from me.

I also knew I couldn't ask Abbie to leave. Her family's business—the store her mom and dad built from the ground up—was here. People who had watched her grow up supported her at every turn. I couldn't ask her to leave all of this behind. I wouldn't do that.

I also knew I couldn't go back to the life I had before. Now that Abbie was back in my life, I would do everything in my power to keep it that way.

"I need another day or two to wrap things up," I said, trying to sound as nonchalant as possible. Abbie's shoulders visibly relaxed, but Imogen's face fell.

We were once again saved from having to discuss this further when our food arrived. To my surprise, Lonnie Watley, the owner and operator of the diner, came to deliver our food to us.

"I wanted to thank you guys personally for the work you did on the festival," Lonnie said. "One of the couples that attended loved our waffles so much, they want us to cater their wedding. Can you imagine? Waffles! At a wedding! This new generation's something else, isn't it?"

Lonnie bumped my arm with his, as his booming laugh filled the space. Abbie smiled into her coffee, and I gave a small shrug.

"That sounds like a great opportunity, Lonnie. I'm glad the festival could help you make some new connections," I answered.

Lonnie nodded, appeased with my response, and turned to Abbie.

"How's your dad these days, sweetheart?"

"He's doing fine, Lonnie. Thanks for asking."

I respected the hell out of Abbie for always being respectful. She tried her hardest to take the most generous interpretation of people's questions.

Lonnie turned back to me, and I braced myself for what I knew was coming.

"I'm glad you came back here, kid. Always knew you'd make something of yourself."

My jaw twitched, but I gave him a tight-lipped smile. He clapped his hand across my back one last time before walking back to the kitchen, shouting orders as the brunch rush started. Kam let out a small snort, and I glared in his direction.

I didn't understand why everyone in this town continued to brush over the fact that Ellis was a horrible human being and that I was the one who had to live with him. The more time I spent in Watford, the more conversations I had with people who knew Ellis and what kind of man he was.

Yet none of them had ever stepped up to help me. And now that I was back in town, all they wanted to talk about was how proud they were of me for rising above it.

I didn't want their amends.

The rest of the meal passed with random conversations and huge mouthfuls of good food. Lonnie's relatives excelled at one thing—American comfort food—and they hadn't made any updates to the menu in years. One didn't mess with perfection.

Kameron paid the bill, citing one last expense for their festival sponsorship. I slid out of the booth and followed him to the door. I looked back and saw Lucas talking to Abbie while she waited for Imogen to come back from the bathroom. I frowned, confused about what Lucas would need to say to her he couldn't say in front of the rest of us.

"Everything okay?" I asked when Abbie stepped out onto the sidewalk just outside the front door.

"Yeah," Abbie said, though she didn't meet my gaze. "Yeah, I'm good. I need to check on my dad before we head out."

Chapter 24
Abbie

Lucas's words from the diner rang in my head as we walked the short distance from Watley's to Watford General.

Your dad's going to need you a lot in the coming months, Abbie.

Rationally, I knew he meant well. He worked in the addiction recovery space. He knew just as well as I did that recovery wasn't linear. But it didn't land as the encouraging, hopeful statement he surely intended for it to be.

Instead, it sent me spiraling into doubt about how all of this was going to work. If my dad got sober, what would that mean for Watford General? Could I finally start my business? Would I be able to move away?

That was a dream. I knew it was an unrealistic dream, because recovery was hard. If my dad was serious about getting sober and making amends, that meant years of hard work, and I'd need to be here to support him while he did that. There would be no running away with Connor, or doing something truly ridiculous, like finding a plot of land near Winding Road, so I could be closer to him.

Those were childish ideations. I was needed here. It would be months still before my father was ready to take over the daily operations of the store, and there was also the IRS to worry about.

There would be no leaving for me. Not now, at least.

We arrived at the storefront after a few brief minutes. I fished my key out from the bottom of my purse, unlocking the front door and stepping inside.

"Dad?" I called out, throwing my purse onto the counter. "It's Abbie. I was just coming by to check on you."

No response came. Unease pricked my skin, and I turned toward Connor.

"I'm going to run upstairs and check on him," I said, even as my chest constricted. I silently prayed that I wouldn't find him dead. I could handle it if he started drinking again. I would manage it, just like I always did.

I climbed the stairs one at a time, keeping my gaze on the step ahead. I tried hard to keep my breathing even, and as the loft opened before me, I was stunned to see that it was clean.

There were no empty or half-drunk bottles of beer littering the floor. Someone had clearly swept and mopped the place. The bed was made up with clean linen sheets, and there was no dust on his nightstand. My lips parted in surprise as I took the last step into the loft space. I took another step forward and something crinkled beneath my foot. I crouched down to investigate and frowned when I saw it was a picture.

I picked it up and gasped in surprise. It was a crinkled picture of my mom, the one my dad always kept in his wallet. It was a picture of her from the early days of their marriage. She was grinning at the camera, her eyes creasing at the corners, radiating joy like she always did. I looked around the room once more, but his wallet was nowhere in sight. I set the picture back down on the freshly made bed, assuming it had just fallen out. If he'd also cleaned out his wallet, it made sense that he may have forgotten to put the picture back inside.

I took one last look at the space and tried to stomp out the hope taking root in my chest.

Maybe this was it. The moment where things got better.

"He's not here, but his space is clean," I said as I descended the stairs.

"That's good," Connor replied, giving me a reassuring smile.

"Do you have plans for today?" I asked, fiddling with the daisy necklace against my collarbone.

"I just want to spend time with you," Connor said.

I considered this for a moment. The image of my mom's smiling face appeared in my mind once more.

"Want to go for a hike? It's only fair, since I made you sit through *This is Us*."

Connor groaned at the memory. "I will accept time in nature as your apology."

I smiled and reached for my purse and his hand.

We arrived at the base of Westfall Peak, aptly named for its position west of Watford, and because it was one of the small mountain peaks that boxed the town in. I hopped out of Lucy and grabbed my jacket. It wasn't cold this time of year, but there was enough of a chill in the air that I wanted my windbreaker.

"I know it's probably hard for you to imagine staying here," I said. I wasn't sure why I said it. I hadn't intended on striking up a conversation until we hiked deeper into the woods.

"I have terrible memories of Watford. That's not a secret. But none of those things have to do with you," Connor said with a small shrug. "I don't think I'll ever find the words to explain what your presence in my life means to me. I can *try* to imagine staying in Watford, and it's because of you it's even on the table."

I swallowed tightly and pulled my phone from my back pocket. I put it in airplane mode. Connor raised his eyebrows at me.

"I assumed you were taking yours with you," I said, putting my phone in the glove box and locking it there.

"You assume correctly. Not scared about leaving your phone behind before hiking into the woods with a strange man?"

A loud laugh escaped me.

"I think if you wanted to murder me, you've had plenty of chances already. Besides, you're not strange. I don't think there's any cell service once we get higher up Westfall."

Connor shrugged and grabbed his pack from the truck bed. "Being prepared is important."

He insisted on bringing a full medical kit, as well as extra snacks like energy bars. I wouldn't be carrying the bag, so he could bring whatever he felt was important.

"We're just going a little way up," I said, squatting down to lace my right boot. "I said hike, but it's more of a strenuous uphill walk."

"I've been up this way before," Connor murmured once we'd got everything squared away.

I hesitated as I pulled my hair back into a ponytail. Connor likely already knew where we were going, but at least he wasn't calling me out on it.

"Lead the way," he said.

He locked up the truck, and we headed off.

The first few minutes we walked in silence, listening to the wind rustling the multicolor leaves on the trees. Sounds of distant bird calls floated in our direction. We listened to the sound of small creatures running along the forest floor, rustling the leaves that had fallen to the ground.

"Do you think you could be happy here?"

I spoke the words so quietly I wasn't sure he heard me over the soft forest sounds enveloping us.

He hesitated.

"I don't know," he answered.

As much as I appreciated his honesty, it still hurt.

"The work we do at Winding Road feels like my purpose in life. I'm able to channel my experiences in a healthy way, and I get to help teach others. I wouldn't want to give it up."

"I wouldn't want you to," I blurted. "It's such important work, and you're good at it. You have more passion for Winding Road's mission than I could hope to have for anything. I guess I was trying to figure out what things would look like between us, living separately and all that."

Connor said nothing, and my stomach dropped. He'd been distant today, and it was like being doused in ice water after how close we were last night. It felt like a sign that something bad was coming.

I upped my pace, channeling the anxiety I was feeling into my feet, pushing us further. I knew the path leading up this hill better than any other.

"Where are we going?"

Connor's voice was distant, and I pushed harder. Everyone had their ways of channeling anxiety, and this was mine.

"Abbie," Connor called, but I didn't stop. The damp, leaf-strewn path was all I could focus on. Every time I visited this place in the years since my mom died, I came on my own.

"Almost there," I said, even though Connor clearly knew where we were headed. He finally stopped trying to talk to me, understanding that this was something I needed to do alone. I wanted to hike with him alongside me, but I didn't want to talk. Not until we got to the clearing, which we came across after a few minutes.

Iron fences closed in the small clearing, weathered by time and rain. It was the cemetery where most Watford locals were buried. There were very few plots remaining, and most of the locals had already chosen to be buried next to their loved ones.

This was the place where we buried my mom.

"Truth," I said, not bothering to phrase it as a question as I pushed open the iron gate. "I haven't come up here with anyone else since the funeral. Most of the time, I come up here when I need to think. And sometimes, I ask her questions, even though she can't hear me. And I know that most people who haven't lost a parent won't understand why I would want to talk to a dead woman about my problems because it's morbid and weird, but it's the only way I feel close to her. It's been five years, and I miss my mom—" My voice cracked on the last word. I sank to my knees in front of my mom's gravestone, running my fingers along the engraved letters.

"It's not stupid, Abbie," Connor said softly, taking a seat beside me. "I'm glad you found something that helps you."

"Grief is this wild, crazy thing," I said, pulling my knees up to my chest and resting my chin against my arms. "Some days, I feel like I have it under control, and other times, I feel like I'm drowning under the weight of it."

Connor put his arm over my shoulders and pulled me into his side, letting me rest my head on his shoulder instead. We sat in silence for a few minutes, and I let the wave crash over me.

"Is there a particular reason you wanted to come up here today?"

"I wanted her to know that you came back," I whispered. "After you left, I spent a lot of time up here talking to her about everything. My dad was either at the Roadhouse or staring blankly at the wall. Even after we sold my childhood home and he moved into the loft above the store, he used to spend hours just staring at the wall. I'd asked him what was wrong, or if I could do something to help him. I never got a response."

Connor rubbed his thumb along my shoulder in a comforting circle.

"Sometimes, silence cuts deeper than words ever could. There was a time I would have given anything to have him show some kind of emotion, even if it involved him yelling or telling me to go away. Anything would have hurt less than the quiet."

A chilly breeze swept past us. I inhaled deeply, steeling my heart.

"And now it's the opposite. Grief is funny like that. There was a time I practically begged for him to be out of control, because at least I'd know he was still fighting. But I'm exhausted. I haven't slept through the night in years. I'm always terrified I'll get a phone call that something terrible has happened. I'm constantly in damage control mode, trying to make sure that the store stays afloat. It's all up to me. I don't get to take days off, even when I need to."

I looked at my mom's gravestone, exhaling shakily.

"I miss you, Mom," I said. "I don't know what to do. I don't know how to help him. And I'm so tired." My voice cracked again, and my chest ached. The full weight of everything I had been given to handle in the last few years choked me. It wasn't fair.

The worst part was I was good at handling things under pressure. I'd abandoned my plans of leaving Watford in the weeks after my mom's death, because I knew where I was needed. I didn't know the first thing about running a general store, but I used every search engine and video I could find to figure it out. When the debt collectors started calling the store, trying to get in touch with my dad, I was the one who stepped up.

I always stepped up. And I was so fucking tired of always being the dependable one.

"Hey," Connor said, tilting my chin up so our eyes met. "Thank you for bringing me here. Thank you for trusting me with this."

"It's nothing."

"It's not nothing, Abbie. It's everything."

I *love you*, I wanted to scream. As he leaned in to kiss me, I let some of the weight roll off my shoulders. I clutched his face tighter, as if he would vanish if I let go.

I had never stopped loving him. Even when I'd tried to forget him, I couldn't.

As we prepared to hike back down to the truck, I realized I couldn't stop this now. I was so tired of fighting everything in my life, and that included the feelings I had for Connor.

I hopped into the passenger seat and cranked Lucy to life while Connor secured his pack in the truck bed.

"What do you want to listen to?" I asked when he slid into the driver's seat.

"You're not asking me that because you care about my opinion. You've already decided."

"True," I said, smiling. I put on the playlist I made with my favorite songs, thinking it would give us a healthy mix. It was less than a twenty-minute drive back to Watford. Connor reached for my hand and pulled it to his lips, pressing a kiss to my knuckles.

"You've got to stop," I chided, pulling my hand back and smiling. "I'm going to get a complex."

"I'll never stop," Connor said, and I believed him.

When we pulled onto Main Street, there was a small crowd gathered on the right side of the street.

To the left of the sheriff's office, a tow truck was parked. The lights were on, drawing attention from the onlookers. A pair of officers were speaking with the truck driver on the sidewalk outside of the station.

"Wow, that looks bad. I wonder what happened."

It took a minute for Connor's words to register, and my gaze moved from the people conversing on the sidewalk to the back of the tow truck. There was a dark blue sedan. The front half of the car was obliterated, with the hood bent in half and pushed toward the windshield. The driver's and passenger's side mirrors were shattered. It looked like the vehicle had been involved in a nasty head-on collision at high speed.

"Abbie?"

"Does that car look blue to you?"

My voice sounded distant. The world moved in slow motion as my gaze locked onto that car.

It was the long white scrape across the back left tire that took my breath away. I put that scrape there when I was learning how to drive. I clipped a cement barrier when learning how to back out of my parents' driveway many years ago.

"It's . . ." Connor trailed off as I continued to stare at the scene in front of us.

I unlocked the glove compartment and slid my phone out, switching it off airplane mode. I didn't know how I forgot to check my phone when I first got back in the car.

Dozens of missed calls immediately flooded my phone, with even more missed texts from Imogen:

bffl

> SOS call me now

> Where the hell are you???

> Abbie please answer your phone it's important

> Call me as soon as you have your phone on.

My stomach dropped. Imogen never texted like this, and she certainly never called me twelve times in a row.

Not unless it was something urgent.

And there was no denying the color of the crunched-up car on the back of the tow truck.

"What's wrong?" Connor asked. "You're pale."

"I think something's wrong," I whispered. It was all I could think to say.

I dialed Imogen's number with shaky fingers.

Chapter 25

Abbie

I mogen answered on the first ring.

"Where the hell have you been?" Imogen cried. "We've been trying to get a hold of you for hours."

"Connor and I went for a hike. I left my phone in the truck, and Connor didn't have service," I said. "We just got back into town. What happened, Imogen?"

There was rustling in the background, like Imogen had covered the bottom of her phone with her hand while she spoke to someone else.

"Your dad was in an accident," Imogen finally said. "Officer Ludgate and I both tried to call you. He's at the hospital in Brighton."

I closed my eyes.

The other shoe always drops.

I don't know what I had expected.

Connor was already putting Lucy in drive as the phone slipped from my hand. I leaned forward and pressed my fingers to my temples, trying to wrap my mind around this.

"I've got her, Imogen. We'll head there now," Connor told her after he grabbed my phone from my lap.

My fingers trembled.

"Call me when you get an update. John could only tell us it was . . . The scene didn't look good," I heard Imogen say, and I felt sick. I hung up the phone. I didn't have the words to tell her I saw his car.

We barely made it a minute down the road before I clutched my stomach.

"Stop the car," I ordered, my chest heaving.

Connor did so almost immediately, and I pushed the door open as soon as we were stationary. I stumbled my way into the tree line and threw up, then leaned against the nearest tree for stability, a sob escaping me.

"I've got you," Connor said, pressing a kiss to the top of my head as he wrapped his arms around me. I cried against his chest. "I've got you, Abbie."

I didn't remember most of the drive. I only remember listening to Connor's music and rubbing my thumb over the leather seat, staring out of the window.

Connor found us a parking spot in the middle of the visitor lot at Brighton Regional Hospital, throwing Lucy into park to gently idle in the dusk light.

I leaned my head against the cool glass, grateful for the sensory distraction.

"We'll sit here as long as you need."

"Right," I replied, my warm breath fogging up the window. Rain fell gently against the pane. My fingertip traced the path of one drop, and then another.

"When they called to tell me Ellis died, I laughed."

I turned to face him, grateful for the distraction.

"The notion that this person—who had hated me, abused me, broken me down until there was nothing left—was no longer on this earth . . . it made me laugh. Because where was the justice in that?" Connor shook his head and crossed his arms, leaning back in the driver's seat.

"For years, I dreamed of all the things I'd say to him if we ever came face-to-face again. All the insults I'd scream, the demands I'd make. I had delusions of making him see what a good man I'd become, despite what he did to me. But with that phone call, all of those visions of revenge, of closure, vanished in an instant."

Connor blew out a long breath, resting his head against the back of his seat.

"I realized in the coming weeks it wouldn't have mattered," Connor said quietly. "It took me a long time to come to terms with the fact that I would never get closure. I would never understand how he could do all the things he did to me; someone he was supposed to love and care for. I would never know his history. My therapist helped me see it wouldn't have changed anything. The conversation I thought would give me closure . . . it wouldn't have made a difference. Because Ellis was a sick man, who did terrible things, and never once apologized for anything. I would never make him see reason. He was who he was, and there was nothing I could ever say or do to change him."

Tears pricked at my eyes, and my heart broke for Connor all over again. Connor, who had been my rock and my strength throughout high school. Connor, who had shown me love during my mom's treatment, who had supported my family in the most personal ways. Connor, who was still with me now, even as my world unraveled once again.

"Do you wonder how life would have been if you had different circumstances?"

My voice trailed off as Connor shook his head suddenly.

"No," he said with conviction. "I don't wonder for a second if my life would have been different. I did that enough when I was younger. Now that I've been through my addiction and come out on the other side, I don't imagine. I don't wonder. Because I know how badly you have to want to change. Sobriety is a struggle some days. At the beginning of the journey, it feels damn near impossible. But the decision you make at the beginning . . . well, some people might struggle with it. I won't speak for everyone.

"But for me, it was easy. When Kam came and practically scraped my disgusting, bloody, vomit-covered form from the sidewalk outside a bar in Okinawa, I'd been on a two-day bender. Kam dragged me back to the barracks, made sure I was safe, and stayed there the entire night so I wouldn't choke to death on my vomit. The next morning, he gave me a choice. I could go talk to the SACO and start sorting my shit out, or he'd cut me from his life entirely."

My mouth dropped open a bit. "He was going to leave you?"

"I realize that sounds juvenile. It wasn't because he wanted to leave me, nor was it an idle threat," Connor explained, sensing my hesitation. "It was because he loved me enough to stop enabling my self-destructive behaviors. He saw how bad my alcoholism had become, and he was willing to step out of my life entirely, if that was the push I needed to get straight. Needless to say, the choice was an easy one. I went to the SACO as soon as I was well enough to stand and started a never-ending journey of staying sober."

I let Connor's story float in the air between us. When Connor had first spoken, I'd been grateful for the distraction, but now I was grateful to have this last piece of his story. The rain fell harder, the familiar *plink, plink, plink* filling the truck cab with a comforting sound. I looked through the rivulets racing down the hazy windshield to the hospital beyond.

"And my father? Do you think he would change, given the chance?"

Connor looked up at me, eyes searching, and I held my breath, terrified at what his answer would be.

"Your father *is* sick, and he needs help, but in a very different sense. Whatever happens next, it will be his choice. But I need you to know, Abbie, that his choices have always been his own. Nothing you did could have stopped him from tumbling down this path. Addiction is a nasty, angry beast, and once it has its claws in you . . . well, sometimes it takes an experience like this—" he gestured to the glowing light of the hospital in front of us "—for an addict to realize just how bad it's gotten. The choice they make next is theirs and theirs alone. To leave their old way of living behind and take a leap of faith. Or to turn away from the people who love them and continue spiraling into their own self-destruction. I will be there for you, no matter what he chooses. But he will have to make a choice."

It should have scared me, the knowledge that I could very well lose my father today. Not physically, but in every way

that mattered. A distant part of me also knew that the way
he and I had been existing these past several years was far
from living. He would choose, and I would make my peace
with his decision.

One way or another.

Chapter 26

Connor

I really hated hospitals.

I'd been an inpatient more times than I cared to admit. I'd visited Tilly with Abbie in this very hospital dozens of times before her death. The clinical walls, the wallpaper colors, and strange, generic waiting room paintings designed to be soothing, but really just reminded you that you were here because something awful happened—I hated all of it.

Abbie paused outside of the hospital doors, gazing into space.

"I'm here with you," I said, giving her hand a tight squeeze. "You're not alone."

She rolled her shoulders back and readjusted her purse strap.

Abbie walked through the revolving door entrance and strode straight to the information desk.

"Hello. I received a call that my father, Malcolm Collins, arrived by ambulance a few hours ago."

"Of course," the receptionist nodded, and began keying information on her computer. "Let's get the two of you some visitor badges and figure out what floor he's on."

A few signatures, ID checks, and strained smiles later, we both had visitor badges and information that Malcolm was in the ICU. On the elevator ride up to the third floor, Abbie sighed, knocking her head back against the wall.

"Truth?"

I nodded.

"I'm about two seconds away from turning tail and leaving him here to navigate this by himself. How awful is that? My dad's in the hospital, and all I can think about is whether he hurt someone else."

"Would knowing if he hurt someone change whether you wanted to be here?" The question slipped out before I truly realized what I was asking.

Abbie considered this for a moment.

"No," she finally admitted. The elevator dinged, and the doors opened. "I'd want to see him one last time."

I cleared my throat and gestured for Abbie to walk to the check-in desk first.

"I'm Malcolm Collins's daughter. We were told he's on this floor?"

"I'm glad you're here, Ms. Collins." A nurse behind the nurse's station waved us forward. "Your father is at the end of the hall. He's sleeping now after an extensive surgery, but you're welcome to come sit with him after you speak with the police. They have a few questions for you," the nurse said. Her name was Hadley, according to her name tag.

"Right," Abbie replied shakily, tightening her grip on her bag. "The police."

Hadley gave her an awkward smile.

"They were in the waiting room last I checked. Give me a few minutes to find you someplace private to talk."

Abbie rubbed her temple as she turned to face me.

"I'm not looking forward to this conversation," Abbie murmured. I said nothing, opening my arms. She leaned into me, wrapping her arms around my waist, and I felt some of the tension drain from her body.

"I'm here with you," I whispered into her hair, pressing a kiss to the top of her head. "You're not in this alone."

It was all I could think to say in the moment, and I'd repeat it as many times as was necessary for her to feel safe.

At that moment, two officers appeared from the waiting room.

"Hi, Ms. Collins?"

"That's me," Abbie said, turning away from me in the officer's direction.

"Mind if we talk with you?"

"As if we have a choice," Abbie muttered before plastering a small smile on her face. I bit the inside of my cheek to keep from chuckling. Not even the direst of circumstances would stop Abbie from being sassy.

We approached the officers. The officer who called out to us gestured for us to take a seat in the waiting room, which was empty at this time of morning. I didn't miss how the shorter man looked me up and down briefly before deciding against asking me to leave.

"My name is Officer Powell. This is my partner, Officer Laramie. We work with John Ludgate down in Watford. Your father was involved in a pretty ugly car accident a few miles outside of Watford," Powell explained. "He slammed his car into the bridge over Highway 54, going thirty over the speed limit."

Abbie put her head in her hands. Her shoulders trembled as the weight of the police officer's words settled over us. I let out a long breath.

I don't know what guardian angels were looking out for him, that he avoided harming anyone else. My anger didn't belong here, but that didn't stop me from being mad. I was angry with Malcolm for endangering the lives of others in this way, and I was angry with whoever let him behind the wheel.

"It's also important for you to know that he was operating his vehicle under the influence, and that his blood alcohol panel came back at over three times the legal limit," Officer Laramie added.

Abbie sucked in a sharp breath. "*Three times?*"

Laramie gave a firm nod of his head. I fought to keep my expression neutral, even though questions as to how this man had been allowed to get behind the wheel swirled within me.

"Does your father have a history of alcohol abuse?" Powell asked, pulling a notebook and pen from his chest pocket and flipping it open.

"My mother died of cancer a few weeks after my high school graduation," Abbie said, fiddling with her hands in her lap. "After that, my father changed. It's gotten worse over the years, but I never would have guessed he'd be this reckless and stupid."

"Was there anything this week that would have triggered him?"

"Oh my God," Abbie croaked. "My mother received her diagnosis in October. The anniversary would have been a few weeks ago. I was so busy with the festival and everything else I didn't . . ."

She looked at me helplessly. I pulled her in for another hug, and she sobbed into my chest.

"It's my fault," she whispered. "I should have been there. I don't know how I forgot."

"It's not your fault, Ms. Collins." Officer Powell shook his head. "Your father's actions are his own."

Abbie only shook harder.

"Thank you for speaking with us," Powell continued. "We appreciate your insight. The nurses and doctors can apprise you of his condition."

The officer paused. "Your father will be formally charged with driving while under the influence, Ms. Collins. I'm sure you're aware of that."

"Good," Abbie murmured, wrapping his arms tighter around my waist. "He deserves to be finally held accountable for his actions."

I met Officer Laramie's gaze over the top of Abbie's head, giving them a slight nod to let them know I had her.

A knock sounded at the door.

"I'm sorry to interrupt, but Mr. Collins is awake. You can see him now," Nurse Hadley said.

Officer Powell slid his notebook back into his pocket and stood to leave.

"We'd like to speak with your father. We'll let you know when we're finished. In the meantime, here's my card. Please call me if you need anything."

I took the card from his outstretched hand. When the officers left the room, Abbie let out a high-pitched groan of true agony. She sobbed into my chest, and I held her like the world would fall apart if I let go.

Less than an hour later, Officer Laramie came back to the waiting room to let us know we could see him. As we approached the room, Abbie paused at the door.

"You don't have to do this if you're not ready."

"I'll never be ready," Abbie said, and pushed the door open.

Malcolm wore a blue and white hospital gown and sat up in bed, with a thin white sheet covering the lower half of his body. His face was covered in scrapes and bruises, and it looked like he'd been through hell.

"It's Abbie, Dad."

"I can see you perfectly fine. I can see the asshole standing behind you, too," Malcolm said, and dread filled me at the harsh words. I had a feeling this wouldn't go well.

Abbie bristled beside me.

"We've already had this conversation. Connor is here for me, not you. Now, do you want to talk about what the hell happened the other night?"

"I just spent thirty minutes talking to the cops. No, I don't want to talk about it. I don't owe either of you an explanation," Malcolm replied harshly. "If you came here to berate me, you can leave."

"Do you understand how badly you fucked up?" Abbie asked, trembling with how hard she was holding herself back. "You could have *killed* someone. There's no turning away from this."

Malcolm flinched, and he bared his teeth in a snarl.

"You're going to yell at me about family when you're running around behind everyone's back with the man who destroyed yours?"

Abbie shook her head, letting out a frustrated groan.

"He has nothing to do with this. You're deflecting your issues onto someone else, just like you always do."

"Like hell he has nothing to do with this," Malcom shouted. "You're going to let him waltz back into your life like you're some cheap whore he can use and then discard? For the *second* time? You're smarter than that."

"Dad," Abbie said, and I watched the blood drain from her face. All the anger vanished from her body, replaced by dread. "Don't talk like that."

Malcolm sat up straighter in the bed, raising a pointed finger at his daughter. I acted on instinct, stepping in front of Abbie, as if I could also shield her from the emotional blows her father landed.

"You know how those military men are, Abbie. You're not stupid. You've never been an idiot, so why are you acting like one now? Because he came back and gave you his sob story about how his uncle was horrible to him, as if that somehow excuses the mess he left you in? I raised you better than that."

"Dad, please," she whispered.

"And you." He turned his attention back on me, eyes blazing. "Don't think I'll ever forget that you pulled your little stunt mere days after they buried my *wife*."

I inhaled sharply, but I forced myself to meet his gaze. I could handle whatever bullshit he wanted to throw my way. At this moment, Malcolm was just like every other addict I'd ever worked with. He was going through the initial stages of withdrawal. Angry, scared, and terrified; he dreaded the prospect of never having alcohol again. He was lashing out at everyone to get them to cave.

I was no stranger to this. Malcolm had hurled insults at Abbie in drunken rages for years now, but attacking her sense of judgment was a new low, even for him.

"Your mother would be ashamed of you if she were here," Malcolm said, and Abbie crumpled. Tears streamed down her face as she swayed on her feet. That was a step too far, and based on the way Malcolm seemed to recoil slightly at Abbie's reaction, he knew it too.

"You can be mad," I told him, taking a step forward. I slid past Abbie, who had wrapped her shaking arms around her body, her eyes boring holes into the floor. "You can be angry that you've dug yourself into a hole you can't drink your way out of. You can feel scared about facing all of the shit you've buried so deep—and having to do it sober. But you don't get to take it out on her," I said. I leaned over his hospital bed, making sure he had no choice but to meet my eyes.

"She's been your emotional punching bag for long enough. Throw whatever you want at me, tough guy. I can take it. But leave her out of this."

"You're just as much of a shitbag as your uncle was," Malcolm seethed. "Get out."

I paused, still invading Malcolm's space as I glanced over my shoulder at Abbie, waiting for her to decide what she wanted to do here.

"Get out!" he roared. I fully turned to Abbie, who was staring at her father with such a sorrowful expression that it made my chest tighten. I wrapped my fingers around her arm and pulled her out with me.

"I'm so sorry," Abbie said as soon as we were in the hallway. The door to Malcolm's room slammed shut behind us with a loud thud. "I didn't think . . . He's never—I didn't expect that."

"He's lashing out because he's scared. I'm honestly glad he is."

Abbie's eyes flared brightly.

"You're glad that my father is acting like that?"

"That came out wrong," I said. "I meant that it's common for addicts to lash out at loved ones when they come face-to-face with reality. That he's angry can sometimes be a good sign. It means he hasn't given up completely, that he still cares."

"Right," Abbie said, her jaw twitching in annoyance. "I forgot that you're a professional."

"I don't know if that was a reference to my job, or to my past struggles, but I promise you I'm not trying to overstep. I just want to help."

"We don't need your help, Connor."

We. The word clanged through me.

"What he said to you was awful, but he's still your dad. I know you love him despite the mistakes he's made. Out of all the people in your life, I know that. Don't push me out. Not now."

"You know, I'd actually deluded myself into thinking that we could do this."

My face fell. My mouth hinged open, as if I could stop what I knew would come next from happening.

"But my father makes a good point. I'll give him that. We know nothing about each other, except for what we enjoyed when we were seventeen. What was true when we were teenagers isn't true now. Other than a few funny stories, I have no idea what you did during the last five years."

Her words landed like a physical blow to my chest. Had the last six weeks meant nothing to her?

"There hasn't been anyone else, Abbie," I said, exasperated. "I was never interested in having that kind of physical relationship with anyone else but you. I know it might be hard for you to trust my words, but ask Kameron, or Lucas, or anyone I served with. They'll tell you that, as much as I drank and partied, I never went home with another woman. *Never.*"

Abbie considered this.

"I'm sorry," she said, tears spilling out from her eyes. "I didn't mean to attack you like that. I think . . . I think I need to be alone now. Lucas was right. This is too much."

"Lucas? What did he say to you?"

Fucking Lucas. I would kill him for this. For planting that seed of doubt in Abbie's mind, making her think she had to deal with her father on her own.

"It doesn't matter," Abbie answered.

"What? Abbie, don't push me out."

"I just need some space. Look around, Connor, for God's sake," Abbie said, gesturing wildly to the hospital corridor. "I can't have you running around getting me coffee and food and letting me cry on your shoulder when my focus needs to be here. I need to *fix* this, and I can't do that if I'm distracted. I can't do this with you right now."

My heart beat wildly in my chest as panic threatened to pull me under.

My thoughts kept stopping and starting, like an old truck engine trying to turn over and failing. A faint mechanical buzz filled my ears as I tried to make sense of Abbie's words. I tried to reconcile the distant person in front of me with the woman who had bared her heart to me just that morning.

"You're breaking up with me?" I asked incredulously. "What is this, some terrible romance movie? That's not how things go."

"We aren't dating, Connor," Abbie snapped, and my insides twisted. "It's not a break-up because we never put a label on this."

She gestured flippantly between the two of us, and awareness slammed into me as I realized what she was doing. I could see her rebuilding those walls, brick by brick. The walls I'd spent the last month and a half tearing down were now back in place, and there wasn't a damn thing I could do about it. I would have to wait her out. I had been prepared for this possibility since the minute I stepped foot in Watford again.

But I hadn't expected it to physically hurt like this. I was no stranger to pain. Between Ellis and the Marine Corps, I'd experienced my fair share of ass kicking. But the pain that now radiated from my chest was all-consuming. There was no comparison. Purely physical pain, I could handle. This pain, born from having someone you love push you out of their life, was something wholly different.

"I need space. Please give me that."

"Abbie," I said, slightly shell-shocked.

"I was an idiot for this," Abbie said, fiddling nervously with her hair. I wanted her to look at me. I wanted her to remember that, despite everything we'd been through, she couldn't pawn me off that easily now. "My father might be an asshole going through withdrawal, but he's not wrong. We've been moving way too fast. And Lucas—he was right. I'm needed here. My focus has to be here. I just can't right now. I *can't*."

I knew at that moment, this went far deeper than our history. This was about the story Abbie had woven in her mind about the men in her life and how much she mattered to them.

My hands went limp at my sides as I released a long sigh.

"Call me when you're ready to talk," I said, trying to keep my tone light, even while my chest cracked down the middle.

I had promised her I would walk away from this, from us, if she said the word. I expected her to shut me out in those early weeks, but I hadn't expected it to come now, when we're so close to having it all.

But I was a man of my word. On this, I wouldn't push her.

Abbie said nothing as she wrapped her arms around her torso and turned away from me. I let my fingers hang loose at my sides, clenching and unclenching my fists the entire way out to my truck.

I wrenched open the driver's side door and climbed in, slamming the door shut with more force than necessary. Lucy groaned in protest, and I ran my hands over the steering wheel in a soothing movement.

I stared at the neon lights of the hospital sign, trying to figure out how two days ago I had everything I could ever want, and now it had all gone to crap.

Chapter 27
Connor

D riving back to the cabin in Watford was a blur.

I was so zoned out I didn't spare a second to put my music on. I white-knuckled the steering wheel the entire way back to Watford.

I was *angry*—pissed in a way I hadn't been in years. Every minute of therapy I attended over the last few years vanished the minute I saw that Kameron's car was still there.

I slammed the front door open. Lucas and Kameron were in the kitchen, putting their dirty breakfast dishes in the sink. Both of them jumped back at the sudden noise. Lucas cursed as he spilled hot coffee down the front of his shirt.

"You had no right," I shouted.

Lucas immediately whirled in my direction. "Dude, what the hell is your problem?"

"My problem is *you*," I said, stalking toward him. "My problem is you putting your nose into other people's business. You had no right to say that to her. To say *anything* to her."

"What are you talking about?" Lucas asked, scowling. "I haven't done anything."

"The little *conversation* you had with my girlfriend at Watley's," I said, using air quotes for emphasis. It didn't matter that we hadn't formally put a label on things. She was still my girl, especially where he was concerned.

Lucas shook his head. "I didn't say shit about you."

"What *exactly* did you say to Abbie?" Kam asked Lucas, wary of his answer.

"I told her that her dad would need help from her in order to stay sober," Lucas blurted, throwing his hands up in defense. "I meant he would need her support in the coming months, because that's when shit is the hardest. That's all I said."

I groaned, feeling the urge to rip my hair out.

"That was the *worst* thing you could have possibly said to the daughter of an addict. You think she doesn't know that? She's in her own head all the time about how much her father needs her. Add that to the fact that her mother is dead, and she's responsible for keeping them both afloat financially, and you just reinforced the idea that she can't have anything for herself."

Lucas grimaced. "I didn't mean it like that."

"Well, she took it as a license to push everyone away. I don't understand why you opened your mouth. It wasn't your business. *None* of this is your business."

"I'm sorry, man," Lucas said.

Kameron leaned across the counter with his arms crossed, clearly annoyed by this turn of events. No one said anything for a few moments.

"Want to crack open a non-alcoholic cold one?"

Lucas's suggestion cut through the awkward silence. Kameron's cough sounded suspiciously like he was trying to cover up a surprised laugh.

I sighed. "Yeah."

It's not like there was anywhere else to go. The last thing I needed to do was alienate the two people I had left.

Chapter 28

Abbie

My father would need to stay in Brighton for at least a week. I was encouraged to go home shortly after my conversation with Connor in the hallway. Given that it was less than an hour between the hospital and Watford, I took that advice.

If my life was going to fall apart, I at least wanted the ability to curl up in my own bed.

It had been two days since I ripped my heart out of my chest and stomped on it, and done the same to Connor.

I tried my damndest not to think about it. Not because it didn't hurt, but because there was no point in expecting things to change.

This is how things went: things were good, something terrible happened, and I put my nose to the grindstone to fix things.

It was back to business as usual.

Rain came down in droves outside, so I tugged on my rain boots and grabbed my jacket as I packed up my things to head out to the coffee shop. As much as I was glad to be home, I was also going slightly stir-crazy.

Everywhere I looked, I saw Connor. I remembered the times he brought me coffee or cooked me breakfast. I remembered the night we fell asleep on the couch together, and the kisses we shared in the kitchen. I couldn't allow myself to think about the things we shared and confessed.

I damn near had a panic attack when I realized his toothbrush was still in my guest bathroom. I needed to get out of the house.

Kevin was definitely getting a raise for how much he'd stepped up to run the store recently. Most days, I felt like Kevin was doing a better job of running things than me. He seemed to have a passion and drive for it I lacked. During the time I spent working on the festival, Kevin had figured out how to fix many of the physical problems the store was having. He even showed me the research he'd done on growing and maintaining a consumer base. All things I never did when I inherited the store, and I had no intention of doing now.

I felt less guilty about texting him and telling him I needed a few days to get my bearings after my father's accident. His nineteenth birthday was fast approaching, and he wanted the extra hours so he could take Kyrie on a trip upstate.

As I stepped into Blackbeard's, I pushed my hood back and wiped my boots on the entry carpet. I smiled when I approached Kyrie at the order counter and wondered if she'd been by to see Kevin.

"Hey, Abbie! What can I get you on this dreary morning?"

She giggled like it was funny, not knowing how accurately the weather outside reflected how I felt.

"Vanilla latte, please. And a chocolate chip croissant, if you have any left."

"Gotcha," Kyrie said, tapping away on the tablet before turning it toward me. "I'll have it up in a few."

"Thanks."

I a beeline for the booth that lined the far wall. I wasn't in a mood to talk to people more than necessary, and sitting in the front booth—or worse, the one closest to the entrance — would open the conversation to questions I didn't care to answer.

I pulled out my laptop, along with the manila folder with letters from the IRS and their various requests. I didn't know where to start with fixing this mess. I tried to read the most recent correspondence, but the black lines blurred against the white paper. I couldn't focus.

Kyrie called my name, alerting me that my order was ready. I looked up to find that Phillipa was now working the register, and there was a short line. I grabbed my latte at the pick-up counter when Kyrie appeared with my croissant.

"Where's Connor today?" she asked and pushed the croissant toward me. She inclined her head, waiting for the gossip.

"He headed back to his farm."

"Aw," Kyrie said with an exaggerated sigh. "Long distance sucks. If you ever need to talk, my sister is in a relationship with this military guy, and they—"

"We're not together," I exclaimed, more harshly than I intended.

"Oh," Kyrie said, cheeks reddening. "I'm so sorry for assuming. Let me know if you, um, need anything else."

She gave me one more smile before turning back toward the espresso machine. I wanted to apologize, but the damage was already done. I added it to my mental list of things I screwed up in the last week.

I felt everyone's eyes on me as I sat back down at my table. Jamming my headphones into my ears, I turned on my instrumental Taylor Swift playlist to distract myself. I took a sip of my coffee and turned my attention back to the slew of emails I'd been ignoring.

Many of them were from small businesses that wanted to stock their goods in Watford General. There were a few requests for press interviews, a few thank yous, and even one from a social media manager who wanted to help us expand our online presence. On any other day, under normal circumstances, I would have been ecstatic. This is exactly what I set out to do with the Founder's Day festival. I'd put Watford—and, by extension, the store—back on the map.

It didn't matter.

I'd done everything people had asked of me. I coordinated the festival. I found new vendors to invite to the fair. I re-established community connections. I encouraged people to do things differently. Even business owners that had been doing things the same way for the better part of fifty years had been willing to try.

And I had nothing to show for it.

The store was still going to be in debt. Even with these new initiatives to bring income into the store, it wouldn't be enough to get us back in compliance with the IRS *and* the debt collectors.

The stares of the people standing in line burned into me like a brand. I needed to get out of here.

I grabbed my things and shoved them back into my backpack. I slung my jacket on, pulled my hood over my head, and stepped out into the dreary gray, without so much as a look back at the people who had once supported me through thick and thin, and now looked at me like I was a stranger.

The bell above the front door of Forest Grove Books jingled, and I felt some of the tension leach from my shoulders.

"Hi, Mari," I said, breathless. "I was at Blackbeard's, and people were staring. I just needed some. . ."

What the hell did I need?

"Sorry," I said, giving her a tight smile. "I'm not in the best headspace right now."

"Pick a book," Mari suggested, gesturing to the packed shelves full of cracked spines and foxed pages. "Sit down and read for a bit. Then we'll talk."

I nodded gratefully and slung my bag onto one of the two teal velvet loveseats that framed an antique side table. It was a quaint space where people could sit and read, or in my case, escape the world for a few hours.

And that was exactly what I did. I walked to the romance section, closed my eyes, and blindly ran my fingers along the spines of the used book section until one felt right. I pulled the book out without looking at the cover and began reading without so much as glancing at the blurb.

"Brought you some tea, in case you were thirsty."

I looked at the clock behind her desk. My eyes widened.

"I didn't realize it was almost three in the afternoon," I said, closing the book and giving her my full attention.

"Interesting choice, considering your circumstances," Mari said, gesturing to the book in my hands. I flipped it over to look at the cover, and sure enough, it was a romantic comedy.

"I didn't read the blurb before I started reading," I admitted.

Mari smiled, and the two of us fell into a comfortable silence as we sipped our tea. Greystone, Mari's cat, and Forest Grove's unofficial mascot, came to rest at my feet. I reached down to scratch behind her ears and gave her a pet.

"Did I ever tell you about my husband?"

I shook my head as I leaned back in my chair once more, taking another sip of tea. In all the years I'd been coming to visit Forest Grove Books, Mari had never volunteered that information, and I never felt like it was my place to ask.

"He served in Vietnam," Mari said, leaning back in her chair. "He was one of the few from our hometown that made it back. It was only a few months after homecoming that his symptoms started. At first, it wasn't anything that couldn't be attributed to returning home from war—fatigue, fever, insomnia—but they got worse over the years. My husband had a gut feeling that something wasn't right. A few weeks after our daughter's fourth birthday, he finally had his answer. His cancer was advanced. The doctors gave him three years, and Jim lived for six. Several years after his death, the Veterans Administration finally classified his death as service-connected."

"Agent Orange," I breathed. Mari nodded.

"He's buried up on Westfall. People look at my shop and wonder how it survives, given how small our customer base is." Mari let out a small sigh. "It's because of my Jim. I named it Forest Grove Books because it reminds me of the place we met, at the base of a tall evergreen tree on the outskirts of the Washington forest. I loved him almost my entire life."

My eyes welled with tears. I took a moment to look—truly look—at the woman in front of me, who had more stories and experiences than I ever stopped to realize.

"You've been through so much."

Mari took my hand in hers.

"Life can be unkind to those of us who love so deeply," Mari said. "But that doesn't mean the love we share isn't worth it."

I glanced away, unable to meet her eyes.

"You love your books where the hero gets the girl in the end, and you can't see when your knight in shining armor is right in front of your face," Mari said. I looked back up at her, ready to defend my actions, but she held up a hand and tutted under her breath.

"No arguing. Life has already separated you once. Go get him, Abbie. Love isn't supposed to be easy. More often than not, it's about learning how to make sense of the mess you've inherited. You were kids when you fell in love for the first time. That doesn't mean you can't have it now, when it's heavy and exhausting, beautiful and *real*."

Mari reached up to wipe away the tears cascading down my cheeks. "Your mother loved you. She loved your father, too. The two of you were her entire world. She would want you to be happy. If you're asking me, she would have been over the moon that the two of you ended up together."

I let out a small, strangled noise and put my free hand over my mouth to stop a full sob from escaping.

"And one last thing, while I'm imparting all of my hard-earned wisdom on the younger generation . . . You don't have to earn Connor's love, Abbie. He has already given it to you, freely and without restraint. Go to him."

I didn't need to be told twice. I grabbed my bag and kissed Mari on the cheek as I stood to leave.

"Be careful, Abbie. There's a storm coming," Mari called after me. I frantically waved my hand.

Sure enough, I looked at the sky, and looming rain clouds darkened the horizon. I had less than an hour before the rainstorm arrived, and it would render many of the back roads impassable for the rest of the day. It was a risk taking my car on unpaved roads, but it was a risk I had to take. Time wasn't on my side for this.

I probably looked like a crazy woman, dodging people on the street and muttering apologies, as I forced my way through the early morning crowd to get to my condo, taking the stairs two at a time. I burst into my apartment, and as I threw my bag down and grabbed my car keys from the dish, I quickly realized that I didn't know what I would say when I got there.

I was going to barge into Connor's cabin and say what? I'm sorry I'm an idiot? I love you and I never stopped? I need you to stay with me because I don't know how to walk this path without you?

I couldn't say any of that. I needed to get this right. Because this time I had been the one to leave. Instead of fixing this like I was used to fixing everything else, I needed to show up.

There was one person I needed to talk to first.

Chapter 29
Connor

"What are you doing?" Kameron asked.

It was later in the day. The three of us had spent the better part of the afternoon on the back porch of the cabin, cracking jokes, and just existing. Once we were back at Winding Road, it'd be all hands on deck. The new cohort would arrive in the next few days, and we needed to make sure we were in the right headspace to guide them.

I had just finished packing up the random assortment of crap I'd left in the kitchen before I spent the night at Abbie's house. I grabbed my duffle bag and strode for the bedroom.

"I'm packing up my crap so I can head back with you and Lucas."

"What happened to needing a few days to tie up loose ends?"

My chest tightened, and I tried to play it off with a shrug.

"I'm getting ready to do my job," I said, shoving the last pair of shorts into my duffle bag. I headed into the bathroom to continue clearing my belongings. "At the hospital, she told me she couldn't do this, referring to our relationship that isn't a relationship."

"Have you perhaps considered that history might repeat itself?" Kameron asked, and I groaned.

"Drop it, Kam."

"No," Kameron said firmly. "You left her all those years ago because you couldn't sort your shit out. Correct?"

I sighed warily. I could see where he was going with this, and I didn't have the emotional capacity to deal with it.

"Yes," I bit out. There was no sense in lying now.

"So what if she's doing the same thing?"

I grimaced.

"Hear me out," Kam said quickly, sensing that I was about to tune him out completely. "I don't think she's doing it intentionally. But from the outside looking in, it sounds a lot like she feels completely undeserving of you and the beautiful life the two of you might have together. That fear is crippling her to where it was easier to rip her own heart out—and by extension, yours. There's a lot of crap going on right now. Her dad was in a terrible accident, and he's at a crossroads with his addiction. She probably has freaking whiplash from everything that's happened in the last few weeks."

"What did we say about psychologizing each other's partners?"

"It was merely an observation. What exactly did she say when you asked if she no longer wanted you?"

"She said she needed space." I gestured between me and an invisible Abbie.

"So, she didn't say she doesn't want you. She said she needs space, and you interpreted that as her telling you to get lost. She just went through something traumatic,

Connor. Traumatized people often think in shorter terms. I'm willing to bet she didn't mean she wanted you gone. You know her better than I do, but she looks at you like you hung the freaking moon. I don't believe that she no longer wants you in her life. She's *scared*, and I don't think it has anything to do with you. It's about the sins of your pasts or whatever. Look," Kam said, letting out a frustrated sigh. "What I'm trying to say is that she loves you, Connor. It's plain as day that the two of you care about one another. Maybe what you both need is a clean slate."

"I can't wipe away our history, Kam. Maybe that would make things easier, but honestly, I don't want to. I've felt more myself these last few weeks than I think I ever have." I sighed, rubbing a hand down my face. "I told her to call me. Whenever she's ready to talk, I'll be there. And if she never wants to see me again, I'll respect that, and I'll find a way to be okay with a life where Abbie Collins doesn't exist to me at all."

"Abbie won't do that. She's overwhelmed, she's scared, and all of those long-buried fears of abandonment, and her one remaining parent almost dying, are circumventing everything else in her brain. She needs some space, and she needs some time. But what she doesn't need is to come home to an empty apartment."

"What are you asking me to do?"

"I'm telling you, for the second time in your life, to get your crap together and show up. There's a fine line to walk between giving the people we love space and also holding them accountable when they do stupid shit. Stick around.

Show up. You've never been the man to back down from a fight. Don't start now."

I promised myself there would be no more running. I promised *Abbie* there would be no more running. And I'd be damned if I broke another promise to the woman I loved. I would be there for her when she was ready. I'd go back to Winding Road, but I'd make it clear the door was open.

There was just one more thing I needed to do.

Chapter 30

Abbie

T hunder rolled in the distance as I made my way up the familiar mountain path leading to Westfall Cemetery. I prayed the rain would hold off long enough for me to say my piece and work up the courage to confront everything I spent the last two months trying to run away from. The damp earth gave easily beneath my boots, weeks of early autumn rain having softened the ground beneath me. I took a deep breath, taking the earthy mountain air into my lungs, calming my heart rate and my mind along with it.

When the wrought-iron fence of the cemetery came into view, I exhaled.

I took a moment to examine the other headstones in the cemetery. I recognized some of Imogen's relatives, as well as some of the original founding members of Watford. And then I found Jim Pearson's.

I pressed my fingers to the top of his gravestone. The stone bore his dates of service, rank, and a quick note about being a devoted father and husband, etched in the style of a traditional veteran grave marker. My chest ached as I felt the weight of all that was lost when this man died. It was the same weight I felt when my mom died.

"I wanted to say thank you. Mari is a gift, and so is Forest Grove. I'm sorry I didn't get the chance to get to know you."

The words didn't suffice, but my mind was already scattered. I made a silent promise that I would come back and speak with him at a later time.

"I messed up, Mom," I said, kneeling in front of her headstone. "I messed up, and I don't know if I can fix it."

"Dad's been sick," I went on, wrapping my arms around my chest as I stood and began pacing. "I know we've talked about this before. He misses you so much. I don't think he knows how to live in a world without you. To be honest, I don't really know how to either. I feel like I've just been floating for the last few years. I put everything on hold and learned how to run the store. I made sure your hard work didn't go to waste. But now . . . there's so much more I want to do, Mom."

Then I saw them.

A small bundle of fresh daisies, tucked behind the bouquet Connor and I had left during our visit a few days prior.

In my years of coming to visit my mom's grave, I never saw another soul here with me. There was only one person who would have taken the time to come up here and place flowers at my mom's grave.

Connor had come *here*. Not to my apartment. But to talk to Mom.

I picked up one daisy, holding it between my fingers.

"I won't ask what he came to talk to you about," I said, drawing in a shaky breath. "But I love him, and he loves me, and even though we're not teenagers anymore, we've still been idiots about this. Did it have something to do with that?"

A gentle breeze rustled the trees around the cemetery. It was the forest warning me of an approaching storm, but I also believed it was my mother's way of saying yes.

"I'm scared," I admitted. "I don't know if you ever felt like this with Dad, but I'm scared. This love feels more intense than what we had when we were younger, and I don't know how that's possible. But there's a voice in my head reminding me that this feels right. No matter how many times I try to convince myself that I can't have this, I can't stop myself from wanting it. I'm tired of fighting it."

I took in a deep breath, tucking the wilting petal into the pocket of my jacket.

"I love you. You would want me to live my life. And that's exactly what I'm going to do."

Even if it meant confronting those fears head-on.

Mari's words rang in my head as I made my way back down the mountain.

We were kids when we fell in love. For the longest time, I'd thought we had it all—loving parents and a future together.

But that wasn't true. I'd had that. Connor'd had *me*.

I was long past, holding his departure over his head. I didn't want to waste time arguing about the past or what we could have done differently. We'd already been apart for five years. Five years of memories and experiences we missed out on. Just because we needed that time to grow and learn didn't mean I wanted to waste another second.

Thunder clapped as I slid into the driver's seat and cranked the engine to life.

The sky opened up, and rain came down in droves as I sat there, contemplating what the hell I was going to say.

The car was moving toward the Watford campsite before my brain had caught up.

I couldn't think or rationalize my way out of this, because love *wasn't* rational. Running through the woods to talk to my dead mother minutes before a massive storm hit, and subsequently driving through the storm to hopefully intercept the love of my life, before he left town thinking I didn't want him? That wasn't rational either.

It was ridiculous. It was the kind of stuff you see in movies.

But at that moment, I wanted nothing other than to be in the arms of the man I loved. The man I hoped would see me through this next chapter of my life.

I didn't want to be alone for what came next. I wanted Connor. I wanted him in my life, however that looked.

I slowed down as I rounded the last curve coming down Westfall and continued straight toward the campsite.

And what I hoped would be the beginning of a new future for us.

The storm worsened as I slowly made my way down the highway that connected the Westfall peak with the rest of Watford. What would be a twenty-five-minute drive under normal circumstances had turned into an almost forty-minute drive. I passed the sign for the Watford camp-site and turned right, immediately feeling the gravel road shift in protest.

I only made it a mile down the road before pulling off to the side of the road. It was no longer safe to drive. My car would get stuck, and I'd be far worse off than when I started.

"Damn it!" I shouted, banging the wheel in frustration. The boys' cabin was less than a quarter mile away. Storm clouds darkened the sky, and lightning crackled in the distance, illuminating the clouds. The rain poured relentlessly, creating a symphony of rhythmic pitter-patter on the ground.

I realized that if I was going to do this, I would need to walk the rest of the way to the cabin.

Determined, I braced myself for the wet journey ahead, feeling the rush of cool air and pounding rain as I stepped out of the car and onto the muddy excuse for a road.

I wrapped my jacket tighter around myself, feeling like a complete fool for having started this process in the first place.

My boots slid in the gravel and mud, and my legs grew weary. I reminded myself of what was at stake and took a few more steps, finally seeing the faint glow of a porch light.

I ran toward the cabin, pounding my fist against the door.

"Connor? Kam?"

The closed curtains made it impossible for me to determine if there were any lights on. The small kernel of hope I'd been clinging to faded as my gaze landed on the parking space, now devoid of the one blue Chevy I'd been praying to see.

They had already left. I was too late.

I knew it had been a long shot. Kameron and Lucas had told everyone of their plans to leave Watford. I was foolish to hope that they stayed after learning what happened with my dad.

I was an idiot. A complete idiot.

A hysterical sob escaped me.

I'd abandoned my car on the side of the road and walked here, in the middle of an unseasonably horrible storm, and he was already gone. I leaned against the porch beams for support.

I would find a way forward, just like I always did. I'd live my life, even if that meant living in a world without Connor. Even if that meant I spent the rest of my life wondering what would have happened if I'd made the right choice.

"Abbie?"

I whirled toward the door, and Connor stood there, a towel in his hands, wearing a fresh pair of jeans and a blue t-shirt, concern etched into every line of his face.

My entire body slumped forward in relief as I stumbled toward him.

"I'm so sorry," I cried. "It was a mistake, all of it."

Connor's face was full of concern as he reached for me.

"You're soaking wet," Connor said, running his hands down my shoulders and arms. "How long have you been out here?"

I let out a desperate laugh.

"I thought you were gone," I said frantically. "I drove all the way here after I talked to my mom, and then my car got stuck, so I walked, and Lucy wasn't parked in the driveway, and I thought I'd lost my chance to explain."

Connor shook his head and took a step back. He slid his hands into his pockets, leaning against the door.

"We decided to stay one more night. It's not safe to drive in the storm. We parked the cars around back, so they wouldn't get stuck in the mud. Kam had his headphones on and didn't hear you knocking while I was in the shower. Now come inside before a tree falls on you."

"Before you invite me in, I need to say my piece," I said. Connor glared at me, clearly not pleased with my decision, but inclined a hand toward me.

I opened my mouth to speak, and the words tumbled out.

"I'm a mess, Connor. My life is a mess. I don't know what to do with my dad or the store or anything, but I know I want you. I want you in my life, whatever that looks like. I'm so tired of living a life you're not in. I'm tired of running from you and the beautiful life we could have together if we just try."

Connor smiled at me, soft and warm and understanding. Those familiar butterflies of hope and desire fluttered low in my belly.

"I told you weeks ago, Abbie, I'm here for you. Whatever you need," Connor reminded me.

He stepped forward and took my face in his hands, stroking his thumbs over my cheekbones. With the rain, there was no deciphering the difference between the water and my tears, but he wiped them both away just the same.

"I don't want you to love me because you pity me," I whispered.

Connor chuckled and took another step closer to me. The pine and citrus smell of him enveloped me. I knew in my bones that I would never let this man go again.

"You are the most stubborn, oblivious, infuriating woman I've ever met. I don't love you because I pity you. I love you because even after all these years, you are the one person I want to see at the end of the day. You're the person who feels like home. Even when we're apart, the memory of you wakes me up, reminds me to push forward. I love you, Abbie Collins, not because I pity you, but because I admire you. I admire every part of you, even the dark things you keep hidden from everyone else. Because you've seen the darkness in me, but never turned away."

A sob escaped me, and I closed the distance between us, pressing my face into his neck. He let out a low hiss at the damp cold now soaking his shirt. My apology came out muffled as he pulled me closer, resting his cheek against my wet hair.

"Sometimes you think I have things all figured out, but I don't. I don't have *any* of this figured out. Despite everything we've been through, we're still young. We're not supposed to have it all figured out. We still have time, and we can figure things out together. But I need you to trust me. No more pushing me out. No more hiding. No more running."

"No more running," I agreed, pulling my face away from his neck to meet his gaze. "Never again."

"Never again," he repeated, and lowered his head to kiss me.

I'd been kissed by Connor many times, but nothing had ever felt so full of promise, light, and acceptance. This was a kiss of truth, deeper than teenage promises and whispered dreams in the back of a pickup truck.

My hands sank into his hair, pressing our bodies closer together.

"Now, will you please come inside so we can finish what we've started?"

"First, I didn't start anything, and second—"

Connor cut my words off with another kiss, walking us toward the door.

"Should have known you would argue with me," Connor said, and lifted me up to spin me around. I threw my head back and laughed.

"You're stuck with me, unfortunately."

Connor put me back down on the porch, though his hands remained on my hips. "I wouldn't have it any other way."

Connor

"Hi, Mom," Abbie said as she knelt on the picnic blanket.

We had spread our picnic out beside Tilly's gravestone. It was a beautiful February day—the earliest hints of spring approaching hung heavy in the air, a promise of warmer, longer days. Abbie wore a maroon, long-sleeved dress, and black lace tights that were becoming increasingly distracting. She reached for the basket and pushed it open, pulling out a tub of fruit. I laid down, facing Abbie, my legs crossed at the ankles, my tan utility jacket unzipped and hanging loose around my chest.

"I brought strawberries, your favorite," Abbie said as she removed the lid and pulled out a ripe berry. Her engagement ring glittered on her finger as she did so, and I smiled at the sight.

"So," Abbie started, turning to Tilly. "We have some news to share. But first, I wanted to tell you about Dad. You already know about his accident. But I wanted to tell you he's currently working through a recovery program and performing community service hours. He lucked out with an understanding judge and only had to spend a week in jail to help him 'get his perspective straight.'" Abbie used air quotes for emphasis as she let out a quiet chuckle. "I've never seen him so excited about anything as he was when we went to pick him up after his release to take him to his recovery program."

I smiled at the memory. I was the one to have a separate conversation with Malcolm about the resources that were available to him. He didn't qualify for Winding Road, given that we primarily serve veterans and first responders, but he attended another program Kam recommended. The program was located on the Oregon coast, only a few hours by bus from Watford.

"Dad and I are working on things," Abbie said quietly. "There's a lot to unpack, but we're both trying. I'm hopeful."

Abbie ate another berry, her fingers twitching nervously as she reached for a napkin.

"There's something else we came here to tell you. Connor and I are getting married, Mom," Abbie whispered, and my chest tightened. I know she wished more than anything that her mom could be there for this.

"Imogen is beside herself with excitement over getting to plan a wedding from scratch. Not because she gives a crap about the intricate details of the wedding itself, but because she gets to be in control of organizing it. She has a brand-new spreadsheet and everything. We're getting married at the new Winding Road barn. Our ceremony will be the grand opening of the venue."

"Multipurpose space," I corrected. She smacked my hand playfully.

"You'll be happy to know that I went wedding dress shopping with Imogen and Kyrie. Imogen was her usual honest self, and Kyrie was beside herself with excitement about being surrounded by lacy white princess-y things. I think she'll be next to get married if she can get Kevin on board."

"I think Kevin will run away screaming and crying. Not because he doesn't love her, but because he's commitment-phobic."

Abbie looked at me, a soft expression gracing her delicate fingers. I reached for her hand and gave them a reassuring squeeze.

"I could have said the same about you, once upon a time."

I shook my head, crooking one finger and encouraging her to lean in closer so I could whisper in her ear.

"Play nice," I said, my breath grazing the shell of her ear, and Abbie shivered, sticking her tongue out briefly before turning her attention to the rustling forest beyond.

"You called it," Abbie said with a quiet laugh, looking back at her mother's headstone. "I distinctly remember you telling me not to screw this up after that first family dinner with Connor. You had more faith in Connor than you did in me."

I laughed at that, laying down flat on my back so my face was to the early afternoon sun. A gentle breeze caressed my skin as I did so.

"If it makes you feel any better, she had the same conversation with me after senior prom," I chimed in. "If those conversations before and after prom were supposed to be private, Tilly, I'll apologize now, because I definitely told Abbie."

Abbie pinched my arm, and I batted her hand away.

"We love you, Mom. I wish you were here with us now. You would be so proud. Imogen's business has taken off after the festival, though I'm not sure she has the same passion for homesteading as she did when she first came back to Watford. I think she might want something more. Watford General is back on its feet, and we've got an accountant who's working with us to get our books straight. Kevin really has a knack for running the store, too. He's knowledgeable about social media marketing and maintaining a customer base. He's been doing everything I should have been doing the last few years, but didn't have the capacity for. I've already promoted him to General Manager while Dad is in recovery. All of your hard work is safe, Mama."

Abbie paused then, setting the bowl of fruit on the picnic blanket and reaching out for her mother's gravestone, fingers brushing over the engraved letters of Tilly's name.

"She's smiling down on you, Abbie."

"She's smiling down on *us*. She loved you too, Connor, and always wanted to see you do good things."

I smiled, tucking a stray piece of hair behind Abbie's ear and stroking her cheek with my thumb.

"The most good I'll ever do is show up for you and fight to protect what we have. I love you," I murmured.

"And I love you."

Abbie leaned down to kiss me, and I pulled her closer, settling her hips over mine as our lips met.

It had all been worth it.

Acknowledgements

U nder *Pink Skies* is a story of many parts. There are parts of my story and my family's story. All parts are deeply meaningful and personal to me. I've always joked that my first book was always going to be more self-insert than the rest, and suffice to say that's true. I needed to tell this story of redemption and healing before I could tell the other stories that live in my head.

In sum, I am honored that you picked this book up out of the millions to choose from. *Thank you.*

Barb, Jeff, Willie, Matthew, Liz, and Little Justin: our story is complicated and rough around the edges, but it's ours. I love all of you more than I can put into words.

Chris, you are the reason I can write about true love, because I live it with you every day. Thank you for the all-day writing days, for relentlessly believing in me, and for holding me accountable to my goals. Thank you for being my go-to male-gaze beta reader, and for letting me borrow your brain when I hit a plot hole.

Kiddo, you are the light of my life. Being your mama is simply the best. I love you beyond words.

To my in laws, thank you for welcoming me into your family. I hit the lottery with you. Thank you for spending time with your favorite grandson so I could get some words in, and for being my unofficial nursing/medical fact checkers.

Eve, you've read most of my stories, fanfiction, and other ramblings that really shouldn't have seen the light of day. We've seen each other through good times and bad. I am grateful to have a true friend in you.

Nana, I love you. I hope you're with Jim, and that you've found peace.

To all the members of S. K. Dwyer's Discord community, especially Steph, Katrina, and Devon: thank you for all the encouragement, sprints, and livestreams. Milli, Maddi, and Jen, thank you for beta reading.

To my editor, Alyssa, some authors go their entire careers without finding their "soulmate" editor, but I'm lucky to have found mine in you. Thank you for all your hard work making this book the best it can be.

To the authors of my favorite books, your stories have inspired me to never give up on my dream of having my book in my hands.

To my church community, who has seen me grow up and encouraged me to follow my dreams: thank you.

To the daughters of fathers who have struggled with addiction: you are not alone. I pray you find peace on your journey.

The story continues...

Imogen Phillips learned long ago that letting people in only leads to heartbreak.

Kameron Miller has poured his heart into helping others heal, but never stopped long enough to mend his own.

An unplanned kiss lays bare the feelings they've both been trying to ignore, but letting go of the past is easier said than done.

NOW AVAILABLE AT ALL RETAILERS

About The Author

Hallie Anne writes romance stories with complicated characters working through tough problems and the love they find along the way. She lives in the Carolinas with her family. When she's not writing, she's curled up with a cozy blanket, a cup of coffee, and a romance book. Connect with her on Instagram at @hallieanneauthor, and join her Discord server for behind-the-scenes snippets and exclusive online events!

Sign up for my newsletter
to stay up to date!

Join Hallie's Heartstrings

Sick of the constant social media scroll? Me too. That's why I created a Discord server where we can hang out and connect on a deeper level—without being buried by the algorithm.

Join the Discord server

www.ingramcontent.com/pod-product-compliance
Lightning Source LLC
Chambersburg PA
CBHW010740310726
48971CB00010B/2885